WINTER'S KNIGHT

KNIGHTS ARE FOREVER SERIES BOOK #3

Debbie Boek

Copyright © 2019 Debra Boek

Wolf Rider Publishing

Publisher's Cataloging-In-Publication Data
(Prepared by The Donohue Group, Inc.)

Names: Boek, Debbie, author.
Title: Winter's knight / Debbie Boek.
Description: [Lafayette, New York] : [Wolf Rider
    Publishing], [2020] | Series: Knights are
    forever series ; book #3
Identifiers: ISBN 9780960077595 (paperback) | ISBN
    9781734248203 (ebook)
Subjects: LCSH: Knights and knighthood--Europe--
    History--To 1500--Fiction. | Normans--Europe--
    History--To 1500--Fiction. | Women, Romani--
    Europe--History--To 1500--Fiction. | Man-woman
    relationships--Europe--History--To 1500--
    Fiction. | Great Britain--History--Medieval
    period, 1066-1485--Fiction. | Normandy (France)-
    -History--To 1515--Fiction. | LCGFT: Historical
    fiction. | Romance fiction.
Classification: LCC PS3602.O42255 W56 2020 (print)
    | LCC PS3602.O42255 (ebook) | DDC 813/.6--dc23

ALSO BY DEBBIE BOEK

If Not For The Knight
Knights Are Forever Series
Book #1

When The Knight Falls
Knights Are Forever Series
Book #2

Sommers' Folly

<u>THE DEVEREAUX CHRONICLES</u>

Devil's Bait

Devil's Retribution

Devil's Gathering

Visit the author at:
debbieboek.com
debbieboek.blog

CHAPTER 1

London, England 1111

The young woman lifted her head and ceased what she was doing, pushing her thick, black hair back away from her face as best she could while she listened. She waited for a couple of moments, but there were no further sounds from above deck, so she continued gnawing at the ropes that were securing her wrists.

She did not know where she was, the ship had docked a short while before, but she could not see anything from the dark hold that she had been thrown into before their journey across the water began.

Slowly, the sounds from the ship and its crew had subsided and all she could hear were the waves lapping gently against the side of the boat. She could only assume it was some time in the early morning hours and that her captors would wait till daylight before doing anything further with her.

Realizing that this may be her only chance at escape, she tried to shred the rope with her teeth. It was made of hemp and, although secured firmly around her wrists, the actual strands were not twisted together very tightly.

The rough fibers rubbed the corners of her mouth raw as she continued to tear at them and her frustration mounted until, finally, the strands separated and she was able to pull them apart the rest of the way and release her hands.

Reaching down to undo the ropes around her bare feet, she stood and walked quietly around the hold. The blood rushed down her legs and she had to wait until the prickly, sharp pains abated somewhat before taking the next step towards her escape.

Slowly, and ever so quietly, she opened the hatch and climbed up onto the deck, the sky was overcast and there was little light shining through the darkness. She took a deep breath of fresh air, but then had to stifle a cough as her lungs filled with bitter cold sea air, and the smells of dead fish and unclean sailors bombarded her nostrils.

The flat bottomed ship had been able to dock along the wharf and she sighed in relief that she would not have to jump into the frigid water in order to gain her freedom, she only had to avoid detection until she could make her way off the ship and onto the docks.

She did not know why these men had kidnapped and brought her here, but it was obviously naught for anything well-intentioned.

The boards of the ship creaked when she stepped on them, but the noise was muffled somewhat by the wind whistling through the sails that were tied back to the masts, and the loud snores of the sailors asleep below deck.

Her heart began to race in her chest, she was so close now to freedom and only had to stay calm for a bit longer and she would be well away before they woke.

She looked over the side and the wharf was just a few meters down, she would be able to jump to it easily enough. She climbed over the side rail of the ship and stepped onto the wooden pieces of the frame. Looking down once again so she could gauge the distance, the woman was unable to bite back the scream that escaped when someone grabbed a handful of her thick, black hair, trying to halt her escape and pull her back up.

She fought like a banshee, ignoring the pain that came when it felt as if he might actually be pulling a chunk of hair loose from her head. Her feet were just a few meters from the dock, but she could not get him to let go of her and now she could hear scuffling and other noises coming from the deck and knew they would all be upon her momentarily.

The sailor was leaning very far over the side of the ship as he tried to retain his grip on her and, at the same time, was yelling out an alarm to the others. Squirming violently, trying to force him to loosen his hold on her, she reached up and was able to grab hold of one of his hands.

Prying his pinky finger back, she twisted it with all her strength until she heard it snap. The man let out a shriek of pain and pulled his hand away, releasing her abruptly.

Naomie fell heavily onto the wharf but quickly leapt back to her feet, ignoring the shouts coming from the ship, refusing to look back and see how close the other men might be, she sprinted off into the dark, sleeping city which sprawled out in front of her.

At approximately that same time, a single priest was riding slowly through the moonlit French countryside. He was tall and thin, slight of frame but not frail. His normally clean-shaven face was now covered with several weeks' growth of hair, he'd not taken the time to worry about such inconsequential considerations on this journey.

Besides, it helped protect his face from the harsh winter chill that was strong enough to bite through his mantle, as well as the black wool robe he wore underneath it.

He could see both his own and his horse's breath waft through the night air as they made their way across the frosted ground. They still had over a hundred kilometers to go before reaching Normandy and safety, so he tried to ignore the cold that was seeping into his bones.

He would only remain in Normandy for a short time, just long enough to rest a little and prepare himself for the next phase of his journey.

Gwyn turned to look back frequently, but with only the moonlight to illuminate the roads and the thick trees growing along either side, he could not see far. He thought he may have lost his pursuers along the border between the Kingdom of Germany and the Kingdom of France, but he could not be certain.

The sword bumping uncomfortably against his leg as he rode led his thoughts back to how he came to be here, cold and frightened and far from his home.

Despite the numerous church doctrines forbidding clerical participation in warring activities, more and more warrior bishops were being created since the Crusade ended in 1099. At that time, the Knights Hospitaller, a military order, had been established. It was a Christian religious society of knights in the Kingdom of Jerusalem, whose purpose was the care and defense of the Holy Land.

They were the first of the warrior bishops and, although Pope Paschal had not recognized the society yet, it was anticipated that he would do so in the near future, creating an entirely new realm for some of the clergy.

Gwyn was not a member of that society, however, he had recently been appointed as a bishop by the Pope himself. And, somehow, he also managed to be drawn into the new warrior aspects of the bishopry, although fighting, or battles of any kind, were not at all in his nature. He had no intention of using the sword unless he was forced to, and he could not foresee any reason for that to occur.

Slowly plodding along the frozen ground, Gwyn thought back to the unexpected private conversation he had with His Holiness after the ceremony appointing him as Bishop.

Just he, the Pope, and Robert I of Capua were present at the time. Robert was the papal protector, as his father and grandfather before him were, and Gwyn had been surprised to find him a party to the meeting.

"My son," the Pope began, "I cannot stay for this conversation, however, I need you to know that Robert has my full blessing for what he is about to charge you with. It will be a dangerous assignment, yet I have full faith in the Lord that he will protect you on your mission."

Gwyn had looked at the Pontiff in confusion, having no idea what this mission could possibly involve.

"God be with you, my son," Paschal said, holding out his hand. Gwyn took it in both of his own and, kneeling before the Pope, he kissed his ring.

"Thank you, Holy Father," he murmured, as the Pope withdrew his hand and made his way out of the room.

Robert watched him go and then turned to have a long, frank conversation with Gwyn.

"As you know," he began, "there is an ongoing dispute between the Pope and King Henry of Germany over the investiture issue."

Gwyn nodded his assent.

"Henry will be riding to Rome in the near future and we fear the Pope's life could be in danger when he arrives."

"How so?"

"If Henry does not get what he wants, he will not hesitate to respond in any manner that he feels he must."

"What does he anticipate happening?"

"He has renounced the right of investiture in return for a promise from Pope Paschal to coronate and restore the Empire of all Christendom to him."

"He would no longer be the King of Germany, but the Emperor of the Holy Roman Empire?"

"Correct, Germany has been in the middle of a civil war for half a century over the conflict between church and state. In return for his agreement on investiture, Henry wants the Pope to coronate him, then the Bishops, Abbots and Princes of Germany will have to restore all the fiefs of the crown to him. The issue would thus be resolved in Henry's favor."

"How will the Pope get them to go along with that?"

"They won't, that is what Henry is counting on, so he does not have to keep his word regarding the investiture. If that happens, the coronation may not go forth."

"What could I possibly do to help?"

"For now, you must keep your priest robes, no one should know you are a bishop. It will be safer for you. There are several distinguished knights in your family, are there not?"

Gwyn nodded his agreement and Robert continued. "We fear there may be a battle coming and need as many men as we can draw together for the Pope's safety."

"You want me to collect my brothers to fight on behalf of the Pope?"

"If that is what needs be, speak to the knights in your family and see who is willing to risk their life for His Holiness. We must have a care because spies are everywhere and it is difficult to know who we can trust. But we have little time to prepare, and your family may also know of others who are willing to come and use their swords to protect the Pope."

Gwyn's musings stopped and he was jerked back to the present when he heard a branch snap in a thicket of trees, just slightly off to the side of him. He pulled back on the reins of his horse, needing silence to determine if there might be a nearby threat, but when the horse blew out loudly through its nose, he knew there was no longer any way to hide his presence.

With a sharp crack as another frozen branch was stepped upon and broken, Gwyn had no further doubts and kicked his horse, urging him into a gallop.

Turning his head, he could see the two men hurrying out to the roadway behind him. Gwyn held on tight and lowered his body further down onto the saddle after seeing one of the men pulling back on his bow.

The man was a good shot and, although it only sliced through the flesh of Gwyn's upper arm, the burning pain almost caused him to fall from the horse's back. Had that happened, he knew they would be upon him and he would not live to see the sun rise.

Ignoring the searing pain, Gwyn held tight to the reins and gripped his thighs securely around his horse's body as they continued to speed along the frozen roadway, praying he could maintain his seat until they were out of range of the brigand's arrows.

Beorn groaned in response to the incessant banging against the door of his bedchamber.

"Milord, are you awake?"

He groaned louder still and rolled over onto his back on the featherbed, his hand grazing the backside of the woman still asleep beside him.

"What is it, Verne?" His voice cracked due to the dryness in his throat and he barely managed to pry open one dark blue eye to look around the room. Spying a cup on the table to the side of the bed, he slowly sat up, hoping his pounding head did not explode from his shoulders as he did so.

Grabbing hold of the cup, Beorn was relieved to see there was a bit of cider still left in it and gulped it down, hoping a little hair of the dog would help ease the painful throbbing in his head.

"Milord," Verne said again, opening the door a sliver now that he knew Beorn was finally awake.

"Yes, what do you want? Why are you waking me at such an ungodly hour?"

"The sun is full risen, Milord. Besides, you have a guest."

"A guest?" Beorn said, looking around the room again, this time searching with bleary eyes for his sword. No guests came to visit this time of year, so this person's motives were immediately suspect.

"A priest, Milord, he says he is your brother."

Ignoring the pounding in his head, Beorn allowed a slight smile to crease his face. "Gwyn is here?"

"Aye, Milord."

"See to his comfort, I shall be down anon."

He ran his fingers through his hair, trying to tame the chaotic light brown mess, but only left it in further disarray. Beorn turned to the woman lying beside him on the bed and slapped her bare bum. The linen sheets had been torn from the bed during their drunken antics in the wee hours of the morning, and she lay on the featherbed as naked as the day she was born.

"Wake up, Mimi, time to leave."

"No," she said, rolling over and stretching her arms up above her head, "it's too early yet."

"Apparently, it is not," Beorn said, admiring her swelling breasts and lightly pinching one of her nipples. Mimi squealed in a very unladylike fashion and sat up on the bed, immediately grabbing hold of her throbbing head.

"That cider of yours is too strong, I won't recover for days," she whined, her long blonde hair was now a mop of snarls and her eyes were puffy and red-rimmed. "Where are my clothes?"

"All over the floor where they fell, my love. I have a guest and must leave." He quickly donned a pair of loose linen pants and threw an undertunic on over them. "See Verne before you go and he will be sure you receive enough coin for your favors from last evening. Which were commendable, I might add."

"Of course," she replied, "don't you always get what you pay for, Beorn?"

"That I do, Mimi, and you will be well compensated, as always. Ah, here it is," he said, reaching under the bed for his rumpled wool overtunic which he donned before leaving the bedchamber.

Mimi watched him go, headache or not, she smiled thinking back to the night they'd shared, which was much better than the ones she usually spent. If wasn't often that a handsome, strong man like Beorn had need of her services, but she was always willing to make time for him when he did.

"Be sure that Mimi is well paid," Beorn said to Verne, as he reached the bottom of the stairs and passed him by, "and have food and ale brought to me and my brother."

"Yes, Milord."

Beorn was still adjusting his belt around his waist and placing his sword into its scabbard when he entered the Great Hall and spied Gwyn.

"It is you, brother," Beorn said, extending his arms out towards Gwyn. "Welcome, it's been ages since I've clapped eyes on you."

They hugged, but Gwyn stepped quickly out of his embrace. "Good to see you, as well. But what have you been ingesting to give you such malodorous breath? It's frightful."

"Apologies, brother," Beorn said. "I had quite an evening and I fear your arrival woke me from a drunken sleep and I've had no time to freshen myself, as of yet."

Just then two servants arrived with ale, cheese and bread. They sat at the long table on the dais and neither of them wasted any time before beginning to help themselves to it.

"What brings you here, Gwyn?" Beorn asked, after draining his cup of ale and finally getting a little relief from his pounding head.

"I have need of some knights."

"Whatever for?"

Gwyn looked around, some of the servants were lingering in the event they were needed further, and he was not comfortable speaking in front of them.

Beorn saw the look and waved his servants away. Once they were the only two left in the room, he looked a little more carefully at his younger brother.

His brown hair was a well-trimmed tonsure, a ring around the outer edge of his scalp with the inner portion shaved to his bare head. His dark blue eyes, so like Beorn's, stood out starkly on his thin, pale face.

"Is their aught amiss? You do not seem well."

Gwyn began to shrug his shoulder but stopped, wincing in pain. Beorn stood and moved to his side, removing Gwyn's heavy wool mantle, Beorn could see the blood-soaked robe underneath.

"What happened?"

"I was set upon and hit by an arrow. It hit only the outer flesh of my arm, so there should be no worrisome aftereffects."

"Who set upon you?"

"I cannot say for sure. I've an assignment on behalf of the Pope. The German King may be causing trouble for him shortly and I've been bound to collect as many knights as I can to help protect him. I do not know if I was set upon by brigands or if these were emissaries of King Henry sent to prevent me from accomplishing my mission."

"If they were, we should know shortly."

"How so?"

"If they are Henry's men, they will know that you come to me. If they attempt to strike at us here, we shall know for sure."

"What should we do?"

"Have you filled your belly yet?"

"I have."

"Verne," Beorn bellowed, and the squire quickly returned to the room. "Have the servants prepare a room for my brother, he will need some sleep after his shoulder wound is looked after. Be sure his robe is cleaned and repaired while he rests. You will come with me, we need to take a ride and check for possible trouble."

"Yes, Milord," the young man replied, as he hurried off to see to his duties.

"Don't worry, Gwyn. We'll be ready for them if they do show, so rest easy for a bit, you look peaked."

Gwyn was already fast asleep inside the Manor by the time Beorn and Verne headed out. As they rode, Beorn shared what little information Gwyn had provided him with.

"I may need to go with Gwyn, help him find knights to aid the Pope. Have you any interest in coming along?"

"Aye, I do."

"Could be nothing more than a fool's errand, and a dangerous one at that."

"True, but if I'm not there, who the devil would look after you? We both know you are not capable of doing so."

"You forget yourself, boy. Best shut your gob before I reconsider taking you with me."

"Yes, M'lord," he responded, managing to bite back his smile, but he couldn't keep the amusement from shining out of his warm, brown eyes.

Beorn allowed no one to speak to him in such a manner, except Verne. The young man had been his squire and, in truth, also his friend, for many years. They understood one another and the boundaries of their relationship.

"Hold up," Beorn said, raising his hand and pointing into the distance. "And now we have our answer."

The two men were on high ground and the barren trees that stretched out along the frozen fields below allowed them a view for a long distance and, although they appeared to be as small as ants, the group of riders heading in their direction was unmistakable.

"Come, Verne," Beorn said, rubbing his fingers through the short, well-trimmed beard covering his chin as he contemplated this turn of events, "we best get back and prepare."

CHAPTER 2

Gwyn woke up later that afternoon, feeling warm and well-rested for the first time since leaving Rome. He took some time down on his knees to converse with God and thank him for giving him so many blessings in his life.

"Most importantly, my Lord, I thank you for letting me reach my brother's estate safely, and for watching over us all as we take on this task to protect the Pope." He was about to make the sign of the cross and stand up, but hesitated. "And thank you, for letting me spend time with Beorn, and get to know him as the man he has become after all these years we have spent apart from one another."

Finishing up his prayers at that point, Gwyn washed his face and loosened up his wounded shoulder. He was pleased to find his cleaned and mended robe waiting for him. Drawing the heavy wool garment over his alb, a white, linen garment, similar to a tunic with long sleeves, he returned the chain with the heavy cross on it around his neck.

The robe was still a bit damp and cast the soothing scent of applewood, which must be what was used to feed the fire and ensure it would be dry by the time he woke.

Patting his tonsure into place, he headed down to meet with his brother. Beorn's squire, Verne, was waiting for Gwyn in the Great Hall and handed him his mantle before leading him outside where Beorn was sitting on a wooden deck at the far side of the Manor house.

Beorn had designed and helped build it himself shortly after he bought this estate, preferring always to be out of doors whenever possible.

The Manor was a large stone building with two wings which formed an ell shape. The deck was built along the one end of the ell that allowed Beorn to view the outlying buildings and the orchards that sprawled out for acres.

He was leaning back in a chair with his feet propped onto a small table in front of him, sipping a cup of something, no doubt some type of alcohol, Gwyn assumed.

The air was brisk but not frigid, and Beorn wore only a woolen tunic and woolen hose as he waved Gwyn over to his side. A thick belt secured the tunic around his waist, it had several small sheaths attached to it with a sharply honed dirk nestled within each one of them, as well as the scabbard holding his broadsword.

That was not something he wore every day since no longer being in service as a knight, however, the circumstances of this particular day called for a great deal of prudence.

On this day, Beorn chose to sit with his back to the glorious view that he usually appreciated so much and, instead he situated himself so that he could keep an eye out in the direction that he anticipated any unwelcome guests might approach.

"Have a seat, brother. Are you well rested?"

"I am, thank you."

"Share some cider with me, we make it here on the estate."

Gwyn started coughing after the first sip.

"It is strong," Beorn said proudly. "If you can't handle it, we do make apple juice for the children, I can have that served to you instead."

"No need," Gwyn replied, his voice was hoarse from coughing, but the warmth of the brew was already spreading through his insides and he cautiously took another small sip.

"Why do you sit outside in the middle of winter when you have a fire roaring within the Manor?"

"It is too large and too quiet in there. I prefer being out of doors, breathing the crisp fresh air and letting the cold winds clear my head. What do you think of my estates?"

Gwyn followed his gaze, off to the left were an assortment of buildings and straight ahead orchards spread as far as the eye could see, the trees were all dormant now, waiting for the warm spring sunlight to bring them back to life.

"Very impressive, are all of the outbuildings a part of your estate?"

"They are, there is a great deal that goes into the making of cider and each building has a particular use. That one out there, just before the orchard begins is for fermentation and storage, and the one off to the side of it is for milling and pressing. We also have smaller buildings for equipment, building and storage of casks, as well as obviously having need of stables and a barn for the cows."

"You hire locals to harvest the apples and make the cider in season?"

"Mostly, some are employed all year round to care for the equipment and the stock, see the cattle milling out under the trees? We not only make cider and perry, but cheese, as well. I have more coin now than I know what to do with."

"I am not familiar with perry, what is that?"

"It is a type of cider made with both pears and apples, quite tasty, I'll have them bring some out for you."

"I'm fine for now," Gwyn replied, still afraid to take more than a tiny sip from the potent cider in his cup.

"Tell me more about the troubles that are coming," Beorn said, stroking his beard as he continued to gaze out onto his lands.

"Are you familiar with the investiture controversy?"

"Nay, I pay no attention to politics."

"It's been an ongoing issue for Pope Paschal, first with King Louis and now with King Henry of Germany. His Excellency sided with Henry over his father, hoping Henry would abide by the papal decree about investing bishops, but he has not done so."

"Hold that thought," Beorn said, as the faint clinking of chainmail reached his ears. He stood up and casually stretched his shoulders. "Verne, come here."

The squire had been standing just inside the doorway, waiting for this moment, and hurried over to Beorn's side. The young lad was tall, but not as tall, nor anywhere near as broad as Beorn. He listened closely as Beorn leaned down, his lips almost touching Verne's ear as he gave his orders. The young man nodded his head and hurried inside the Manor.

"Mayhap, you might want to step inside now, Gwyn."

"Whatever for?" Gwyn asked with a frown.

"Too late," Beorn replied, as he withdrew one of the small dirks from his belt, turned slightly and threw it with deadly accuracy at the knight who had just slunk around the corner of the building.

The man was not in full armour and wore no helmet. He lifted his hand toward his throat, trying futilely to pull the knife from it, but then fell to the ground, his broadsword clanking against the stones as it dropped from his lifeless fingers.

Beorn pulled his own from its scabbard and held it ready as he rushed in the direction that the man had come from. He'd taken only a few steps before three other knights turned the corner, all battle ready with their swords raised, wasting little time before engaging Beorn.

The suddenness and fury of their attack startled Gwyn and, as he attempted to jump up out of his chair, his foot got tangled in the leg of it and he fell to the hard, wooden floor.

The clang of metal on metal echoed in the vacuous winter air. Beorn had been a knight almost all of his life and was a master with a broadsword, striking out at the first one and disarming him, his sword hand now useless.

Turning quickly towards the next man, Beorn parried his thrusts effortlessly, however, he was aware that there was a third man who was trying to make his way towards his blind-side while the second kept him engaged.

He heard Verne and several others approaching, but so did the other knights and the third man realized he hadn't much time, so he made his move at Beorn, hoping to deliver a deathblow before the others reached them.

Raising his razor-sharp broadsword, ready to deal the final blow, the man took one step forward, then grunted in pain and fell onto his face, his sword rattling harmlessly to the ground beside him.

Both Beorn and the second knight stopped momentarily to look at the dead man and then up at the ashen face of Gwyn, who was still holding his bloody sword in both hands.

The German knight recovered first, saw that he was now the outnumbered foe and turned on his heel and ran. By then, Verne and the others had arrived and Beorn indicated his head in the direction of the fleeing knight, sending them off in pursuit.

"Well done, brother," Beorn said, slapping Gwyn on the back and almost knocking him off his feet.

He raised what was left of his glass of cider and handed Gwyn his. "Here's to more adventure soon to come."

Gwyn had never killed a man before and was shaken at the realization of what he had done. He knew that he must confess his sin as soon as possible, however, since that could not be done at this moment, he finished the cup of cider, feeling its warmth spread through his body and calming the tremors he felt both inside and out.

Verne returned, his blond hair was blowing around his face as he shook his head towards Beorn. "They had horses waiting and the one knight escaped. Our men are giving chase, but I do not think they have a chance of catching up with him."

"Well then, it appears we must join this fight whether we want to or not."

"Why do you say that?" Gwyn asked.

"The Germans know who you are, they know who I am, and they will know of our family in England. We must go there as soon as possible and warn them. London should be a good place to enlist the mercenaries you need, as well. We obviously haven't much time, so we must leave anon."

"I need to find a church first."

Beorn frowned at him. "No, brother, God will wait for a time before he requires your penance. You have a mission to fulfill which must be your first priority."

Then Beorn looked Gwyn over critically from head to toe. "It will be even colder in England, have you no boots or warmer clothing?"

"No, only these clothes and sandals."

"I shall find some of my own for you. We cannot have you falling prey to the cold on this journey. Verne, have the horses saddled, I will tend to my weapons and grab warmer clothing for us all. Gwyn, head to the kitchen and see that some food is prepared for our journey."

Gwyn's blue eyes were clouded like a stormy sky as he struggled with the conflict that filled him. He stared hard at his brother and would do as he was asked, but would insist on stopping at the first church they passed or he would not continue on. He had his mother's stubbornness instilled within him and he would not rest easy until he was able to unburden himself by confessing his mortal sin as soon as possible.

"And be sure my flask is filled to the top with cider," Beorn bellowed after Gwyn, as he walked away.

Beorn stood for a moment, looking off into the distance, a half-smile formed on his lips. He rubbed his calloused hands together, relishing the thought of being back on the battlefield again.

It was what he had known for most of his life and, although his orchards were a lucrative business, the lifestyle was boring and left him with naught to do but drink himself silly to while away the time. Now he could get back to what he did best, back to the business of killing.

When the preparations were completed, the three of them set out on horseback, with Verne pulling an extra horse along which carried their supplies.

Gwyn was exceedingly grateful for the woolen hose and boots that replaced his caliage, the open sandals had provided no protection at all from the cold.

Beorn seemed to not even notice the bitter temps, throwing his mantle over his shoulder in order to keep his sword arm free at all times.

"We'll stay the night here," Beorn said, when the sun had almost made its final descent. "We should reach the coast on the morrow and from there I have friends who can get us across the channel to England."

The temperatures remained above freezing and no snow or rain fell, so the night was almost pleasant as the three men sat around the small fire eating the roasted rabbits that Beorn had shot with his bow and arrows throughout the afternoon.

They shared some cheese and apples to round out their meal and washed it down with a stout ale.

"Tell me more about this investiture of bishops, why is it so important?" Beorn had no patience and little interest in anything relating to Kings or to the church, but if he must ask others to put their lives on the line for it, he must understand it himself.

"Investing of any clergyman, particularly a Bishop, is a religious appointment and should be a task completed by clergy, not by a royal or a nobleman. However, many bishops and abbots are appointed by rulers or willed to the eldest male heir through primogeniture; sometimes the positions are even sold."

"Sold, how?" Verne asked, licking his fingers clean.

"Through a practice known as simony, used by wealthy landowners to obtain the titles. A substantial amount of wealth is associated with the office of a bishop. It is a lucrative position and, with a ruling noble making the investiture, they have purchased the loyalty of that bishop, regardless of whether or not they are suitable for the position, or if they will follow the appropriate papal decrees."

Beorn drank some more ale as he pondered Gwyn's explanation.

"What of the danger to the Pope, I'm not clear on that."

"King Henry plans on making his way to Rome for his coronation and ratification of the treaty he forced on Pope Paschal."

"Which was?" Beorn asked impatiently.

"He will renounce the right of investiture in return for a promise of a coronation and restoration to the Empire of all Christendom."

"All Christendom?"

"He would become the Emperor of The Holy Roman Empire, which is currently the Kingdom of Germany."

"What would change other than his title?"

"There has long been a civil war in Germany between the State and the Church. If this happens, the church must restore all of the crown's property to Henry, and he will then be the sole ruler."

"You said that the Pope already agreed to do this, correct?"

"Yes, but part of that agreement was that the Bishops and Princes of Germany must agree with this and they will not do so. Henry will rely on that to violate the agreement and continue with the investitures after he is crowned."

"I'm not a simple man but, I still don't understand what the danger to the Pope is," Verne said, his brown eyes almost black against the darkness of the night.

"The danger will arise should the Pope refuse to coronate Henry until they've arrived at an agreement about the investiture."

"Let me be sure I understand this," Beorn mused. "Pope Paschal agreed to crown him as Emperor and, in return, Henry agreed to forfeit the right of investiture, leaving any future appointments of bishops to the church."

"Correct, but not all of the German clergy are agreeable to the coronation of Henry as the Emperor and the Pope must take all of their concerns into account."

"The Pope may not go through with the coronation then?"

"Correct, and that is where the danger lies. Henry will insist upon it and, if the Pope refuses, Henry will withdraw his agreement regarding the investiture, and no one knows what he may do to the Pope to force the coronation."

"I must enlist men to defend the Pope who is reneging on a deal already made with a German King?"

"With the strength of his forces, Henry left Pope Paschal no choice but to accept an impossible treaty."

Beorn shook his head silently, taking a long stick and poking at the fire, watching as sparks flew high into the sky above them.

"A deal is a deal, whether made by a Pope or a poor peasant, a man needs to stand by his word."

"He was forced into the agreement by Henry, who was backed up by an army. He did not enter into it voluntarily." Gwyn was surprised at Beorn's rigid attitude about the issue.

"Regardless, a man should not break his word and then expect others to forfeit their lives to keep him from having to live up to its terms. I've seen it happen too many times in the past."

"Are you refusing to aid the Pope?"

"I do this for you, Gwyn, not for your God, not for your Pope. I am struggling to understand how best to convince any other men to fight for this cause. I can find naught but for coin alone. We will have to look to mercenaries only, not knights with any noble affiliations."

"I do not understand."

Beorn caught Gwyn's eyes across the fire. "Greed, my brother, is an all motivating factor. Only knights who care about coin will bother to get involved in this fray.

Those others who report to their own Barons will have no loyalty to the Pope, they will do as their Barons instruct them, which could very well be to disrupt the chances of this investiture no longer being an option for them. It takes away from them, as well as from Henry.

We find those who give their loyalty to the highest coin. I hope you have plenty as this looks to be all the fun of the faire."

"I do have a great deal of coin, no expense will be spared in this endeavor. There will be others to help protect the Pope, as well, so I pray it will not be an overly difficult task." Gwyn replied, relieved that, even though he was struggling with doubts, Beorn was with him on this most unusual journey. His brother's knowledge and experience in this situation were priceless and Gwyn knew he would be floundering uselessly without Beorn's assistance.

"Verne," Beorn said, stirring the fire a little further and sending off another cluster of sparks into the night air, "this battle has no honor as far as I can see. I must go forward, but you need not risk your life for it."

Verne was due to be knighted as soon as Beorn deemed him fit, he was anxious to prove his skills and his courage and would not miss out on this opportunity.

"Thank you, M'lord," he replied, "but, at the close of play, a battle is a battle, and I'm ready for it."

Beorn simply nodded his approval at the boy, there was no sense doing otherwise, he fully remembered how he'd felt when he was Verne's age and knew there would be no changing his mind about this.

They sat quietly for a few moments, then Verne stepped off into the trees to take care of his personal business.

Finally having a chance to speak to Beorn with no one else around, Gwyn asked, "How are you keeping, as far as Anna and the babe?"

Gwyn actually felt a shiver go down his spine in response to the cold gaze Beorn threw in his direction. He could have sworn Beorn's eyes had somehow turned to chips of ice in that moment.

"We will not discuss that, ever."

"But, Beorn, please let me help."

"This is not negotiable, Gwyn. Bring it up ever again, regardless of where we are or what is happening, and I will be gone and damn the consequences."

Beorn swallowed the last of his ale, pulled his mantle up tight around his body and laid down near the fire, closing his eyes and hoping that the normally elusive sleep would finally find him this night. And, if so, with any luck it would not be filled with nightmares.

CHAPTER 3

The young woman slowly made her way along the quiet early morning streets of London.

The cold wind bit through her thin linen and silk clothing and blew her thick, black hair around her face. Her bare feet were so cold that they burned as she was forced to place them, one after the other, onto the frost covered dirt roadway.

She stopped frequently, hugging her arms tight to her body and trying to hold in what little heat remained, as she looked over her shoulder and listened for any evidence that her pursuers might still be nearby.

But all remained quiet, other than the sounds of the city beginning to wake for the day. Turning a sharp corner, Naomie was startled by a large pig that was rooting through one of the garbage heaps.

She gave it a wide berth and continued on, the smell of wood burning fires now filling the air, as more and more people began to rise and prepare for their day. Her stomach grumbled loudly as the scent of freshly baking bread wafted out through the vent holes of some of the cottages.

But she had no time to think of her hunger just now, she was still not confident that she was free of her pursuers and lost herself further down the winding narrow alleyways.

Eventually, she had no choice but to stop and make time to do something about her feet. Her captors had taken her leather boots from her, hoping to ensure she would not escape, but they were very wrong.

She had often gone barefoot back home and there were hard callouses on the soles of her feet. But she was not used to this climate and even the callouses could not prevent the burning pain from the cold.

The young woman removed a couple of the brightly colored silk scarves from her waist and from her throat and wrapped them as best she could around her feet. They did little to protect her from the frost-bitten ground, but she would have to make do as best she could.

She was not from this city, not even from this country and knew not where to turn next. Her captors were down near the docks where they still held the other women they had taken, so she knew she must avoid those areas at all costs. Following her instincts, she made her way out of the bowels of the city, towards the richer neighborhoods that lie on the outskirts.

The sun was just beginning to make its way up into the sky, allowing Naomie to continue traveling in dim light and away from prying eyes.

She heard someone hurrying up the street and hid behind a large bush along the edge of someone's property. She waited quietly as she watched the servant girl approach.

Violence was not in Naomie's nature, but she would do whatever she had to in order to survive.

As the young servant, Julia, approached, Naomie stepped out in front of her. The girl stopped abruptly, trying to take in the appearance of the young woman in front of her in the dimness of the light around them.

Even with as cold a January as they were having, this woman wore only a skirt made of several layers of thin material, most of them brilliant and colorful. She had on a white, long-sleeved undertunic made of linen which was covered by a sleeveless purple or black vest, she couldn't be sure of the color in the dim light.

Julia had heard stories of a tribe of people who wandered from place to place, homeless and without values. But they lived far away on the continent, not in England, so Julia could not be sure that the girl in front of her was a Romani, even though the various colorful scarves tied around her hair, neck and waist indicated she might be.

But, with all the stories she'd heard about these homeless gypsies, no one ever revealed the fact that they also tied scarves to their feet to use as footwear.

"Good day," Julia said, trying to regain her composure as the other woman continued to stare at her. "Can I help you, Miss?"

"Yes, you can," the girl replied. Her voice was low and tinged with an accent that Julia had never heard before.

"How so?"

"May I have your mantle? And your boots?"

"What? Nay, of course, you may not."

Naomie did not want to plead with this girl, she had neither the time, nor the patience to do so. She could not share any information about being kidnapped and brought to this awful place against her wishes.

She did not know who the girl was or if she would report Naomie's whereabouts to her captives. There was no one that she could trust, including this young servant.

"Please, it would be for the best, for both of us, if you would give them to me."

Julia stared at her in disbelief, hugging the heavy wool mantle tighter around her body. "I am sorry, I cannot help you."

She began to walk past, but Naomie swung around with a sharp rock she had been holding behind her back and hit Julia in the head with it. She caught Julia as she began to sink towards the ground and Naomie pulled her away from the street and closer to the bushes, relieved that Julia was just dazed, but not seriously injured.

Naomie took advantage of her condition and removed the girl's leather boots and let loose the pin securing her mantle. It was heavy, made of wool with a fur lining, squirrel, Naomie suspected by the feel of it. She slid it off Julia's shoulders and hastily ran away with her stolen treasures.

Julia was fortunate to be near her employer's residence and was able to reach it safely before the cold impacted her too severely. Her teeth were chattering noisily, and blood dripped from the wound on the back of her head as she tried to explain her encounter with the unusual gypsy woman.

As soon as they docked in London, Verne and Beorn headed off to round up the requisite mercenaries for their cause. Much to Gwyn's consternation, he had never had an opportunity to give his confession along their way and hurried to Canterbury Cathedral, where he was fortunate enough to be granted a private audience with Archbishop Ralph d'Escures.

The archbishop agreed to hear his confession and once Gwyn provided him with the details of what had happened and why, the Archbishop gave him his penance and then took Gwyn by the arm.

"Walk with me, my son," he said, as he led Gwyn out into the gardens. Gwyn had been there in the past and had seen them in all their spring and summer glory. They were well tended, and it was a place of peaceful contemplation when the flora was in full bloom.

However, that was not the case at this time of year and Gwyn could not fathom why the Archbishop would bring him out to such a desolate location.

Not only was the scenery barren and forlorn, but the temperatures were frigid and the Archbishop wore only his mozzetta, a short cape that covered his shoulders, over a white cassock. The mozzetta had a silk lining and trim which would not have provided any protection from the cold.

"Forgive me for the subterfuge, however, I would not want anyone to overhear our conversation. Tell me more of your mission for the Pope."

"I must collect as many knights as possible to defend the Pope because Henry has threatened violence against him. There are many other clergymen who are older and more experienced than I", Gwyn confided to the Archbishop, "so I am not sure why I was chosen for this mission."

"I do not wish to distress you unduly, Gwyn, however, you are not the first that His Holiness has sent to our shores for this purpose."

"Then he has already been collecting knights for his protection?"

"He has been trying, however, Henry seems to stay always a step ahead of Pope Paschal. He may have a man inside the Vatican, he always knows who is being sent and when.

To the best of my knowledge, none of the priests or bishops sent by the Pope have returned to him. Time is now running out and Henry will be riding into Rome in the very near future.

Pope Paschal and I have not always seen eye to eye on every subject, but I would never wish him harm. It is all up to you, Gwyn, you cannot fail or the Pope's life could be forfeit."

The Archbishop had other duties to attend to and took his leave shortly after that grim declaration.

Gwyn made his way back inside the church and, after reciting his act of contrition and asking for forgiveness for the heinous sin that he had committed, Gwyn stayed in a kneeling position for quite some time.

His head was bowed as he sought guidance, praying for the success of his mission as well as the safety of the Pope and all involved, as he contemplated the heavy weight of the burden he now carried.

Gwyn was so engrossed that he never felt the eyes staring at him from the shadows at the back of the church.

He finished his prayers so that he could meet up with Beorn and then make ready to travel to Wyndymshire. It had been many years since he had last seen his mother and he was grateful that this mission would require them to make their way home once again, albeit just for a short time.

With any luck, Radolf, his oldest brother, could provide the services of some of his own knights. Gwyn had no doubt that he would be able to trust any knight from Wyndymshire, regardless of what Beorn thought.

He made his way to the side-altar in the bay of the nave and lit a candle for his father, gone these many years now.

Gwyn stopped short as he turned to leave the church and found a young woman standing just in front of him, staring at him curiously.

Their eyes met and, not even realizing he was doing it, Gwyn made the sign of the cross.

The girl, her head a cloud of thick, unkempt black hair, actually hissed at him as she grasped her mantle tighter around her shoulders. She had the most mesmerizing eyes that Gwyn had ever encountered.

Even in the dim candlelight of the church, chips of black onyx intermingled with the silver flecks in her eyes and glittered brighter than any gem he'd ever seen. Their allure was emphasized by thick, black lashes and a heavy dark brow, and Gwyn knew not what to make of her.

"Can I help you?"

The girl simply stared at him, doing a quick once-over, noting his ecclesiastical clothing and hairstyle. The simple black robe indicated he was not of high stature within the church and her face relaxed a modicum, but still she hesitated to respond.

"Are you looking for someone?" The girl remained mute. "Do you speak English?"

Naomie nodded, still undecided. She'd been wandering most of the morning and was no closer to finding an answer to her current dilemma. She understood what a church was and, although not a trusting soul, Naomie could only hope that she might find an honest clergyman to help her.

The warmth inside the building was also a welcome change as she had wandered through the enormous structure and contemplated her next move. She had never seen anything like it and was overwhelmed by its beauty.

The church was several stories high and the stained-glass windows alone were breathtaking, the stone columns, the carvings scattered inside and out, all were more than she could ever have conceived.

Gwyn was the first clergyman that she had run across inside the church and she had to decide now if he was the one that she would place her trust in.

"Are you in danger?" Gwyn was not sure why he asked that, but suspected there must be something amiss for the girl to look so afraid, particularly in church.

"Yes, I must leave but have no coin."

Her voice as low, tinged with a pleasant, but unfamiliar, accent.

"I am leaving for northern England, a place called Wyndymshire. I can take you there with me, would that alleviate your danger?"

Once again, she looked him up and down as if assessing what, if any, threat he might be. "I need to cross the water, to go back to my home."

"Where is that?"

"Wherever the rest of my people happen to be."

"Are you Romani?" he asked. More people were filtering in and he did not want their conversation overheard so, before even allowing her to answer, Gwyn took her elbow and escorted her towards the back of the church.

She pulled her elbow out of his grasp before they reached the front doors and he stepped off to the side, out of the way of incoming traffic, so they could continue their conversation without having to stand outside amidst the biting winter wind.

"Are you Romani?" he repeated. He knew of them but thought they mainly resided within the Byzantine Empire, he had never heard of them being in England before.

"I am."

"And how did you get here?"

Her silver eyes continued to watch him studiously, she took her time answering his questions, still not feeling safe with him.

"I was taken."

"By whom?"

She simply shrugged her shoulders. "Does it matter?"

"How did you get away?"

Naomie was done providing him with information. "Can you take me back across the water?"

It was Gwyn's turn to hesitate. As a clergyman, he would do whatever he could to help this lost soul return to her own people, but he was in the middle of a life or death situation and was not sure it would be appropriate to get her involved in the midst of it.

"Where I go there will be much danger. Mayhap, it would be best if you found someone else to help you."

"Do you go back across the water?"

"I will, yes, but I have other duties to attend to first."

"Then I go with you."

"It will be very dangerous and I do not think it is a good idea. Someone else should help you."

"No."

Gwyn was undecided, he hated the thought of leaving her to possibly be taken advantage of or even sold by some bad hat, but he was not sure they could protect her if she came with them.

"Please," Naomie said, for the first time showing a bit of emotion as tears shivered in her silver eyes.

Beorn grabbed a sharp dirk off of his belt and threw it at the large man approaching him. It cut a part through the thick, dark hair along the top of the man's head but caused no other harm and Beorn swore heartily as he prepared for the attack.

He had no time to retrieve his sword from its sheath before the oversized man was upon him, lifting Beorn into the air and dropping him onto a nearby table.

Beorn shook his head to clear it and scrambled around the room, trying to keep other tables between him and the brute that was bent on dispatching him. Sliding under one of them, he managed to grab another of his dirks and ran it through the top of the man's foot as he approached.

The monstrous berk let out such a loud, painfilled roar that men grabbed for their cups of ale that were trembling and threatening to fall off any table in the vicinity, then they all scattered back along the walls, not wanting to be involved in this particular fray, their cups now gripped firmly in their hands.

Beorn stood and looked into the behemoth's grimacing face. "Truce, my friend?"

The man growled and glared at him, then bent over to pull the dirk out of his foot.

Beorn did worry that he might heave said dirk in his direction and considered making his way out the inn, but he needed this man, as well any others he could enlist, so he stood his ground.

"Daegal, I did not know she was your sister. How could I know, how could anyone? How could the likes of you come from the same loins as that beautiful piece of fluff?"

"You treated her like a doxy from the street." Daegal's voice was deep and his dark brown eyes bored down into Beorn's.

"Not exactly," Beorn said, "she came to me, I did not go to her."

Daegal just growled.

"That's long past, friend, and I may have a job for you. Can we let that be in the past or do I look elsewhere for men to give my coin to?"

Daegal hesitated, particularly when he saw the interest from the other men around him at the mention of coins.

"She is married now and lives off in the mountains, no longer sullied because of your randiness. I can listen to what you have to offer."

"Excellent, barmaid, bring my friend and I some ale."

Beorn's eyebrows went up in surprise when Daegal's large paw took him by the throat.

"Ne'er call me friend again, Beorn, or we pick up where we left off."

"Understood." Daegal's grip was so tight on his throat that Beorn barely managed to spit the word out.

Daegal slowly released him, picked up an overturned table and, pulling over a stool, he sat down to hear what Beorn had to offer.

CHAPTER 4

As agreed, the three men met up at the stables located not far from the Palace. Beorn worried about Gwyn being on his own and thought it best for him to remain in the safest part of the city, which is why that particular stable was chosen.

Verne had arrived first to prepare the horses and was waiting impatiently.

Beorn arrived last because the inn was quite a distance from their meeting place, and because he was slightly sloshed. The consumption of much ale had been required for the negotiations between he and Daegal until both were satisfied with the resulting agreement.

Verne and Gwyn were waiting for him with the horses saddled and ready to go.

"Who is that bit of fluff and why is she holding one of our horses?"

Gwyn took a deep breath. "This is Naomie, she was brought here forcibly and will be with us until we can get her back to her own people."

"And who might they be?"

"Romani."

"Romani, what are you doing in this country, lass? You don't belong anywhere near here."

Naomie watched him carefully, knowing he must be the leader of this small band of men. Him, she did not trust a whit and he stunk of ale.

Her silver eyes were narrowed, and her mouth was set as she tried to determine how best to deal with this particular non-gypsy, this gadje.

"I told you," Gwyn began.

"And I asked her, not you," Beorn replied, turning back to meet the girl's glare. Her eyes were like nothing he had seen before, but even they could not dissuade him from his suspicious thoughts.

"They took me and brought me here." She spat on the floor of the stable, showing her contempt for her captors.

"Who are they?"

She simply shrugged her shoulders as she met his gaze.

Beorn continued to watch her as he weighed the pros and cons of taking her along with them.

"I've heard tell that the Romani can steal a shirt from someone's back and be long gone before they even know it is missing. Is that true?"

"We are not thieves."

"If I need you to pick up an item for me," he said slowly, sure she would understand what he was truly asking, "could you do it?"

"Need be, of course, I could." If that was how she would have to pay for this journey, she could pinch anything she was asked too. It was her specialty, but no one need know that.

Beorn continued to watch her for a moment, then nodded his assent, mounted his horse and headed out of the stable, leaving the others to follow along behind him.

The overcast sky also followed for a bit, then the cold, winter rain began. Naomie pulled the hood of her mantle up over her head but her hands were red and raw from holding the reins.

The men also pulled up their hoods, all but Beorn, who kept on as if he hadn't even noticed the change in the weather. He wore chainmail over his tunic, which gave him some additional protection from the wind, but Verne did as well, and he still seemed to suffer from the cold and rain.

Beorn's long, dark hair had rivulets of water dripping from it and even his beard seemed to be filled with water. He did not notice though because his mind was churning restlessly.

"Gwyn," he called, and his brother cantered up beside him.

"Yes?" The rain was starting to taper off, but the drizzle was cold and Gwyn, not used to this inclement weather, felt quite miserable.

"Did the Archbishop have any information to share about our duties?"

"Yes, he did." Beorn looked over at him curiously. "Not good news, brother. Apparently, others have been sent on this mission before but have not returned. The Archbishop intimated that Henry might have spies within the Vatican, telling him who would lead and when these missions would take place."

"I was afraid of that," Beorn said, looking forward but not seeing the roadway in front of him.

"Were you successful in finding some mercenaries?"

"I found one."

"Just one?" The high pitch of Gwyn's voice reflected his dismay.

"A big one, though, a very big one. And he has other friends and will be making inquiries while we go to Wyndymshire. There should be a number enlisted by the time we return."

"Will we have enough?"

"It isn't always the number of men, but the quality of the men that matters, Gwyn."

"I am not a knight, Beorn, but even an exceptional warrior cannot defend against a hundred foe."

"True, little brother, but you, of any of us, should have some faith."

Beorn continued staring ahead, but there was a whisper of a smile on his face now. He reached under his mantle and pulled out a flacket, a small leather flask, and took a long pull of cider from it, feeling the warmth of it spread throughout his body.

Verne rode next to Naomie, a small distance behind the two brothers. He was intrigued by the girl, although he was having trouble getting her to even acknowledge him.

Seeing how red and raw her hands were, Verne peeled off his own gloves and moved his horse over closer to hers, holding them out for her. Naomie eyed him suspiciously and refused to touch them, until he said, "I have another pair, please, take these."

After a sidelong glance at him with her mysterious silver eyes, Naomie took the gloves and slid her cold, chapped hands inside of them. They were leather but the insides were fur-lined, and she sighed in relief at the comfort and warmth she found within them.

Turning towards him once again, she whispered, "Thank you. What is your name?"

"Verne," he replied with a blush, staring down at the frozen ground in front of them.

He was normally more gregarious but she was different than any woman he'd met. He was afraid he might start stuttering and sound like a ninny if he talked too much.

Verne had been trying to surreptitiously study her out of the corner of his eye, she was a stunning beauty, with an oval face and full, pink lips. Her cheeks were also a deep pink hue, at least partially due to the cold, no doubt. The corners of her mouth looked like they'd been rubbed raw somehow but were beginning to heal, and even that could not detract from her beauty.

Her eyes were something unto themselves, they were silver with tiny black chips sprinkled throughout them, and a thick black lining around the outside edge. Most of her dark hair was hidden by the hood of her mantle, but her long, black eyelashes and thick, black brows emphasized her beauty, as well as any emotion that she allowed to show on her face.

The rain became a light drizzle and then stopped completely, but the air still carried a chill that would not leave them.

"He is your king?" Naomie asked, inclining her head towards Beorn.

"He is not a king, he is a knight of the realm."

"A knight?"

"Yes, a warrior."

"He is your leader?"

"I am his squire, I do his bidding." He loved the lilting accent in the girl's soft voice and vowed he could listen to her talk all day.

"He has wives?"

"No, he did have one, but she died."

"How?"

What a blunt lass, she is, Verne thought, glad she had asked him and not Beorn. It was a subject he would not allow any discussion on.

"I will tell you, but do not mention it around Sir Beorn, understand?"

She lifted a dark eyebrow at him, then nodded.

"He had a beautiful wife, lovely woman, her name was Anna. He bought a property in Normandy when he met her, so he could stop traveling as a mercenary and could stay in one place and share his life with her."

"She did not want to stay?"

"Of course, she did. She cared for Beorn more than words can say."

Verne had loved Anna like a second mother, his own having died when he was very young, and his eyes got misty at the thought of her.

Naomie looked over at him again, waiting for the rest of the story.

"She died giving birth to his first child."

"Did the child die, as well?"

"No, it did not."

"Where is the child now?"

"He sent it off to live with another nobleman's family. He could not keep it around him, it reminded him too much of Anna."

The look of disgust on Naomie's face did not exactly surprise Verne, it was the same reaction as that of many others.

No one, save himself, was able to understand how deeply Beorn was devastated when he lost Anna, and so they could never understand his actions towards his infant child.

"Family is the only thing that is important in life," Naomie said. "I cannot fathom how a father could do such a thing."

"It is not for you to judge and please do not ever mention it around him."

Her eyes narrowed as she turned forward to stare at Beorn's broad back.

"He is the leader, the other a priest. What are you?"

"My father sent me to be Sir Beorn's squire many years ago, when I was a young lad. He has trained me well and I anticipate being knighted shortly."

Verne looked on Beorn as his own father and had, indeed, learned many things from him, but sometimes questioned whether or not the time might ever come when he would actually be knighted.

Currently, he acted more as a man servant than a squire, and he could only hope that they would run into enough trouble on this mission to let him show Beorn that he was worthy to be a knight.

Verne was tall and slim, with light blond hair and golden-brown eyes. He had no problem getting a lass' attention when he wanted it, but this Romani girl was proving to be quite vexing to him. From the look on her face, she was obviously much more intrigued by Beorn, than by him.

Naomie had already dismissed Verne in her own mind and, as he suspected, was thinking about Beorn, although not in the way he assumed.

Know your enemies. Naomie had been taught that at a very early age. Her tribe was always traveling, they had been far and wide and, in many places, they were mistrusted and mistreated. The only way to survive was to know who you were dealing with and what to expect from them.

Naomie was still learning about these gadje, but now she knew what could hurt their leader the most. She would keep the secret but, need be, she would use it like a dagger to bury into his heart.

They were forced to sleep out of doors that night and Beorn led them into a hilly area to get set up. The path to get there was narrow and sharply winding.

"Verne, you can start the fire, I'll try to find some game."

Once the fire was roaring, Gwyn, Naomie and Verne sat as close to it as they could bear, the dampness had seeped into their very bones, it seemed.

Naomie propped up some long sticks on one side of the fire and hung her mantle from it, steam immediately beginning to rise as the moisture escaped and it began to dry out.

Gwyn handed her a wool blanket when he saw her begin to shiver violently on the other side of the fire. There was no more precipitation, but the temperature was dropping, and the ground would most likely be covered in frost by morning.

Beorn was gone quite a long time and Gwyn made use of the time by closing his eyes and saying his evening prayers.

Once Beorn finally did arrive, he handed his reins to Verne and the dead rabbits to Naomie to finish cleaning and to put on a spit over the fire.

At first, she refused to take them and simply glared at him but, when even her own stomach grumbled, she knew they all needed food. Conceding to his wishes this time, Naomie grabbed the rabbits from his hands and began to prepare them.

"We'll keep the horses saddled tonight and everyone needs to rest lightly. Methinks, we may have visitors before the sun shines in the morn."

Gwyn's eyes opened wide with fear as he glanced around, although all he could see was darkness.

Beorn tried to reassure him. "They are still a distance away and may lay up for the evening. If not, if they choose to have a bash at us tonight, we must be prepared, is all. Verne and I will take turns watching.

Do not concern yourself, Gwyn. If trouble appears, we'll be ready."

Beorn then turned his attention to Naomie as she arranged the rabbits onto spits and placed them over the fire. There was no denying that her beauty was stunning but, being of a suspicious nature, he wondered how it was that she came upon Gwyn, rather than anyone else that might have come to her aid.

Gypsies roamed closer to the Kingdom of Germany's borders than they did to England and he couldn't rule out the possibility that she had been sent to spy on them.

Naomie felt Beorn's dark blue eyes following her every movement and turned towards him, her eyes reflecting the flames of the fire and her face unreadable as she met his gaze.

"Tell me about your people," Beorn said, his eyes still holding hers prisoner. He admired the fearlessness that she exuded and wondered if it was real or just for show.

"What of them?" she asked.

"I'm not familiar with the Romani people, I've heard very little, only that they have nimble fingers and are in league with the devil."

"Yes," Naomie replied, noting Gwyn's horrified expression with amusement, "I've heard that, as well."

"It's not the truth then?"

"Nay, not even close. We are a family, a large family that travels together, and people do not even try to understand who we are."

"Doesn't one family ever go their own way?"

"Sometimes," she acknowledged. "Only a few wagons might travel together depending on where we are. Some villagers are scared when there are too many of us together.

Yet, when there are not enough of us, sometimes it is our lives that are at risk."

She looked across the fire at him again and the flames made the silver chips in her eyes glitter like stars and Beorn found himself completely mesmerized by them.

"If you have no set path of where you will go, how do join back up with the others in your tribe?"

"Each tribe has its own signal. Its own way of pointing it's members in the right direction."

"What is yours?"

"We take small sticks and wrap them in brightly colored ribbons and leave them at a crossroads, pointing in the direction we are heading. Eventually, we all find our way back together."

"How do you support yourselves?" Verne asked, trying to get that scintillating gaze fixed on himself, rather than on Beorn.

Naomie did not play into his hands, however, instead she turned her attention back to the rabbits, turning them to assure they were cooked through properly.

"We have many ways of earning coin, most of the men craft items made of metal and sell them. We also have bear-keepers and snake charmers, which the gadje expect to see from us, being as simple and evil as we are."

She raised her eyes to meet Beorn's again at that point.

"What of the women? What do they sell?" he asked, and even across the fire, he could see the anger that flashed onto her face, but it remained for just moments until she was able to get her emotions in check again.

"We are fortune tellers and we sell herbs and magic amulets."

Gwyn made the sign of the cross and whispered a silent prayer.

"I, myself, am a drabardi."

"What is that?" Verne asked.

"A seer, a clairvoyant, I can tell events of the past and the future."

She saw the smile that threatened to break out on Beorn's face and was not offended. Few people understood the divination abilities of she and others in their tribe. What people did not understand, they laughed at.

"Can you divine you own future?"

"The Roma never use our divination abilities with our own people, only with the gadje."

"That wouldn't be because it's all bent, would it?"

"There are many reasons, the most important being that there is no need. We follow our laws and our rules. We live clean lives and it is the unclean that contaminate others and cause misfortune."

"How do you divine our futures?"

"There are many ways, many signs that a person gives without even knowing they are doing so, and the universe itself gives us signs. If we do not heed them, it is to our own peril."

Gwyn cleared his throat loudly. "Naomie, I know that you believe everything that you are saying, and I hope, before our journey has ended, that you and I can speak more about many things, God in particular. For now, please desist in talking about your powers of divination any further. It goes against everything that I believe, and I am very uncomfortable with the discussion."

The men all watched Naomie closely, wondering how she would respond.

"Father, I respect your beliefs, but I am curious as to why it is that no one feels they have to respect mine?"

A spark was set off in the fire, drawing Naomie's attention, and she turned back to attend the roasting meat.

There was no further discussion, none of the men would pick up the gauntlet she had thrown down, and Naomie now turned to study the three men.

If a wood fire makes any kind of noise, it means a quarrel is in the offing, and she wondered which of them it would involve. In the back of her mind, she suspected that it may be her and Father Gwyn at some point soon.

It wasn't long before the three rabbits were ready. They were each on their own roasting stick and Naomie handed one of the sticks to the three men and sat back and waited for them to eat their fill.

Neither Gwyn nor Verne noticed that she had not kept any for herself and eagerly tore into the meat.

Beorn did not know what she was playing at now but ripped off a hind leg for himself and walked over to the girl. Her eyes were large with wonder as he handed the bulk of the carcass to her.

"Thank you," she whispered, and with a nod of acknowledgement, he made his way back to the other side of the fire.

CHAPTER 5

It took a long while for Gwyn to control his shivering and finally fall asleep, and it felt as if he had just done so when Beorn was shaking his shoulder and whispering for him to wake up.

Verne had the horses prepared and was stepping onto the last of the embers. Naomie was walking back from behind a clump of bushes and seemed completely at ease as she mounted her horse.

Gwyn hastily took care of his own needs and then joined the others, quietly assuring God that, although he couldn't perform his usual prayers this morn, he would make up for that once they'd reached the safety of Wyndymshire, if he managed to keep his horse under him until then.

Verne led the way and Beorn took up the rear of the motley group as they meandered down the steep trail. At one particularly narrow area, he stopped and took out several caltrops from his bag and scattered them on the ground behind his horse. The small spiked pieces of metal were crafted of sharp nails twisted together, with at least one sharp edge always facing upward.

The Germans were still a bit of a distance away, as far he could tell from the faint sounds of their horses and clinking of their chainmail, but this would slow them up even further. It was still dark enough that they would not spot the caltrops lying in their path before some of their horses stepped on them. Anything he could do to slow down the brigands would be an asset.

He quickly caught up with the others and let out a low whistle. Verne heard and understood its meaning, picking up his pace as much as he dared on the treacherous path. The sky was lightening but still the sun had not broken the horizon and the ruts in the pathway were frozen, causing the horses to stumble and slide periodically.

Beorn was pleased to see that the girl was able to handle her mount, but he worried about Gwyn. When his brother's horse stumbled, Gwyn was almost unseated, and this hard ground could cause a serious injury should he make unexpected contact with it.

The wound from Gwyn's prior altercation had not yet healed completely and they could not risk him sustaining more injuries.

They all breathed a sigh of relief when they hit flat land. None of them had spoken, not wanting their voices to carry, but when Beorn heard horses whinnying up high on the trail, he knew that this was their opportunity to put as much distance between them as possible.

"Now, Verne," he called out, "have that horse run as if all the hounds of hell were on its tail."

Verne obeyed and the four of them sped across the open ground. Tension still ran high, the area was level, although not completely flat, and there was always the risk of one of the horses stepping into a hole or onto an uneven piece of frozen ground.

They ran hard until the horses' chests were covered in foamy sweat and Beorn knew they must rest or lose them. He let out another sharp whistle and Verne pulled back on his reins, slowing his horse to a walk as he looked back at Beorn for further directions.

Gwyn hadn't realized he'd be doing that and his horse almost ran over Verne's, just barely swerving to his right and avoiding a collision. The horse swerved so sharply that Gwyn kept going straight and landed in an ungainly pile next to the hooves of Verne's horse.

Verne quickly moved it away so that Gwyn was no longer within range of its great hooves and Beorn shook his head in disgust. Fortunately, the horses were tired so he had no trouble catching Gwyn's. Had he not, someone would have had to ride double and that could have seriously affected their chances of escape from the Germans.

The riders were almost as tired as their mounts. Naomie flopped onto the hard, cold ground, grateful for even a few minutes of rest.

Beorn stared back at where they had just come from for a few minutes but saw nothing amiss. The scattered trees blocked him from seeing very far, so it did not ease his mind overly much.

He grabbed some chunks of bread from his bag and tossed a piece to Gwyn and Verne. He walked over to Naomie and squatted down beside her, holding out a portion for her.

"You've done well," he said. "I was worried that you might hold us up, but your horsemanship is excellent, and you are no chattermag, you know when to keep your mouth shut. It is good."

Her silver eyes met the dark blue of his as she reached out to take the bread from him. She didn't speak, just nodded her acknowledgement of his words.

Gwyn, on the other hand, had much to say. "Beorn, how far back are they? How much longer till we reach Wyndymshire? Will we make it before they catch up to us?"

"Rest easy, Gwyn," Beorn said, clasping his brother on the shoulder. "Time will tell and, methinks, you must have it in good with the man up above because someone has kept us from breaking our necks so far. I can only assume he will continue to keep us safe whilst we have you with us."

"Can you tell how far away they are?" Verne asked.

"Nay, I cannot see them, and the wind is picking up and blowing the wrong way, so I cannot hear them. Some of their horses would have injured their feet so they could not all ride full out as we did. We should have a bit of a lead on them, although they may have sent some ahead of the others."

He grabbed a handful of oats from his bag and held it out for his horse, who ate them greedily. Then he walked the stallion over to the small stream babbling nearby and allowed him a long drink of the cold water.

"If you intend to make the rest of the journey safely, I'd suggest you do likewise and care for your mounts."

The three of them followed his example and then they got ready to continue on.

"Shall we head into one of the villages?" Verne asked.

"I've been thinking on that but I'm not sure it's a safe bet," Beorn replied, pulling at the hair covering his chin. "I worry it would give them the time they need to reduce the distance between us. And we cannot trust anyone, we could be sold out by just a few coin."

"We will spend another night outside in the cold then?"

"I fear so, but dark comes early this time of year. We will cover as much ground as we can without taxing our mounts overmuch. Once the sun sets, we'll stop and eat, rest for a couple of hours and then be on our way again. If we travel in the darkness, we should reach Wyndymshire sometime in the morn."

There was no disagreement, no argument, but the drooping heads and slumping shoulders spoke volumes about his fellow travelers' frame of mind.

Beorn smiled to himself as he got back up onto his horse, thinking back to many of the missions he'd been on in the past. Compared to them, this ordeal was of no consequence, but he would do his best to be patient, after all, they were not knights and could not be expected to respond any differently than they were.

They continued on throughout that afternoon with only one circumstance arising to delay them.

Verne was still leading the way and Gwyn and Naomie rode side by side after him. Beorn brought up the rear, staying back a bit and frequently stopping to check behind them to be sure the Germans were still nowhere in sight.

After scanning the distant horizon at one point, Beorn turned and his horse almost ran into the back of Naomie's.

"What is amiss?" he asked. The three of them had come to a complete halt and he was unable to see any reason for it.

Verne was clearly agitated, as he replied, "She will not go this way."

"What?"

"Naomie will no longer go forward on this road, and it is the only road which will take us to Wyndymshire."

Beorn got down off his horse and stretched his weary muscles, letting the stallion graze on what little he could find to forage.

Then he extended his hand and helped Naomie down. Her face was set, her head thrown back and her glittering eyes sent him a challenge that he would have loved to respond too, had they not been in such a hurry.

"What is amiss?"

"There is a dead crow in the roadway."

Beorn turned his head and saw the dead bird just ahead of the horses. "Yes, there is. What concern is that of yours?"

"It is an evil omen, we must turn back." She had reached into the pocket of her silken skirts and pulled out a small item wrapped in a colorful scarf. Beorn couldn't see what it was, but she held it tightly in both hands.

"I don't believe in evil omens, a man's fate lies only in his own hands. And today, our danger lies behind us with the German knights, so we must continue on."

"We cannot, we will all be in danger if we go forward."

"You are being foolish and we have no time for it."

She felt her ire rising and was about to spit on the ground at his feet when she realized that this was the quarrel foretold last night and restrained herself, raising her eyes to his.

Somehow, she must get him to see reason, only bad things would happen should they continue on past the dead crow. Of that, she had no doubt, and so she would forgo even her own pride in the hopes she could convince him of how important this was.

"Crows are very powerful, spiritual creatures, they are exceptionally wise and intelligent. They are great portents of the future and to find one dead in your path means grave danger ahead. You must trust me on this."

She reached out and grabbed his muscular forearm and he jumped at the intensity of the jolt that ran up his arm in response to her touch, feeling as if he'd been struck by lightning. "Please?"

Beorn was frustrated, by his reaction to her touch and by the situation itself. But the fear he saw in her eyes was real and, even though he knew it was all foolishness, he felt compelled to ease her mind.

He looked behind them and saw no riders within sight, then turned to scout the area around them.

"Verne," he called out, pointing to a copse of trees to their right, "we will go through there and circle around back to the road. It will only take us a bit out of our way."

"But, M'lord," Verne began, snapping his mouth closed when Beorn turned his fiery gaze upon him. "As you wish."

"Is that satisfactory?" he asked Naomie, as he went over to help her back onto her horse.

"We shall see." She shrugged her shoulders and opened the mantle so she could stuff the little package back into a pocket.

"What is that?"

She hesitated, then unwrapped the item and held it out in the palm of her hand.

"Is that a rabbit's foot?"

"Yes, I took it from one of the ones we cooked last evening."

"Why on God's earth would you do such a thing?"

"It provides protection from evil spirits."

Beorn looked down at it one more time before she wrapped it back up and put it in her pocket. Shaking his head, he mumbled, "I hope it's a strong one because things are just starting to get interesting."

He helped her up onto her horse and then mounted his own. He sat for a moment, watching her ride after Verne, then realized Gwyn was still there and had a most curious look on his face as he stared at Beorn.

"You have something to say?"

"More an observation."

"Of what?"

"God's little miracles still always tend to surprise me." Gwyn could not hide the grin on his face.

"Your God had nothing to do with my decision."

"But a dead crow in the road did?"

"Get knotted, Gwyn," Beorn replied, then kicked his horse and cantered off towards the others.

Several meters back, a German knight, tall, blonde and blue-eyed was staring in their direction, although he could not actually see them from that distance.

He was angry, very angry, and his jaw was set so hard it was surprising he did not crack a tooth. Several men were now without mounts due to the caltrops thrown in their path on the mountainside.

Those few horses who stepped on the metal nails were lame and now useless. He could not have knights double up on one horse so the others were forced to walk and would seriously deplete his supply of men.

They could not wait for them and he'd given them instructions to buy, or steal if necessary, any horses that they came across and to catch up as soon as possible.

He knew Beorn Wyndym well. He'd fought with, and against the man, and respected him as a knight, if not as a person.

Beorn would head to his home, would try to enlist loyal knights from that area to bring back to Rome. Jakob had no intention of allowing that to happen.

King Henry had tasked him with the most important assignment of preventing any additional interference between him and Pope Paschal until the coronation was completed.

Jakob had nullified all of the Pope's attempts thus far and he would not allow Beorn to succeed where all of the others before him had failed. But he also knew that he would have to dispatch them before they reached Wyndymshire.

Once there, under the protection of Baron Radolf, the upper hand would go to Beorn. Jakob and his knights would have to return to London and hope Beorn had not retained more knights than they could quickly dispatch before allowing them to head back to the continent.

Jakob's steely blue eyes hardened as he pulled his mantle tighter around his body to ward off the miserable English winter wind and, spurring on his horse, he knew he would not stop until Beorn's head was in his hands.

Jakob's plans did not come to fruition and Beorn's straggly band managed to enter Wyndymshire about mid-morning the following day.

Beorn was having a heated discussion with the young knight at the gate of the castle when Radolf appeared to see who had arrived and what the fuss was about.

"Beorn," he said, a crooked smile breaking out across his face, "is that you?"

Beorn looked over his way and could not help but smile back at his big brother. "It is, Radolf, it is."

"Well, I'll be jiggered," he replied. "It's been far too long since we've seen you. What brings you to Wyndymshire?"

"I must blame it all on that gawdelpus over there."

Beorn indicated his chin over towards where Gwyn had slid off the back of his horse, so exhausted that he had to lean against it in order to keep his feet. He was excited to be home again, but so bone-tired it was difficult to tell by looking at him.

"Gwyn, that can't be you, is it? If it wasn't for those blue eyes under that ring of hair, I'd never have known."

"Radolf, it is so good to clap eyes on you again." He took a few halting steps towards Radolf, who's smile dropped from his face as he hurried over to his brother.

"What's wrong?"

"We rode through much of the night and this morn, Gwyn is not used to such hard riding and is just knackered. He needs some food and some rest."

Radolf looked back at Beorn. "Is there trouble brewing?"

"Aye, we'll have to talk about it. I was trying to impress that upon your young knight here, but he wouldn't listen to me."

"What do you need?"

"It is what you need to do. This wide reinforced gate needs to come down, now. We may have company from Germany, anon, and if they show, there will be quite a kerfuffle."

"Lonnie, call the other knights to arms and get the villagers inside the gates and have it lowered. Get some of our men up on the barbican with their bows. Have them sound the signal should they see the German knights approaching."

Radolf waved over a couple of boys from the stables and had them take the horses to be fed and cared for.

"This is Verne, my squire, and this is, what is your name, girl?"

The silver eyes flared in anger and her lips pressed together in mute protest.

"She is Naomie," Gwyn interjected, trying to keep their conflict to a minimum. "We are helping to get her back to her own country."

"Is she the reason for the Germans?" Radolf asked.

"Nay, that's a different situation and we're just lumbered up with her until we can get her back home. Gwyn came upon her and couldn't say no."

"Come inside, all of you," Radolf said, looking curiously at the little group. "We'll get you some food and rest."

Beorn grabbed hold of Naomie's arm as she started forward.

"Listen, girl, Naomie," he granted her that when she turned to him with daggers flashing from her eyes and tried, unsuccessfully, to pull her arm from his ironclad grip, "this is the home of my mother and my family. I will allow no disrespect to them, from anyone, do you understand?"

"What do you expect that I will do?"

"Mayhap, nothing untoward, just know that I will be watching you and, at the end of the day, should you pinch anything that doesn't belong to you, I'll throw you out on your arse and let the Germans have you."

He loosened his grip and Naomi pulled her arm away. She stared up into his eyes, the blue glittering so darkly that his true thoughts were hidden, but she knew that he meant every word he said.

She had no intention of stealing anything but, sometimes old habits did take over. Naomie realized she was not dealing with a simpleton here and, therefore, would watch her manners while at the castle.

Stepping back, away from Beorn's broad, muscular body, she turned and walked away without responding.

He watched her go, impressed that, even as tired as she was, her body moved in such a way that you could hear the silk skirts under her cloak undulating seductively.

Word had made its way to Regan and she was waiting for them in the Great Hall, her face lit up with joy because her two boys were home again.

She was hugging Gwyn tightly when Beorn walked into the room, and he could see how deep the lines on her face had become and how grey now washed throughout her red hair.

Naomie watched Beorn's face closely and realized that she now knew another of his weaknesses, the depth of his feelings for his mother. That was as it should be for any man, however, she still wasn't sure what kind of man he was or what gave his life value. This was just another nugget of information to be treasured and used if need be.

Giving Gwyn a kiss on his cheeks, Regan released him and turned towards Beorn, tears of joy glittering in her beautiful emerald eyes.

Beorn strode over and wrapped her in his arms, bending down to kiss the top of her head.

"Mother, it is so good to see you. Are you well?"

"I am, and especially well today. What brings you to us?"

"It is not a pleasant visit, I fear. And we cannot stay long."

"Long enough to eat and get some rest, I hope?"

"Of course," he replied, looking over at his younger brother and knowing he would never make it back to London without a little respite.

"Becca, is that you hiding behind Radolf?" he asked.

"It is," she replied, her thick brown hair tied back and her large brown eyes still making her look like a doe ready to run at any moment. "Welcome, all."

Beorn pulled her into his embrace and then turned towards his fellow travelers. "I would like you all to meet, Verne, my trusted squire, and this is Naomie."

He hesitated, not sure of how to introduce her so Gwyn interjected once again.

"She is our new friend and we are helping her find her way back home."

Naomie's eyes softened as she inclined her head in a brief nod of gratitude in his direction.

For the next few minutes complete mayhem ruled as the guards sounded the call to arms. Beorn and Radolf headed outside to be sure the gates had been secured and that everyone was safe.

The gate was not yet lowered and Radolf demanded to know why.

One of his knights, Milo, responded, although he found it difficult to hide his frustration while speaking. "Your brother and your son rode out and have not yet returned."

"When?"

"Moments ago, they thought to look to find the Germans and let us know what to anticipate."

"The plucky little beggars," Beorn said, not bothering to hide his feelings. "Let me go after them, if the Germans catch them, we're all jiggered."

"Fine," Radolf said, the word barely understandable through his clenched jaw. He turned to call to the stable hand but before the words came out of his mouth, his son, Grant, and youngest brother, Draco, came galloping through the gateway.

The knights immediately began dropping the gate and Godwin, one of the archers along the barbican yelled down.

"They look to be heading off, we'll watch longer to be sure, but they must know they are no threat to anyone inside the castle."

"Thank you, Godwin, let us know if anything changes. You," he pointed to his son and then to his brother, "and you, get to the Keep. I will speak with you alone."

CHAPTER 6

Radolf took Draco and Grant off to the side of the Great Hall, out of earshot of the others, or so he thought.

Draco was twenty and two and Grant just a year younger than he, and they had always been more like brothers than nephew and uncle.

Beorn accepted a cup of ale as he settled into a chair along the Lord's table, up on the dais along the front of the room. He watched Radolf with a warm heart, he had always looked up to his older brother, had always wanted to be more like him, but finally had come to terms with the fact that they were not forged of the same metal.

Radolf was born to be the Lord of the Manor and had an innate sense of justice. Beorn was, and had always been, a knight, a warrior, he did not have the diplomacy or patience required of a Baron or any type of noble, and that suited him just fine.

He continued to watch his brother, whose hands were gesturing hither and yon as he expressed his anger at Draco and Grant. Both boys were just two piss-pots high when he had last seen them, and he was pleasantly surprised at the men they had become.

Time had dulled Radolf's hair and now it was littered with a few grey hairs in amongst the red ones. From the side, he bore an uncanny resemblance to their sire and Beorn could almost believe it was Calder off in the corner scolding the two young men.

He had only met his youngest brother a handful of times and did not know him well. Unlike the other men of the family, Draco looked more like his mother than his father. His eyes were a piercing green and the winter sun coming in through the small window openings reflected the red highlights of his light brown hair.

Draco was not as tall or as broad as Radolf, or of Grant, but he seemed fit and healthy enough. Grant's physique was similar to Radolf's, however, his features also favored his mother, Becca, and his dark brown hair hung long around his face, almost covering his soulful brown eyes.

"Pardon?" he said, as he pulled his eyes away from the little group of men and turned towards his mother.

"I only wanted to tell you how sorry I am about Anna."

Beorn caught his breath and put his finger to her lips.

"Thank you, Mother. I do not speak of what happened, so please do not mention it again."

Regan felt a squeeze around her heart as she recognized the devastating pain that suddenly filled her son's eyes. She understood the agony of losing someone you love dearly, but his refusal to even acknowledge her death was not healthy and caused Regan great concern.

She patted his hand and turned away, honoring his request, but saying a quiet prayer that he would someday come back from his loss and not let himself become hard and jaded because of it.

The serving girls brought their meals just then, so Radolf and the others returned to the table. Beorn could tell Radolf was curious about the purpose of their visit but decided to wait until he could speak with him alone to discuss relieving him of some of his knights.

Regan noticed that Naomie had not yet touched any of the food on her trencher.

"Are these dishes unfamiliar to you?" she asked.

The girl gave her a sideways glance and nodded her head, remembering Beorn's warning about being polite to his mother.

"Please try them, I think you'll enjoy the taste."

Naomie hesitated again, then responded, "But the men have not yet finished."

Regan looked at her curiously. "No, they have not, but we all eat together, at the same time."

"Is that not disrespectful to your menfolk? Our women and children always wait until the men have their fill, then we get what's left."

"That's horrid," Regan said, biting back any further comments when she saw the hurt look on Naomie's face and realized it was not her place to judge their customs.

"Beorn hasn't been making you wait to eat last on this journey, has he?"

"No, but we only made brief stops and he provided me with the food. I assumed the men had already taken what they needed, but that is not the case here today."

Regan smiled tenderly at the girl, wondering at what other curious rituals she and her people shared. "That is not our way, please join us and enjoy your food while it is still warm."

Naomie hesitated for a moment, but she was very hungry and finally gave in and began eating.

Regan then turned her attention to Gwyn, who began sharing story after story about the goings on at the Vatican. As tired as he was, he came full alive while talking about his Pope, his church and his fellow clergymen.

While he took a break to pop a few pieces of cheese into his mouth, Regan turned to Beorn and asked, "Shall I send word to Synne and her family, as well as Lora, to come see you? We so rarely have an opportunity to do so."

"We would love to see them, but I fear there is no time for that, Mother. Those men that followed us will be waiting once we leave and they will only increase in number as time goes by."

"Beorn, can you tell us now what this all about?" Radolf asked, his curiosity finally getting the best of him as the meal came to an end.

Beorn looked around the table and saw how exhausted Naomie and Gwyn both looked. Verne was holding up well, but sleep would be a benefit to him, as well.

"Mayhap, you and I can speak together whilst my fellow travelers get some rest?"

"Of course," Becca said, standing and waving over the serving girls. She whispered orders into their ears, and they scampered off to be sure the visitors' chambers were ready for their guests.

Everyone stood and made their way from the table except Draco, Radolf, Verne, Beorn and Grant. Regan left hesitantly, she wanted to know what was happening, however, the men did not appear to want her input on whatever this particular issue was.

She took Naomie's arm and started to lead the girl down one of the hallways. Naomie's silver eyes widened and her lips pressed together, she stood stock still, refusing to move.

"What is it, dear?" Regan asked.

"Naomie," Beorn called out, and the silver eyes slid his way, "she means no harm. She is only taking you to the guest chamber. Be respectful to my mother."

Naomie was quite a bit taller than Regan and she turned her eyes back to the older woman, but still would not move.

Regan tactfully withdrew her hand from the girl's arm and said, "Please, come this way. We've prepared a bath and we can have your clothing washed for you while you rest."

Naomie had spent her entire life living out of doors, the only roof over her head was the canvas of her family's wagon. She felt stifled, like she could not breath properly within these strong, stone walls.

The men all watched her curiously and, after seeing Beorn nod in the direction his mother was trying to take her, Naomie gave in and walked further into the maze of these stone walls, trying to control her feelings of being a trapped animal.

"Verne, mayhap, you can go along with them, put Naomie at ease a little and get some rest yourself."

"Aye, Milord," he said, hurrying to catch up with the two women.

"So, tell me."

"Radolf, I am here to ask a favor of you. Gwyn," he smiled, assuming his brother was already fast asleep in bed somewhere within the Keep, "has been given a task, by the Pope, and I am providing him assistance."

"What type of task?"

"The Pope has issues with the German, King Henry, and fears he will be invading Rome shortly with many men. The Pope cannot grant what Henry wants and fears for his own safety. He needs protection."

"Doesn't he have his own army of knights?" Draco asked.

"He does, but it is nowhere near large enough to hold off Henry's."

Radolf took a sip of ale and raised his eyes towards the soot singed ceiling as he thought about what Beorn had shared.

"How many do you need?"

"As many as can be spared. I've gotten the word out for mercenaries in London. We'll collect them on the way back through."

"Why mercenaries? I can make arrangements for several other Barons to provide knights."

"No," Beorn said, shaking his head and then draining his cup, "there is treachery afoot and we do not know who can be trusted."

"Yet, you trust mercenaries?" Grant asked, his eyes clouded with confusion.

"They are loyal to coin, boy, they do not care which noble wins, only which is paying them."

"I'll go with you," Draco said.

"Are you a knight?"

"I am," he responded proudly.

"As am I, and I will go, as well," Grant said, if his uncle was going, so was he, or so he thought anyway.

"No, Grant," Radolf said, shaking his head slowly, "you will not be going. Draco is a man and can make his own decisions. He is a knight and it is time for him to make his own way in the world. Your duties are here."

"What are you talking about? I can fight."

"Of course, you can, but you are my heir and your obligation is to Wyndymshire. You are tasked with the protection of this community and you will be the Baron here when I am no longer able."

"That is not fair." His chin lifted and his jaw was set as his brown eyes stared into his father's.

"Grow up, Grant. Life is not fair, you do what needs be done."

"Are there others here that you can spare?" Beorn asked, hoping to dissolve a bit of tension between father and son.

"I will go speak with my knights. We have a few young, newly knighted men that are anxious to dip their swords in some blood, so I will let you know later this day. Would you like to rest now?"

Beorn had never been one that needed much sleep, but he knew the next few weeks would be difficult and that he should take advantage of this opportunity.

"Aye, what room shall I take?"

"Down the main hallway to the right, there are several guest chambers, take any one of them that is empty."

Beorn ambled slowly along the hallway, the sounds of the laughter from his youth echoing in his mind as he recalled happy times here in the Keep. He and his sister, Synne, had been close in age and together they had been little baskets, always getting into trouble.

He suspected that Draco and Grant had been of a similar ilk and would have been quite a handful in their youth. Mayhap, that was why Radolf was ready to send off Draco, but not his son.

He reached the guest rooms off a little used corridor and the first room that he came to was empty so he entered and struggled to remove his chainmail, having a much easier time after that while doffing his undertunic and tunic.

Wearing only his linen pants, he walked over to the washbowl and ewer and vigorously rubbed the water over his face and hair. Shaking his head like a dog, he turned when a servant girl stepped unexpectedly into the room.

"Pardon, Milord," she said, turning her eyes to the floor. "I was asked to pick up the clothing from you and your friends and wash it while you sleep."

"Fine," Beorn said, indicating his clothing in a pile on the floor.

"Hold up," he said, as she walked towards the doorway. Beorn slid out of the filthy linen pants and tossed them to her, ignoring her wide-eyed gaze as she looked over his very fit, naked body before hurrying out of the room.

He blew out the candles and, although there was a warm fire blazing in the corner fireplace, with the wooden shutters closed over the windows, the room remained dim. The thick featherbed seemed to be calling to him and Beorn surrendered to it, climbing in and pulling the warm blankets over his tired and sore body.

Regan had been very patient and kind to Naomie, making sure she had a nice warm bath waiting for her in the bathing chamber.

"Will you be able to find your way back to the bedchamber that I showed you, once you've finished here?"

"Yes, thank you."

Naomie ran her fingers through the warm water in the bath and tried to relax. She waited until Regan was gone and then removed her clothing and slid gracefully down into the wooden tub, sighing loudly as she did so.

She soaked in the warm water for a long while, disturbed only when one of the servant girls arrived to pick up her clothing.

"Stop," Naomie said sharply, thinking the girl was trying to steal them.

The girl's hand froze as she was reaching for the colorful skirt and she looked over to meet Naomie's brittle stare.

"Mistress Regan has asked me to collect all of your clothing and wash it, so it has time to dry while you are resting."

Naomie still did not trust these people, but she looked at the pile of filthy clothing and swallowed her misgivings. Looking back into the girl's eyes, she nodded her agreement and the girl swiped up the remaining clothes and hurried from the room.

Naomie stayed in the tub until the water cooled off. The servants had left pieces of linen for her to dry herself off with and to wrap around her nakedness as she made her way back to the room Regan had originally escorted her to.

The room was lit only by a fire and she made her way to the little table that Regan had pointed out to her. Reaching for the brush that it held, she gratefully ran it through her long, thick hair. It had been some time since she was able to relax and pamper herself in such a way.

Naomie wondered what her family was thinking right now. She had disappeared from their lives so completely, she feared they might assume she was dead. Now that she realized the danger that she had exposed herself to, Naomie felt foolish for running away as she had.

She looked forward to returning to her family, to the life that she knew and was comfortable with. But her eyes clouded as she slowly stroked her hair, the signs were not yet clear to her, but from what she had been able to discern, they seemed to be pointing her in a direction far from home and family.

Naomie knew that she had to be honest with herself and acknowledge that maybe the signs were clear, but the confusion lay in her own mind.

She had no place else to go so, if this knight and this priest could get her close enough to find them and, if old, fat Ninga still wanted her as his bride, she would relent this time. No matter how distasteful the thought of it was, there was no other choice for her.

With a deep sigh and a heavy heart, Naomie set the brush down on the table and turned towards the bed. Throwing back the covers, she slid onto it before pulling them back over her naked body.

Naomi stretched out her long legs but froze when her toes came into contact with the well-muscled calf of another's leg, which was already firmly established on the bed. She rolled over to find out who it was but could only see his broad, muscular back.

Sitting up in bed, holding the blanket over her breasts to cover them, Naomie was unsure of what she should do. Was this a trap? Were they making an offering of her as payment for the food and bath?

With a loud snore, the man rolled over and, even in the dim light cast by the fire, Naomie could see that it was Beorn who was sharing her bed, leaving her even more confused than before. If he was going to take her against her will, why had he waited until now? And why did he believe that she would simply lie here and wait for him to wake up?

Or mayhap, she considered, there was no danger. Mayhap, there were simply not enough beds for all of them to have their own. That had happened many times with her own tribe and it did not mean permission was granted for any type of relationship between the two, or three, who were forced to share the bed.

'Yes,' she thought, *'that is what this is, and he does not trust me so he must have insisted he stay with me himself, to be sure I do not steal from his family.'*

Her eyes narrowed as she stared down into his face, which was partially hidden in deep shadows. Since coming across him and his brother, she had never seen his face so relaxed, so at ease. He seemed always to be on guard and, knowing that he was deeply asleep, she risked taking a long, tapered finger and running it through his beard, along his strong jawline, hesitating as she neared his full, firm lips.

They were opened just a bit and she could feel his steady breath on her finger so she tenderly rubbed the soft skin of his bottom lip, pulling her hand away when he inhaled loudly and she thought he might be waking.

Her heart was hammering in her chest for some reason that she did not understand, but there was no denying the unexpected thrill she felt as she explored his face without his being aware of it, leaving her curious about the rest of his body.

Naomie couldn't help lifting his hand and turning the palm upwards, her eyebrows rising in surprise as she gently traced the lines of it. With another curious look into his sleeping face, she felt emboldened to do even more investigating.

The woman was nothing if not brave and slowly slid the blanket down to the bottom of the bed, exposing his naked body in all its glory. She sat cross-legged on the bed beside him and ran her silver gaze up and down the length of him.

Since the day she was born, Naomie had lived among not only her own family, but among her whole tribe, and there was never any embarrassment or worry about being seen naked by anyone. They lived in too small of a world together to avoid that happening. However, this was the first time she had seen a naked gadje, and she assumed that was what was making her heart race as it was.

His chest was broad and he was well-muscled and well-proportioned, in every way, she realized, her gaze pausing.

"See anything you like?" Beorn murmured, causing her to jump from her sitting position and almost fall off the bed. He reached out and grabbed her wrist, pulling her back to safety.

Naomie yanked her arm out of his grasp and stared down into his dark eyes, which were almost, but not quite, hidden in the shadows.

"Do you?"

"What?" she asked, embarrassment was not an emotion she was familiar with and, instead, she reacted with anger and frustration.

"See anything you like?" He spread his arms over his head in a deep stretch, emphasizing his muscular body, not disconcerted in the least by her gaze.

"Why are you here? Is this some payment that has come due?"

"What are you talking about?"

"Why did your mother have me come to your bed?"

"She did? Did she even know I was here?"

The two of them looked at each other in confusion for a moment.

At first, Beorn thought she had come to him because she wanted him and was willing to do whatever was required, as evidenced by his body's response to finding her in his bed.

However, now it appeared to be just a confusion over which guest room he should be in.

"It's just a cock-up, probably on my part," he said, his passion deflating. He swung his legs off the side of the bed and went to stand up.

"I'll find somewhere else, get some rest."

He was striding towards the door when her voice stopped him. "Please, no."

Wishing he had some way to hide his response to her words, he turned to face her anyway. "What?"

She stared at him and her mouth went dry. Naomie knew that she was walking a thin line here, Beorn's desire was evident as he faced her full on and she was risking much with what she was about to say.

"Please, don't go. I don't want to be alone in this place."

"You want me to come back to your bed?"

"Yes," but when she saw his lips widen in a smile, she added, "to sleep. Just to sleep, please?"

The smile was gone before it even finished forming and his eyes narrowed in contemplation. The thought of sharing a bed with the wench was appealing, but he was not sure he could hold to just sleeping with such a beautiful, naked woman lying next to him.

Naomie sensed the thoughts racing through his mind, and said, "We have a saying that every person is part Judas and part Christ, only luck decides him. Which are you?"

"We shall see, shan't we?" Beorn asked, as he slid back into the bed beside her and pulled the covers up over them both.

At first, they both laid uncomfortably on their backs, trying not to touch one another, but Beorn could only take that for so long.

"Ballocks," he said, his frustration evident as he turned his body towards hers, "may I wrap you in my arms? Twill keep us both warm and, if I keep trying to avoid touching you, I'll naught get any rest whatsoever."

"Yes." Her voice did not give away any of the excitement pulsing through her body at the thought of it and, as he extended his arm, Naomie snuggled up a little closer to him, resting her cheek against his chest. His arm closed around her and he pulled her up tight against his side.

Both of them were more tired than they'd realized and it wasn't long before they fell deeply asleep in each other's arms.

CHAPTER 7

Naomie was being chased in her dreams and her body was thrashing around the bed as she tried to escape her captors once again.

Beorn woke to her terrified moans as she fought some fierce conflict within her own mind. He wasn't sure what to do and brushed the hair off her forehead, trying to calm her down, but the battle continued unabated.

Leaning over her, he then started stroking her face, her closed eyes were blinking rapidly and her thick, full lips were partially open as she dealt with the fear from her dream.

"Naomie," he whispered gently, continuing to stroke her face, "wake up, you're dreaming."

"Ah, God's fingernails," he moaned, clenching his teeth after her knee came up and hit him in a very sensitive area.

"Naomie," his voice wasn't quite so quiet or so tender now, but still she wasn't responding. She moved so that her face was now closer to his and her hand slid down along his bare chest, coming to rest on his stomach.

He inhaled sharply and gazed down at her face, her eyes were still closed, the long black lashes fluttering against her cheeks as the nightmare kept her within its grip.

Her full pink lips were partially open, and it felt to Beorn as if she were offering them to him. He no longer chose to resist and swooped down and took them with his own.

It was just seconds before her groans changed from terrified to passionate and her arms snaked their way up around his shoulders, her silky body sliding up along his as the kiss deepened.

His hands, calloused from years of wielding a sword, roamed freely along her naked skin and she writhed underneath him, her movements igniting an insatiable fire within him.

His lips, followed by his fingers, skimmed along over her soft skin, burning a trail down her throat, her neck, taking some time to explore her breasts before moving lower still.

Naomie's nightmare disappeared as she went swiftly from deep asleep to fully awake and aroused. Her body was on fire with a passion she had never experienced before and was moving of its volition in response to his touch and his kisses.

There was something more that she wanted, that she needed, but she knew naught what that was as the sensations continued to build inside of her, desperately seeking some kind of release.

Beorn continued his sensual torment relentlessly, sliding his lips back up along her torso, feeling her nails raking his back as he took one of her breasts in his mouth then, ever so slowly, he rubbed his body along hers and took possession of her lips once again.

"Are you awake?" he asked, his lips moving against hers as he spoke, his legs gently nudging hers apart.

Her silver eyes glistened in the darkness and she whispered, "Yes."

Her lips were still parted, his touch and his kisses were intoxicating and she yearned for more. Naomie knew she should stop this, but her body would not let her and she gave herself to him freely.

"Are you ready?"

She ran a finger lightly around his lips and whispered, "Be said and just do it before I change my mind."

He crushed his lips onto hers once again and let his tongue plunder as it would. While she was responding to that, he entered her and was surprised to find that he must fight his way through her maidenhead.

Naomie arched up against him, her fingernails once again raking the skin on his back, and he buried himself even further inside of her, moving slowly until she was comfortable.

Beorn believed she must be some type of enchantress, molding her body to fit his, the pleasure building within him reaching heights he'd never felt before.

The tempo increased, the pleasurable friction becoming unbearable as she rose and met each of his thrusts until he could hold out no longer and, with an explosive release, his body shuddered and he carefully lowered himself, using his arm to keep most of his weight off of her, unwilling to be freed from her just yet.

Beorn ran his hand through her thick hair and rained butterfly-like kisses against her lips as she wriggled against him, wringing out the last of their pleasure.

Finally rolling over onto his back, he carried her with him, his arm secured tightly around her shoulder.

"I did not know you were a virgin."

"Why would you think I was not?" Naomie asked, her head was on his chest, her fingers twirling through the dark hairs that grew there. She wasn't sure how she should feel right now, but could not deny a contentment that, heretofore, was completely unknown to her.

"You wanted to sleep in my bed."

"Sleep, Beorn, just sleep." It was the first time she had used his Christian name and he liked the way it rolled off her tongue.

She felt his body move as he shrugged his shoulders. "Are you well? Did I hurt you?"

"You did not hurt me, I liked it very much."

"As did I," he replied, continuing to stroke her hair.

What an odd bird she was, beautiful, obviously brave and intelligent, yet filled with such a simple, refreshing honesty. And that, Beorn appreciated more than anything a worldly coquette could ever offer.

The servants found Beorn and Naomie wrapped in each other's naked arms later that day when they went to wake them, and most of the household already knew what had happened by the time they reached the Great Hall.

There were some curious looks, but no one dared say a word about it when Beorn coldly met their gaze.

It was time for the evening meal and Beorn sat next to Radolf so they could discuss business. Regan entered the room and love blossomed in her chest when she saw her four boys sitting next to each other on the dais.

All were grown men now, but she could see Calder in each one of them. Beorn and Radolf could almost have been twins with their broad, muscular physiques. Radolf's red hair was cut shorter than Beorn's golden brown locks, as was his beard, but their strong jaws and prominent cheekbones were identical.

Gwyn was clean-shaven and had just a ring of brown hair around his head, leaving the majority of it bald. His face was thinner and not so well defined as his brothers', but it was a calmer face also, filled with a serene glow that his warrior brothers would never understand.

The three of them shared the same brilliant, dark blue eyes as their father. Eyes that were so expressive that they could warm a heart or freeze one's blood cold, depending on the bent of the owner's mind at any given time.

Regan had worried about Gwyn somewhat when they'd first arrived, but he seemed much healthier and well-rested now. He had sustained an arrow wound to his arm which had all but healed, and she was relieved to learn that he should have no further trouble because of it.

Her youngest son, Draco, sat to the side of Gwyn, his build more like his older brothers, but his coloring unique to himself. He had Regan's brilliant green eyes and her fair skin, with his father's golden-brown hair. His hair and beard were worn longer but well-trimmed, similar to Beorn's.

Not only did his coloring separate him from his brothers, who were so much older than he was, his carefree and playful approach to life was nothing like any one of the others.

Radolf, his disposition a mirror of his father's, just and kind and wanting only to provide a good life for his family and tenants. Radolf was the protector of all of them at the shire.

Beorn had been sent from her when he very young and she worried sometimes that, mayhap, his being taken away from his mother's love so early in his life had hardened him. But, even so, it was what made him the great knight that he was. Beorn was the protector of all in the kingdom.

Gwyn had the most beautiful spirit and a kind, giving nature. He had also left her side at a very young age but, unlike Beorn, he was raised with God's love shining within him, allowing him to find a peace that he was able to share willingly. Gwyn was the protector of all their souls.

She was proud of each and every one of them and it did her heart well to see all four of her boys together. That was not something that she had ever expected to be able to see again.

Unfortunately, her happiness was overshadowed by the knowledge that there was danger afoot and their lives could very well become forfeit in the near future.

Regan filled her eyes and her heart with the vision of her sons for a moment more, then shook any further maudlin thoughts from her head and made her way to her own seat, so that the meal could be served.

She had discussed the menu with Becca and, although the evening meal was usually just one main dish with some sides, they decided to put out a bigger spread this evening, as it might be some time before the travelers were able to sit down to a real meal again.

At this time of year, most of their food came from the winter stores, but for this special occasion several chickens were butchered and made into Lombard Chicken pasties, chicken in puff pastries with bacon, ginger and verjuice.

Venison en frumenty was also served because that had always been Gwyn's favorite. Radolf had led a hunting party just the day before so the fresh venison was roasted on a spit and served with a thick wheat porridge. The accompanying vegetables were dried peas served with onions and saffron.

Conversation was at a minimum as trenchers were piled high and quickly dispatched, at least by the men. Regan looked over at Naomi who peered at her filled trencher with suspicion, sniffing the various items, but not touching anything on it as she looked up and down the table.

Regan worried that she still was not comfortable eating before the men finished.

"Please feel free to eat, it is acceptable for you to do so, see all of us women are."

Naomie nodded, her silver-gray eyes open wide. "Must I use my fingers for all of this?"

"Have you no dirk?"

Spoons were provided but most foods were generally eaten with the hands, and people brought their own knives with which to cut the food into bite-sized pieces.

"I do not."

"Take mine, please," Regan said, hesitating a bit, the dirk had been gift from Calder many years ago and it was hard for her to let it out of her possession.

"I will give it back to you," Naomie said, seeing the indecision on Regan's face. "I am no thief."

"Apologies, I did not mean to give you that impression. My husband gave me that knife many years ago. He was forever trying to ensure my safety and wanted me to have that to protect myself, need be. I am not used to having it out of my possession, is all."

Naomie chose to accept her explanation and turned the conversation in another direction to ease Regan's embarrassment.

"Your sons all have the same look, I think, mayhap, they resemble your husband, do they not?"

"They do, they are all strong, handsome men and I am so proud of them. Their father was special, he,"

Her voice broke and she was unable to continue. Regan looked down at her trencher, trying to blink back the tears forming in her eyes.

Naomie said nothing, but her hand snaked out towards Regan's and she took the older woman's in her own.

With a little sniffle, Regan looked up and was taken by the depth of understanding that she saw reflected in the girl's silver eyes.

"I fear that having all my sons here makes me a bit emotional," she whispered, patting the girl's hand. "Thank you for your patience with me."

Regan turned and waved over one of the serving girls and spoke quietly into her ear. The girl left the Hall but returned just a few moments later and handed an item to Regan, which she squirreled away in the pocket of her tunic.

"That is all you can spare?" Beorn asked, obviously not happy.

"We have very few knights here now. Many have left for the continent, hoping to make their fortunes. We have quite a few squires, but they are not seasoned and are not yet of an age that they can even be knighted. I need men here to help protect the shire, so three is all I can send with you."

Beorn shook his head in disgust and drained his cup of ale. Setting it down on the table, slightly louder than was necessary, he waved over the page.

"Does that include this blighter?" he asked, nodding his chin in Draco's direction.

"It does not," Radolf responded, "he's an extra bonus for you."

Draco drained his cup, and added, "And you'll learn soon enough that I am no blighter."

Beorn took a pull on his fresh cup of ale, trying to hide his amusement. The boy thought a lot of himself and he looked forward to bringing Draco a taste of real life.

"But not Grant?" Beorn couldn't miss the sulky look on Grant's face and knew there had been more discussion while he was resting, and Grant had not won the day.

"No, he is needed here and knows that is where his duty lies."

"As you wish, but it wouldn't hurt the lad to get some experience in real fighting, instead of just hiding him behind these castle walls all the time."

"He has all the experience that he requires and you can cry off, Beorn. I've given you the knights I can spare, I do not need your thoughts on what happens with my son."

"As you wish," Beorn said, holding his hands up in submission, but neither of the men were looking closely enough at Grant to see the anger festering inside of him.

The meal ended a short time later after the fried fig pastries, cheese and nuts had been served with a spiced wine. Once the tables had been cleared, Beorn went over to speak with his mother.

Naomie stood when he approached and their eyes met. Beorn did not know what would happen between them now, what they had shared was unexpected and most likely would not occur again. But he did enjoy being able to view her beauty and savored the memory of what lay hidden under her silken clothing.

Since the death of his wife, the only female favors he accepted were from high-priced public girls. He had no desire to have a woman in his life and, as beautiful and unusual as this one was, that had not changed one whit.

As a knight, a warrior, one never knew what the next day would bring and so, having this little minx to deal with fit right into that lifestyle, and Beorn was curious to see what lay ahead of them in the next few weeks.

He found himself unable to tear his eyes away from hers, their silver brilliance, framed by thick, black lashes, emphasized her high cheekbones and the breathtaking beauty of her face.

Naomie managed to look away first and turned towards Regan. Handing her the dirk that she had cleaned off with part of the tablecloth, she said, "Thank you, for your hospitality and your kindness."

"You are welcome here anytime, but I hope you find your family and reach your home safely." Regan pulled her into a warm embrace. Naomie withstood the familiarity stoically but did not return the hug.

Regan released her and watched her walk away, then turned towards Beorn.

"Must you leave us so soon?"

"I fear we must. Duty calls."

"Of course, it does." She looked up into his handsome face and rested her fingers on his bearded cheek. "Promise me that, not only will you keep yourself safe, but you will watch out for both your brothers. They are not as worldly as you, Beorn."

"Have no fear, Mother. Their safety is, and will remain, my highest priority."

He engulfed her in a bear hug, happy to have spent this little time with her, sad to think he might not get the chance to do so again.

"You take care, Mother."

"You, as well, Beorn. I love you." She kissed him on the cheek and he turned to make his way out of the Keep.

"Wait, Beorn, there is something else we need to speak of."

"Mother, I told you, that subject is not open for discussion."

Regan frowned at him. "Do not get impertinent with me, Beorn. I respect your wishes and wanted only to discuss Naomie with you."

He narrowed his eyes at her suspiciously. "What did you need to discuss?"

"Do you know much of her people's customs?"

"Nay, I do not, why?"

"The men always eat first, and what is left over is given to the women and the children. Have a care on your travels that you make sure that she eats properly."

Beorn's brow furrowed as he considered what she had shared, and some of what had happened on their travels so far suddenly made more sense.

"Thank you for telling me, I will watch out for her." He gently took her hand and nestled it within the bend of his arm, then escorted her outside to the courtyard where the others were waiting.

"Naomie," Regan called out, "may I have a word before you leave?"

Beorn raised an eyebrow as he stopped and turned, watching as his mother placed some small item in Naomie's hand.

"Please take this," she told the young woman, placing a dirk in her hand. "I would be remiss if I let you go without any means to protect yourself."

"But this means so much to you."

"No, I still have my own dirk, this was my husband's and it served him well. He has no further use of it, so take it and, mayhap, Calder will now watch over you, as well, and keep you from harm. Good luck to you, my dear."

Naomie was taken aback by Regan's kindness and was not sure how to respond. Her interactions with gadje in the past were limited and, in most cases, not at all pleasant.

Since Gwyn had taken her in at the church in London, many of her opinions about them had been tested, but Naomie reminded herself that she must still be on her guard and not get complacent, they could turn on her at any moment.

"Thank you for this," she said, hiding the knife in the folds of her colorful skirts, and turning back towards her waiting horse.

Gwyn, meanwhile, had hugged Becca and said his good-byes to Grant before turning to his mother.

"Mother, I feel so blessed to have had this short time with you. You are a part of my prayers every day, please take care of yourself and, with God's blessing, we'll see each other again before long."

"I love you, Gwyn, and I'm so happy to see you. Promise me that you'll take care of yourself in all this kerfluffle that you and the Pope are mixed up with."

"I promise."

With a warm hug and a kiss on her cheek, Gwyn made his way to his horse, leaving just Draco and Regan.

Although a strong, grown man, he was her baby boy and always would be. She would miss Gwyn and Beorn, but they had spent most of their lives away from her. Draco had never left the shire and Regan felt a tight squeeze around her heart at the thought of the danger he could be walking into.

"Do you have proper clothing packed?"

"Yes, Mother."

"All your weapons, everything you might need?"

"Yes, Mother. I am ready, I've been ready for quite some time and now I have an opportunity to do the things I've trained for all my life. And I get to learn from my brother, Beorn, who better to be my leader?"

"I know," Regan said, unshed tears twinkling in her green eyes. "I will miss you and think of you every day."

"As will I. Please, do not fret, I will be fine. You take care of yourself and know that I love you and will see you soon."

He took her into his embrace and feared for a moment that she might not release him, but Regan drew a deep breath and stepped away, setting him free to go and find his own destiny.

The horses had all been saddled and Draco was just getting onto his when Becca came running from the kitchen area with a heavy sack of food, cold meat, bread, cheese and some oatmeal cakes to tide them over, for at least part of their journey.

"Thank you, sister, for everything," Beorn said, with a grateful nod in her direction. "Radolf, what is our best way back, where we might miss the Germans lying in wait for us?"

"These are the three knights that will be accompanying you, Jay, Millard and Arnell. We've discussed what is happening and they will guide you the back way, through one of the passes, where the Germans would least expect you to go."

"Good, they know who Gwyn and I are. What of Synne and their estates? Has she been warned?"

"We haven't had occasion to do so yet."

"Will we be traveling anywhere near their estates?"

Radolf considered that for a moment. "They are not far from the pass, it would not cause you much extra time to stop there. And your sister would do bodily harm to you if she knew you were that close and did not stop by, even for just a few minutes."

"I know," Beorn replied, a grin spreading on his face, "mayhap, we can take that extra time to warn her about the Germans."

"That would work out well," Radolf responded.

"Father," Grant said, taking hold of Radolf's arm, "may I, at least, ride with them to Synne's estate? Please."

Radolf could see how desperately Grant wanted to be a part of their group and saw no harm in letting him go as far as Synne's.

"You may, but return home as soon as that visit is over."

"I will, thank you, Father," he yelled, already sprinting to the stables to collect his horse and equipment.

"Thank you for everything, brother. It was good to see you again. Stay safe."

"You, as well, good-bye Gwyn, Draco. Have a care for your safety, all of you."

As soon as Grant joined them, the group turned their horses and cantered out of the wide gates and down through the village. It was closing in on the evening hours and most people had already returned to their homes.

Beorn had made the decision to leave under cover of darkness in the event the Germans had not gone far and were watching for them.

Once they were out of the village, they were forced to slow their pace as they made their way through the meandering trails in the forest. Radolf's knights knew the way well, but little sunshine managed to make its way in through the thick trees during the daylight hours and the ground remained frozen in many spots.

The small group had to mentally prepare themselves for another long, cold evening as they snuggled within their woolen mantles.

CHAPTER 8

The little band continued on through the night, the temperatures were frigid but it did not rain or snow. There was an occasional slip by one of the horses, but nothing onerous enough to cause them to go lame.

Gwyn kept wrapping his mantle tighter around his thin body, but still could not keep from shivering. He had lived most of his life in warmer climes and was having difficulty with this weather. The thought that they would soon be crossing back over onto the continent was all that kept him seated on his horse and willing to continue on with this journey.

Verne rode next to him and their shared conversation helped him to forget the coldness seeping into his bones for a short time.

Neither of them had much good to say about the brutal English winter, and so they shared stories of their homes, where the temps never dropped so low and the warm sunlight greeted them most of their days.

Grant and Draco rode on either side of Naomie, sandwiching her in between them. She appreciated that their large, strong bodies blocked some of the cold wind for her, but they were constantly trying to engage her in conversation, and she was in no mood for it.

"Pity you won't be able to come to London with us, Grant. What a fine city it is. Have you been there yet, Mistress Naomie?"

"Yes."

"What a grand city, so much to see and do there, don't you agree?"

When she didn't respond, Grant interjected, "Remember the brawl we got into last year when we visited?"

"What brawl? It was almost of no consequence. Even though we were outnumbered, we handled those blighters in no time, and they did not come back for more once we showed them what we were capable of."

He threw a sideways glance at Naomie to see how much he had impressed her but was disappointed by what he saw. She was staring straight ahead, her face partially hidden by the hood of her mantle and she appeared to have no interest, whatsoever, in their conversation.

Draco looked over her head at Grant, shrugged his shoulders and continued on with only his own thoughts to keep him occupied. He wasn't going to continue blabbing on if she hadn't the decency to even join in on the conversation.

Shortly before daylight they stopped near a stream and fed and watered the horses, giving them all time to rest and eat some of the food that Becca had sent with them.

Naomie also struggled with the frigid temperatures and was grateful for the stockings that Becca had provided her with for the journey. They only went as high as her thighs but did help somewhat.

However, she had to remove Verne's gloves to eat and her hands were so stiff and cold that she had trouble gripping the small pieces of oatmeal cake that were breaking apart as she nibbled at them.

It didn't appear to be by design, however, each time they stopped, Beorn always seemed to be close by her side. When they would eat, he would place the food in her hands and seemed to watch over her until he was sure she'd eaten it all.

Naomie didn't understand why he was watching everything that she did so closely, she wasn't going to run away and there was nothing to steal, so there was no reason for him to do so.

She'd spent much of the dark hours of the night thinking about her tryst with Beorn. He was handsome and an accomplished lover, as far she knew, since he was her only lover.

Naomie had been trained all her life to read people and to read the signs around her. But, with Beorn, her thoughts and senses remained muddled and unclear. He was a hard man to know and she did not think he was looking for a wife, but what she'd seen on his palm the night before left her filled with curiosity about him.

Not that she could, or would, ever consider being his woman, or heaven forbid, his wife. He was a gadje and her people would never except that. They would declare her unclean and she would be turned away, ostracized, and never allowed to be a part of their world again.

Beorn noticed that she was staring at him as she ate and was curious as to what thoughts were hidden behind those spectacular eyes.

When she turned and walked down the stream a bit, looking for a place to fill her flask, he followed and waited quietly until she was done. Naomie gasped in surprise when she turned and found him standing close behind her.

At first, she said nothing, just met his piercing blue gaze, but finally relented and broke the silence.

"Is there something that you require from me?"

"Nay, I just wanted to see how you are keeping. This is, after all, just the beginning of a long, difficult journey."

"I am well enough. Your cold English wind bites through my mantle and I hate this country and its weather. I look forward to returning home soon."

"As does my brother," Beorn said with a smile, one side of his own mantle thrown back over his shoulder, as if the cold could not touch him.

"Where is your home, Naomie?"

"I have no special home, only the Lungo Drom."

"What is that?" Beorn asked, raising his eyes toward the grey sky above as it began spitting snowflakes at them.

"The long road of no particular place to go and no turning back."

"Sounds mysterious."

"Not mysterious," she replied, with a faraway look in her eyes. "Home is everywhere we go."

Shaking herself from the past, Naomie moved forward a step, meaning to make her way around Beorn, but he stopped her by placing his cold fingers under her chin and lifting her face until he could look into those exceptional eyes of hers.

He watched in fascination as miniscule snowflakes landed on her face and quickly melted, leaving a trail of tears along her cheeks.

"Why are you in such a hurry to get away from me?"

"You're are a gadje and I cannot ever forget that."

"A gadje?"

"Yes, a non-gypsy."

"What difference does that make?"

"We can only be with our own people."

"Maybe you should have remembered that before you let me take your virginity. How will you explain that to your people when you return?"

"There are ways."

His eyes narrowed as he contemplated her words. "You will lie but, when he beds you, your new husband will know."

Chickenflesh rose on her arms as she listened to his words and she rubbed them vigorously, pulling her chin back out of his hands. She had also considered that in the dark of the night during their travels.

Proof of the loss of a woman's maidenhead was always provided to the families after the first night of marriage. Need be, a woman would use drops of chicken or lamb blood on their bed as proof.

In most cases, their virginity had been lost to the future husband, who would be complicit in the ruse, so there were no repercussions but, in her case, she was not sure of what might happen.

"How will you explain it to your husband?" Beorn did not know why he was pressing the issue, it was not his concern, but it was eating at him and he wanted an answer.

"When a Romani woman does not provide a child within a year, the man can dissolve the marriage. We have one such man who has dissolved many, he is now old and ugly, and still has no children. He has already paid my parents the ceiz for me. He is desperate for a child."

"What is that, a dowry?"

She shrugged her shoulders, not understanding the word. "A brideprice?"

"Yes, price for me to be his wife."

"Why aren't you married then?"

"I ran away, he was too old, too ugly."

"And that's when you got kidnapped?"

She simply looked at Beorn and he found it intriguing that she did not feel the need to flap her jaws constantly, like most women. The question was self-evident, so she did not even bother to respond.

"Will you marry him when you return?"

"I will. I do not think he will throw me out if he suspects I am no longer a maiden, only if I cannot produce a child for him."

The thought of lying in Ninga's hairy arms made Naomie shudder, but she would do what she had to do.

Beorn frowned, not particularly caring for that thought either. "But will you be safe?"

"Ma-sha-llah."

"What does that mean?"

"As God wills."

Their faces were just inches apart and Beorn's eyes were drawn to her full lips, which parted slightly as he lowered his head towards hers.

She turned her face upward and met his lips with her own, and suddenly the cold did not bother her anymore as the blood raced throughout her body, her heart pounding rapidly in response to the feel of his lips crushing her own.

He wrapped his muscular arms around her and rubbed his hard, ready body up against hers, which was soft and yielding. Naomie had no control of the situation, her arms were wrapped in her mantle, enveloped within his embrace, and she was at his mercy as he continued to ply her with passionate kisses. She moaned loudly and wriggled up against his body.

"Apologies," came a voice from a few feet away. "I don't mean to interrupt but we thought this was to be just a short stop."

Beorn stepped back away from Naomie, swearing under his breath and closing his mantle in front of himself to hide the evidence of his desire.

He turned in the direction of the voice and found Millard standing there, he was the oldest of Radolf's knights, tall and thin, but wiry and strong. Beorn wondered how long he'd been watching them and had a strong desire to smack the smirk off the man's face, but managed to restrain himself from doing so.

"We'll be there, anon. Now bugger off and make sure the horses are ready."

"Beorn," Naomie said, taking a step closer to him and looking up into his sapphire blue eyes.

"Yes?" He could listen to her lilting voice all day and particularly enjoyed the way she said his name. Her soft full lips caught his attention once again and he had to take a step back and force his eyes away from them.

Although snowflakes continued to swirl around them, the sun was making its entrance to this new day, trying to chase away the darkness and snow clouds with its warm rays of light.

As it rose behind Naomie, she was shrouded in an ethereal light that made her seem even more mysterious and unique, and Beorn had to struggle to keep from pulling her back into his arms.

But with her next comment, she broke that spell completely.

"I can still make ugly, old Ninga marry me, even if he realizes I am no longer a maiden. But," her eyes clouded and, for what might be the first and only time, Beorn thought he saw fear in those silvery-gray orbs, "I cannot do so if I am with child. As much as I like to be in your arms and would enjoy the feel of you inside of me again, I cannot get with child or I cannot ever go home."

And with the swish of her colorful skirt under her mantle, she walked past him and joined the others.

By mid-morning, they arrived at the estates owned by Beorn's sister, Synne, and her husband, Wulfgar.

There was some initial confusion as they entered the courtyard, the day was grey and overcast as the horses pranced across the frozen ground, the riders bundled up in their mantles and the residents unable to identify the group approaching their home.

Synne, Wulfgar, and several other men, were waiting for them in front of the Manor with their broadswords at the ready.

As they drew closer, the men on horseback pushed back the hoods of their mantles and Synne threw her sword to the ground and squealed in delight when she recognized her brother, Draco, and her nephew, Grant.

Synne was several months pregnant, but that did not stop her from hurrying toward the group to welcome them.

Once they had all dismounted and she hugged her kinfolk, Synne looked around at the others. A couple of the men she recognized as Radolf's knights, but her blue-green eyes widened in surprise and her mouth dropped open in disbelief as she looked back and forth between Beorn and Gwyn.

"Is it really you, my brothers?"

"That it is," Beorn replied, holding his arms out to her. Synne rushed into his embrace and held tight to him as if he were a mirage that would somehow slip away from her.

"It's been too long, Beorn," she mumbled, not ready to release him yet. "I've missed you."

"And I, you, Synne. You look well, sister."

Taking a deep, calming breath, she stepped back away from him and met his eyes, tears of joy glistening unshed in hers.

"I have been very blessed in my life, Beorn."

"I can see that," he replied, indicating her swelling belly.

"Do you remember, Wulfgar, my husband?"

"Of course," Beorn said, turning to shake the man's hand as Synne stepped over to Gwyn.

Seeing him standing before her, Synne's tears finally escaped down her cheeks.

"Gwyn, I thought I might never have a chance to see you again. I am so happy that you are here."

He wrapped her in a warm embrace, and said, "God works in mysterious ways, Synne, and he has certainly blessed us this day."

"Come," Wulfgar said, brushing back a lock of dark brown hair from his face, "let us go inside and enjoy the warmth of the fire."

"We can stay only a short time," Beorn said, gently grabbing hold of Naomie's elbow and escorting her into the Manor.

The small group sighed in relief as they removed their mantles and stood in front of the large fireplace, letting its warmth soak into their bones and thaw them out a bit.

There was a rush of commotion when two teenage girls ran down the stairs and into the Great Hall, followed by a pack of dogs of varying sizes that all felt compelled to inspect the newcomers.

"These are our daughters, Iva and Holly," Synne said. "Girls, come meet your uncles."

They studied Beorn and Gwyn curiously as introductions were made, their mother had shared many stories about her brothers and to meet them in person was quite an honor.

Once he'd made the acquaintance of his nieces, Beorn introduced the other knights and then turned to Naomie.

"This is Naomie, she travels with us until we can get her back to her family."

"Welcome," Synne said, but her eyes glittered like emeralds and she could not hide the curiosity on her face as she looked between the exotic woman and Beorn, who stood close to her side, as if protecting her.

Food and drink were brought in and Synne sat close to Gwyn, bombarding him with questions on his life and about living in Rome, which Gwyn graciously expounded on.

"But enough about me," he said, as the meal progressed. "What of you, Synne? You have just the two girls, then?"

"Yes," she replied, her eyes sparkling, "for a time, it seemed we would not be blessed with children at all, but then Iva and Holly arrived.

And, after all this time, we now have another babe to welcome into our lives. Wulfgar hopes it will be a boy. We women do so try his temper at times." She giggled and looked fondly over at her husband before taking another bite of food.

The rest of the meal passed quickly. Beorn kept Naomie at his side, so he could ensure that she ate her fill. They would be leaving shortly and would not be able to stop again for quite some time.

Once the trenchers were cleared, Beorn said, "We must leave anon, but we came to warn you of a possible problem."

"What type of problem?" Wulfgar asked.

Beorn hesitated, not sure how much detail he needed to provide, not because he didn't trust them, only because it was not necessary and would only muddle the conversation.

"We are on a mission for the Pope, which is why Gwyn has joined us. The Pope, not Gwyn," he added with a smile, "is in danger from the German king and we go to his aid."

Synne looked around the table. "Draco and Grant are going with you?"

Those two she knew well, as her family frequently visited Wyndymshire. She also knew that the two of them could be quite impulsive and worried about them being let loose amidst such danger.

A smile spread across Draco's face. "I will be going, alas, Grant will not."

There was a sour look on Grant's face as he stared at his uncle, jealously was burning in his chest and he was angry at being treated like a child.

Beorn saw the exchange and sought to quell Grant's ire. "Regardless, you should know that there are German knights on our tail. They've been sent to prevent us from bringing aid to the Pope. They followed us to Wyndymshire and know who we are. They may come here. Have you sufficient defenses?"

"We can bring the villagers here to the Manor. We have enough men to defend our lands. It's good that you've given us notice so we can be prepared."

"If you have sufficient men, why then did you allow my pregnant sister to carry a broadsword to defend your home when a band of unknown knights arrived in your courtyard?"

His voice was cold and his eyes were icy shards of sapphire as he stared askance at his brother-in-law.

Synne frowned and opened her mouth to speak, but Wulfgar caught her eye and shook his head.

"You've been gone a long time," he replied, not backing down from Beorn's gaze, "but, methinks you can still recall your sister's obstinate nature. That has never changed through all these years. I could have argued with her until you'd ridden your horses right through the door of the Manor and still, she would not have changed her mind."

He reached over and took Synne's hand in both of his. "My wife may well worry me to death one day, but she stays true to herself always."

Beorn turned his eyes to his sister. "Then it is you that I must take to task, Synne. Have a care, for yourself and your babe. Do not be reckless by taking its life in your hands."

Synne did not sit still for anyone lecturing her but before she opened her mouth, she remembered that Beorn had lost his wife when she gave birth to his child, and for that, she would forgive his interference this one time.

"I will, Beorn, have no worry on my behalf."

"Good, Wulfgar, gather your men, we must go now. The Germans may be too busy trying to catch up to us to bother you, but you need to be ready for them in case they are looking simply to cause you trouble."

"I will do so, right now, it was good to see you."

"And you," Beorn replied.

Wulfgar shook hands with the men and wished them luck, then headed out to get his defenses in order.

Synne stayed back by Naomie as she put her mantle back on and adjusted it tightly around her body while the others were following Wulgar outside.

Naomie turned her silver gaze toward Synne. "May I see your hand?"

"You're a gypsy?"

"Yes, I would like to see your palm. I know your brother worries for you, but I can tell much from that."

Synne held out her hand and Naomie traced the lines on her palm, a gentle smile on her face all the while.

"You are very much like Beorn," she said softly. "You both feel everything deeply, the good and bad alike."

"Yes, that is true."

"You have a long, solid lifeline, it will continue on as it has always been. If you are happy and are pleased with your life, know that it will continue to bring you joy and fulfillment."

"Thank you, Naomie, you have set my mind at ease about the babe. I am older now and have had some concerns."

"I do have just one warning for you," Naomie added.

"What is that?"

"You have many dogs underfoot and you must have a care to never beat them when they frustrate you."

"I would never do that," Synne replied.

"Good, for if you do, your baby will be born very hairy."

Synne had no opportunity to respond to that comment because just then Beorn bellowed for them to come outside.

They hurried out and, after brief hugs all around, the little band made its way off towards London.

Grant was rigid with anger and his fingers itched to grab his horse's reins and join them, but he knew that Beorn would just send him away.

Synne stood by his side, watching the others get smaller and smaller on the horizon, never feeling the cold, bitter wind swirling around her. She allowed a few tears to fall, knowing there was a good chance she might never see her three brothers again.

CHAPTER 9

They continued plodding on throughout the rest of the day, stopping only periodically to rest the horses. It had rained hard at one point and all of the travelers were now wet and cold, as well as tired.

Beorn or one of the other knights stayed back on the trails to be sure the Germans were not within sight. Arnell had just caught up with them and shook his head in the negative as he dismounted and took a hefty pull from the ale in his flacket.

"There was naught to be seen through that downpour. Methinks that if they were anywhere nearby, they took cover and we should be safe for a time."

"Aye, we'll stay here just a few minutes, then travel on until dark."

"Will we ride through the night again?" Gwyn asked, his face was pale and there were large bags under his eyes, and Beorn was once again concerned about his health.

"If we still see no sign of them by nightfall, we can consider resting around a warm fire for the night."

"Praise the Lord," Gwyn said, his voice so soft that the others could barely hear him.

Naomie had gone off into the bushes for some privacy, but now hurried back into the circle of men, surprising Beorn by taking hold of his arm and pulling him aside.

"Is something amiss?"

She nodded her head, her eyes wide and filled with worry. "The Germans are here."

"What? Where?"

She took his hand and pulled him over into the thicket of trees she had just come from. There was an opening where a tree had fallen, from the singe marks on the trunk, it had most likely been struck by lightning at some point.

Beorn took his hand from hers and peered out from behind one of the tall trees still standing and there they were, probably a dozen or more of them. There were more than they'd encountered back at the castle in Wyndymshire, so the knights on foot must have come across more mounts and caught up with the others.

Turning around, he grabbed her hand and dragged her back over to their group. "The Germans are less than a kilometer away and they have more men with them now. We must make ready, we cannot outrun them at this point, and will have to stand and fight."

He tried to ignore the fear he saw on Gwyn's face as he barked orders at the others.

"We will only prevail if we catch them unawares. They will follow our trail into this clearing, Arnell, Millard, and you, Jay, hide your steeds in the thick of the trees and get to either side of the trail and hide behind those large Scots pines. Once the Germans reach the clearing we can attack."

"Where will you and Verne be?"

"We will sneak down a half kilometer and come up behind them, if we can pick a few of them off quietly before they get here, that may help our odds."

"Have you forgotten me?" Draco asked, still waiting for his own orders.

"Of course not. Radolf tells me you are almost as good with a bow and arrow as Synne, is that true?"

"Better."

"And pigs might fly," Beorn replied. "Get to the trees on the other side of the opening. Find a place where you have room enough to let fly as many arrows as you can and have a care to not hit our own men."

Draco rolled his eyes at the insult and then hurried off to find the best location, which left just Gwyn and Naomie.

Beorn looked from one to the other of them. "Gwyn, it is imperative that you get away safely, so you and Naomie must head out now. We will have them tied up for a time and you should be able to reach London unscathed if you ride on through the night. Do you know how to go?"

"I will not leave you to fight my battles."

"Gwyn, this is not the time for debate. Your safety is paramount, and you need to watch over Naomie." He saw her silver eyes narrow at him in response to his words and he had to bite back a smile.

"Please, head off while it's still safe, Verne and I must go and make ready." Feeling the adrenaline pumping in anticipation of the fight to come soon, he stepped over towards Naomie and buried his large hand into the thick hair along the back of her head and pulled her forward, capturing her lips in a kiss that left them both breathless.

With a nod in their direction, he mounted his horse and headed back down the trail. "Keep your eyes skinned, men, and be ready."

Gwyn blushed at the affectionate display, but Naomie just watched Beorn's back as he rode away, her cheek's flushed and her heart hammering in her chest.

"Come," she said to Gwyn, turning and leading her horse back into a thicket of trees beyond where Draco was setting up his position.

"Why are you stopping here?" he asked, watching her wrap the reins around a strong branch.

"You can go, Father Gwyn. I cannot."

"Why not?"

"You are my tribe for now and we must all protect each other. I cannot leave them in danger. You must stay safe though, so you can go."

"No, I cannot, and if you are willing to stay and join the fray, so I am." Gwyn made the sign of the cross and whispered a frantic prayer to the Lord before following quietly behind Naomie, back towards the danger coming for them.

"We wait here," she said, and Gwyn was quite sure she had already watched or participated in many other battles in her short life. She showed no fear, just a calm resolve that he wished he had.

"Do you have a weapon?"

"I do not," Gwyn replied. "I have a broadsword, but it is in a scabbard on my saddle. I cannot use it against another man ever again."

"No dirk?"

"Well, yes, I have my dirk, that is all." He was a bit nonplussed, he used his dirk to cut food, not as a weapon.

Naomie squatted down amidst the trees while they waited for sounds of the beginning of the battle. The weather was clear right now but the sunlight did not reach these tree-filled areas, it was colder than out in the clearing and there were bits of snow frozen in piles here and there.

Naomie kept rubbing her hands together, trying to keep the cold at bay so her fingers would not fail her if she needed to use her knife. The gloves were too large and clumsy to wear at a time such this and she'd removed them.

She stood up suddenly at the sound of metal clanging against metal coming from a little distance away. Realizing that it must Beorn and Verne engaging the Germans at the back of their group, she stooped under the branches and made her way to the clearing, no longer worried about being seen and giving away their advantage.

The Germans were mounted on horses, riding two abreast and wearing chainmail under their mantles, and helmets to protect their faces.

She heard the hiss of an arrow fly from her right, but it just missed the knight in the front. That knight was about to ride straight at Draco but stopped when Millard, Jay and Arnell rushed out from their hiding spots to take them on.

Their long broadswords clanged violently, but the Germans were on horseback and there more of them, so Radolf's knights were at a serious disadvantage.

Seeing it, Naomie threw her warm wool mantle off her shoulders and grabbed for the bright red silk section of her skirt, cutting a large, jagged square from the material.

Holding it high, she ran straight towards the mounted Germans, shaking the piece of cloth and screaming out, hiyee, hiyee, hiyee.

The Germans were startled, as were Radolf's knights, but Naomie continued on, getting closer to the steeds and continuing to scream while waving the cloth at them. The horses spooked, as she hoped they might. Several reared and unseated their riders, the chainmail was heavy and did not allow the knights to get back to their feet quickly.

One of the horses headed straight into a copse of trees and the heavy pine branches knocked the warrior to the ground as the horse continued running at full speed, as if a banshee was right on its tail.

Radolf's knights regained their wits first and buried their broadswords into the two knights that had first lost their mounts.

Naomie had removed a bit of the Germans' advantage and some of the riders were still having trouble controlling their horses, giving the knights time to take on more of them.

Beorn and Verne had dispatched a couple of the knights bringing up the rear of the group and now rode full bore into the clearing. Both of them were taken aback when they saw Naomie rushing towards some of the other mounted knights with her red silk cloth, screaming all the while as she shook it at their horses.

There was one German knight who narrowed his eyes as he watched the wench unseat his men. His own horse continued to dance uncomfortably, but he held tight to its reins and turned it towards the woman, who was standing fearlessly in the midst of all the massive beasts, and the warriors on their backs.

He started to charge toward her, intending to run her into the ground, but his horse stumbled and he was thrown over its head, landing not far from the wench.

He stood as quickly as he was able and turned, an arrow had taken down his horse and he forced himself to restrain his anger as he looked over the situation.

The girl had moved back out of the center of the action and he took a step in her direction, only to find his way blocked by a large warhorse with Beorn sitting astride, his broadsword at the ready. Jakob lifted his own sword with both hands on the hilt.

The clatter of swords meeting, the grunts of exertion, the moans of pain, all of the noise in the clearing faded in both men's ears as they studied each other.

"Beorn, it has been a long while. Will you fight me like a real man or mow me down with your horse like the cur you are?"

"Like you intended to do to the girl?"

"The wench caused some unexpected trouble, wherever did you find her?"

Beorn did not answer, just stared down at his old nemesis. "I thought you died years ago, Jakob."

"Almost, but you did not finish the job and now it's my turn."

"At close of play, methinks that you are outmatched, as you were the first time."

Beorn slid off his horse's back and took a step towards Jakob, a look of pure anticipation reflected on it. Jakob hesitated, looking around for his men, but they were busy trying to hold on to their own lives. Several had already been killed by Draco's arrows, the others were trying to outmaneuver Radolf's knights and Verne with their swords.

"Scared?"

"Of you, I think not," Jakob replied, then lunged forward with a deadly stroke of his sword. Beorn parried it and brought his own down towards Jakob with all of his strength, but Jakob was able to block it, causing sparks to fly.

They were both strong men, and their muscles bulged and sweat formed on their brow as they repelled stroke after stroke from the other sword.

Beorn could see that Jakob was tiring and felt a rush of adrenaline, victory was nigh. He stepped closer and got ready to deal the final death blow but stopped suddenly when he heard Naomie scream.

He looked away for a moment to see what was happening and Jakob swung at him, Beorn leapt back, almost able to avoid contact, the chainmail prevented any type of deep cut, but the blow to his stomach was powerful enough that it doubled him over in pain.

Naomie screamed again and, this time, Beorn turned and ran in the direction that it had come from, only to find Naomie sitting amongst the frozen pine needles and leaning against a large tree, her silver eyes wide, a single tear slipping down her cheek.

Lying face down next to her was one of the German knights.

"You have blood all over you, where are you injured?"

She raised her eyes towards his, her clothing had been ripped and her breast was exposed, he could see the chicken-flesh rising on her frigid skin and the rapid beating of her heart, and fear gripped him hard.

"Where are you injured?" he asked again.

She shook her head and held up a bloody dirk, then pointed at the man on the ground. Of all the experiences she'd had, Naomie had never taken a life before and was shaken to the core by what she'd done.

Beorn rolled him over with his foot and saw the blood still running slowly out of the puncture wound in the man's throat.

"You did that?" She nodded. "Good, come, we need to see what's still left to be done."

Jakob had grabbed one of the loose horses and had taken off, his surviving knights following right behind him.

Other than the bruise on his stomach, Beorn was fine, a couple of the others had flesh wounds, but none were life-threatening.

"Naomie, why didn't you go with Gwyn?" he asked.

"Neither of us left," Gwyn replied, coming out from his hiding place in the trees. "She wouldn't go, and I wouldn't go without her."

Naomie was standing close to Beorn's side and Gwyn joined them, handing over her wool mantle so she could cover herself up and, hopefully, find some warmth again.

"Thank you," she said, wrapping it tightly around herself.

Draco walked over and clasped her gently on the shoulder. "You are a warrior, woman. I have never seen anything like what you did. Have you no fear?"

"I have fear," she acknowledged. "But, I had to spit in the face of it or we may have lost all."

"The Germans will be licking their wounds for a bit, I think we can stay here for the night. Let's light a fire and get some food and rest. If we leave at first light, we should make London on the morrow.

Men, we will keep watch overnight, two men at time, just in case those bloody-minded Germans want to get upsides with us before we leave this place."

Naomie and the men got busy, the dead knights were dragged off into the brush, assumably to be collected by Jakob and his men at a later time. They scavenged for some usable chunks of firewood and got a blazing fire started, no longer worried about it being spotted in the dark.

Beorn tended to his horse and then stood off to the side, unable to look away from Naomie. He contemplated what she had said about fear and tried to understand his own reaction to everything that had happened here today.

He was a warrior and when it came to battle, it was every man for themselves. You could not save someone else unless you were out of harm's way first. He failed to live by that rule today, he endangered his own life when he heard Naomie scream, which was completely out of character for him.

He should have dispatched Jakob and then worried about her, but he had not been able to hear her scream without responding. It made him angry, made him feel like he had failed himself, yet he knew that he would do it again right now, need be.

As if reading his mind, she stopped adding to the fire at that moment and turned towards him. It was almost dusk and her eyes were luminescent gems as they met his.

Something had twitched inside of him at the words she spoke after all was done and put to rest. Draco was right, Naomie was a warrior and he had never known anyone like her before. A feeling was stirring inside of him, one he could not name or define, and one that he worried may become permanent.

Those not on watch huddled around the warm fire that was blazing, Beorn and Draco rode in a short time later and threw the two hare they'd been able to kill to Verne to clean and begin cooking. They'd hoped for more than that, but the darkness fell too soon.

Arnell and Millard were on watch now, they'd be relieved by Draco and Jay, and then Verne and Beorn would have the last watch at the end of the night.

Once all of them, including Naomie, had filled their bellies with some food and washed it down with ale, they relaxed and let the warmth of the fire seep into their weary bones.

"You're Romani, yes?" Draco asked.

Naomie nodded.

Draco had not had occasion to speak much with her, but was intrigued by her beauty, and now by her bravery, as well.

"Are you a fortune-teller?"

Naomie's glittering gaze focused on his face, its intensity making him a little uncomfortable.

"I am drabarni."

"What is that?"

"I am a healer and a reader of fortunes."

Beorn sat on the far side of the fire, watching her face as she spoke. He could see the change in it and knew she was now play-acting, becoming the mysterious gypsy woman that non-gypsies expected her to be.

Draco and Verne, however, were playing right into her hands. Gwyn was ignoring the entire conversation and was keeping to himself off to one side of the fire. Beorn could see his lips moving and assumed he was having a private conversation with his God.

"Do you read your own fortune?" Draco asked.

"Never."

"Why not?"

Naomie looked back and forth between the two young men, both of them were handsome and a bit older than she was, although she had an old soul and had lived a much different life than they had and, therefore, believed herself to be much wiser than either of them.

"One's own wants and beliefs can affect a reading. We tend to see what we want to see, rather than what is right before us."

Her eyes glided across the fire then and met Beorn's. He had lived a life even more brutal and onerous than her own, and she could relate to him much more easily than these two randy knaves.

"Can you tell us our fortunes?" Draco asked.

She pulled her gaze away from Beorn's and turned to him, studying the flames from the fire that reflected in his emerald eyes.

"Have you any coin?"

'What ballocks this girl has,' Beorn said to himself, after he almost choked on the sip of ale he was taking.

Draco seemed nonplussed, but then plucked a coin from the small pouch attached to his belt and tossed it to her.

She caught it nimbly and squirreled it away in the pocket of her mantle, along with her other valuables, the dirk and the rabbit's foot.

Then she reached towards him. "Give me your hand."

Draco moved closer to her and she held his hand in hers, tracing the lines of his palm.

Draco squirmed uneasily, her touch was gentle and featherlight and was causing his body to react in a way he had not anticipated.

After a few moments of running her fingers lightly across his palm, which had seemed like an eternity of torture to Draco, she looked up and met his eyes.

"There are three major lines in one's palm, the lifeline, the headline and the heartline. Your lifeline is deeply etched and has few breaks."

"Does that mean I'll live a long time?"

"It means you have enthusiasm for life and a willingness to fight for what you want. You are filled with courage and energy and a deep desire to win always."

"So then, I will live for a long time?"

"You will fight to do so." Draco seemed satisfied, but only Beorn noticed that she had never given him a straight answer.

"What of my heartline?" Just her continuing touch on his palm was making Draco's heart skitter around in his chest and he had to keep adjusting the way he was sitting to ease the response of some of his other body parts.

"Your heartline is fainter, not etched so deeply."

Naomie met his gaze again and smiled at the impatient look on his face.

"You don't like to be alone and your heart rules your head. Your heartline is long, meaning you are a romantic but, see here?" she asked, drawing her finger along one portion where the line was broken, and sending a shiver down Draco's spine.

"Yes."

"This means you will have many, deep emotional unions, romantically and as friendships. And you will be devoted and loving to all those you care about."

She released his hand and Draco sat back, contemplating her words.

"Draco, my friend," Verne said, "it does not appear you need worry about marriage for a time then, and when you do, there will be many to choose from."

"And that is how it should be, enjoy your youth Draco, love well and love often," Beorn said, unable to miss the yearning in the boy's face as he gazed at Naomie.

It did not sit well with Beorn, but the girl did not belong to him and if she chose to give herself to Draco, it would only confirm his suspicions about her.

"Best get some sleep now, it will be a short night for us all."

"But I haven't heard about my headline yet," Draco whined.

"Save it for another day, Draco, and get some rest."

The men all wrapped up in wool blankets and tried to sleep as close to the fire as possible, taking care only to avoid being so close that they would be singed.

Beorn made his way back into the shadows and away from the others. Since he'd purchased his estate and was no longer actively fighting, he had grown used to being by himself and needed a respite from being amidst all these other people constantly.

Sleep, however, did not come to him easily. The adrenaline from the battle still roared through his veins and the thought of finding Jakob and finishing him off swirled through his mind.

That vision was swiftly replaced by Naomie's face, her eyes and her lips so clear in his mind that it was if she were right there beside him.

Beorn was deep in his thoughts when he felt someone touch the blanket that he had wrapped around himself and he turned to them, his dirk at the ready to slit their throat, need be.

He paused when he saw Naomie squatting down beside him and sheathed the knife.

"What is it?" he asked, wondering if she might be a true seer, after all, and had been able to read his thoughts.

"I'm cold," she responded. Theirs eyes met, but in the darkness their thoughts remained hidden.

She tossed her mantle on the ground, her breast was still exposed where her undertunic had been torn earlier in the day and she quickly pulled back his blanket the rest of the way, straddling his torso.

Beorn's heart started hammering in his chest as he reached up and adjusted the blanket, pulling it around her shoulders, leaving them cocooned together underneath it.

"My blood runs fast after the today's battle, if you think I will be able to just keep you warm without first ravishing you, you would be very wrong."

Naomie did not speak, but in response wiggled her bottom as she made herself more comfortable. A slight smile creased her face when she felt the response of his body through her silken skirts.

She began to move slowly, lifting her bottom then lowering it again, rubbing it against his already hardened member, Beorn groaned and grabbed her hips, trying to hold her still to keep from losing complete control of himself.

Naomie was enjoying herself, teasing him, tempting him, and she leaned down over his torso, allowing her full breasts to rub against his chest.

He arched up against her and one hand went behind her head, pulling her down close enough that his lips could capture hers, while with the other slid up under her skirts and began its own exploration.

As their lips met, hers soft and sensuous, his harder, more demanding, his fingers continued playing with her and this time when she moved it was in response to his touch.

When she could stand it no more, she slid his linen pants off of him and gently grabbed his shaft, causing Beorn's sharp intake of breath, then she slowly lowered her quivering body onto him and he groaned loudly as he penetrated deep inside of her.

Naomie pulled the blanket tighter around the two of them, forcing their bodies even closer together. They moved in perfect sync, as if their bodies had been designed to fit one another's. Naomie lowered her head towards Beorn's, caressing his chest with her breasts, allowing him to ravage her with his strong, insistent kisses. His beard tickled her face as they moved more and more desperately against one another.

With total abandon Naomie sat up and moved hard against him just as he convulsed inside of her with a loud cry of satisfaction.

Naomie dropped her head onto his chest, her body shuddering pleasantly and Beorn wrapped his arms tightly around her, hugging her close, not wanting to release her just yet.

Feeling the chicken-flesh rise on her skin due to the cold, Beorn finally relented and let her go, rolling her over next to him, then separating from her slowly before reaching for her mantle and wrapping it around her body before covering the both of them once again with his wool blanket.

"Will you be warm enough now?" he asked, tucking her in just a little closer to his side, so she could snuggle her head against the hollow of his shoulder.

"I am at this moment, if that does not last, I will be sure to wake you."

"And I will be ready," he replied. "Best try to sleep a bit first."

The two of them did fall into oblivious darkness a short time later, however, the men over by the fire were still having a hard time trying to ignore what they had heard going on and sleep was not coming as easily to them.

CHAPTER 10

Beorn was gone when Naomie woke the next morning. It was not yet full light and she took advantage of her location in the deep shadows to sit up and languorously stretch her arms over her head, smiling as the memory of the interlude with Beorn ran through her mind.

Naomie sobered when she realized the predicament that she was getting herself into. They would reach London later today, then leave for the continent. From there, she would most likely be on her own to find her people.

Beorn would no longer be warming her nights and she would be at the mercy of old, ugly Ninga. She shuddered in disgust at the thought of it, but there was no other alternative.

Naomie knew Beorn would have her as often as she wanted, but only until it was time for them to part company, then she was on her own. She was the one that must decide if she would share her body with him again or not.

She also knew that with each coupling with Beorn that she risked getting with child, which would forever keep her from returning to her family. Naomie had surprised herself by going to Beorn last night, but her body craved his and she wanted him inside of her at least one more time before their journey ended, she refused to think of what the consequences could be.

Naomie was filled with wonderment at the feelings and emotions that coursed through her whenever she thought of Beorn. He was a gadje, unclean and not worthy of her or her affection.

But it did not feel that way, and left her thoughts battling between her reality now and what she had been taught her entire life.

The thought of never seeing him again filled her with a despair that she could not account for, and she feared that painful spike might just bury itself even deeper into her heart if she spent any more time with him.

Her family would disown her if they found out she had been with a gadje or even, Heaven forbid, had feelings for one. That was something that should never be and she would never be able to speak of it once she returned to her tribe. It was in her best interest to step away from him now, before her situation became irrevocable, but she was not sure she could do that.

Beorn rode into the clearing just then and his eyes were drawn to Naomie, still sitting in the bedding they had shared, her thick, dark hair tangled from sleep. Her silver eyes were positively glowing in the early morning sunlight as she returned his gaze.

He could see her chest heave and knew more was developing between them than was wise. Their time together would be short and he could not send her back to her family if she was with child, yet he did not think he had the strength to resist her should she come to him again in the night.

The group sat around the dying embers of the fire to finish off the last of the food they'd brought with them. There was little conversation, but Beorn could not help but notice the scowl that Draco wore and the sidelong gazes that both Gwyn and Verne sent his way.

They were about to saddle the horses when Beorn held his hand up, demanding silence, then they all heard a horse's hooves approaching and scattered. Only Beorn stood in the center of the opening, his broadsword unsheathed and ready.

With a curse, he shoved the sword back into its scabbard once he saw who was riding in on them.

"Do you have a bit missing? What the devil are you doing here?" Beorn asked, as Grant slid off his horse's back, a wide, satisfied grin splitting his face.

"I came to fight with you."

"Nay, your father will not have it and I will not go behind his back. Hie thee home, you cannot come with us."

"But, uncle," he said, his brown eyes filled with devilry, "I barely survived the Germans while trying to catch up, you wouldn't send me back into their clutches, would you?"

"Where are they?"

"Two, maybe three kilometers away. I was lucky, they were licking their wounds and my appearance caught them by surprise and I was able to pass by unharmed. I might not be so lucky passing them again. Did you have a battle with them? Many were cleaved and bleeding."

"We did." Beorn was happy to hear that the Germans were suffering as a result of their altercation the day before, but he knew not what to do now with this twit.

If he allowed Grant to accompany them, Radolf would never forgive him, yet, would Radolf forgive him if he left Grant alone at the mercy of the Germans? There was no right answer but for now he could keep Grant safe and would do so.

"Come with us to London, once we arrive there we will talk further about your future."

"Thank you, uncle."

The small band mounted their horses and headed out.

The motley crew arrived in London later that day, cold, tired and hungry. After finding a place to stable their horses and have them cared for, Beorn took his odd assortment of followers to a nearby inn.

The others all stepped inside, out of the cold, drizzling rain, but Beorn caught Naomie's arm before she could go in and he pulled her aside.

"What is amiss?" he asked. She had been acting strangely ever since they reached the city limits and he needed an explanation.

Her silver eyes looked deeply into his and Beorn, as always, found himself enslaved by their beauty. When she was quiet and calm, they were the soft grey of a dove's feathers but, when she felt something strongly, as she must right now, the dark rings around the outside of the irises became bolder and darker, emphasizing the silver chips within that sparkled like moonlight reflecting on a pond.

Naomie pulled her gaze away from his and glanced around, she knew they were near the docks, and she feared the men that had taken her may still be here.

"Tell me," he insisted, putting his finger under her chin and drawing her attention back to him.

"The men that took me, they brought me to this place."

"This inn?"

"No, this place." She threw her arms out wide, indicating, as far as Beorn could tell, the entire seaside and then he understood.

"They brought you by boat, so you would have landed somewhere in this area."

She nodded vigorously.

"It looks familiar because its where you escaped."

This time a smile accompanied the nod.

"Have you any idea who they were?"

"No, I was taken by several men near a town on the coast."

"Knights?"

"No, they looked like sailors."

"Do you know why they took you?" The rain continued to drizzle down on them, Naomie's hood protected her somewhat but Beorn was getting drenched.

"I think to sell, they had other women on the ship, as well."

"Did those women escape with you?"

"No, I fought too hard, so they tied my hands and threw me into a hold by myself."

"They didn't know what they were getting themselves into by taking you, did they?"

Her face remained devoid of emotion, but now her eyes glittered with a bit devilry.

He gently drew a calloused finger down her cheek, then around her full, pink lips, feeling himself get aroused as he watched her lips part slightly. He quickly removed his finger and his voice was a little more brusque than he intended when he spoke.

"Someday I would like to hear the story of your escape. For now, they will be long gone and, even if not, you have a bevy of knights at your side, you are safe with us. Now, come inside and let us get out of this rain before we are completely soaked through."

He took her hand and dragged her inside and over to the table where the others were already half done with their first cup of ale.

The small group ate and drank their fill, then Beorn managed to get a couple of rooms for their use. Looking over the group, he began doling out assignments.

"Gwyn, you need to meet with the Archbishop to get any more news."

"Of course," Gwyn replied.

"Take Grant with you. Word needs to be sent to Radolf and Becca that he is alive and will be traveling with us. Grant, have a care for the Germans should they make it into the city, they will still be looking to cause trouble."

"Aye."

"Jay, Millard and Arnell, I need you to check the ships, find one that can take us, and our horses, across the pond as soon as possible. Be sure they are reputable, we don't want our throats slit halfway across just so they can have our mounts and our weapons."

"As you wish," Millard replied. Beorn waited for them to leave the inn before getting back to business. "Verne and I will go to collect our mercenaries."

"Did you forget me again, brother?" Draco asked.

Beorn could not miss the anger in his voice and on his face, and he knew it had to do with Naomie. That particular issue would have to be addressed between them, but now was not the time.

"Of course not, I'll get to that in a moment, but first, how long has Arnell been in Radolf's service?"

Draco frowned. "Not all that long, why do you ask?"

"Keep an eye on him, I still wonder how he was able to miss all those Germans when he was on watch just before they attacked us."

"Could be bad luck."

"Yes, Draco, it could be, but best to not be caught unawares yet again, don't you agree?"

"I do, is that my mission for today?"

"No, I have one much more challenging, you will be responsible for the safety of Naomie. She needs new clothing, so she won't be so conspicuous."

He threw several coins across the table at Draco. Seeing the young man roll his eyes skyward, he felt a rush of anger at the ill-mannered lout.

"Draco," Beorn's voice was sharp and Draco immediately turned his attention back that way. "This is not about Naomie and me, nor your feelings towards her. Grow up and do what I ask of you.

Naomie was kidnapped from her homeland and brought here by sea. Those men are still here somewhere and will risk all to take her back should they come across her. You have the duty to ensure her safety, be sure you understand the importance of that and do not let me down."

Draco met his angry gaze, embarrassed to be called out on his feelings for Naomie. He was tired of being treated like a spoiled child by his brother and they would have this out, sooner rather than later.

"As you wish."

Their eyes remained locked as their mental battle continued but, finally, Beorn turned away.

"Let us get to our tasks then," he said, standing up and striding out of the inn with Verne right behind him.

"It was a blessing to be able to visit with Lora once again," Gwyn said, his face glowing with love. "When we were young, we were so close in age that we were the best of friends."

"It's been like that for Draco and me, as well," Grant replied. "We were quite the little baskets, always getting into trouble. Me, more so than Draco, of course."

"Why was that?"

"My father had high expectations for me as his eldest son, while Draco was the baby of his family and even grandfather went easy on him."

"That surprises me," Gwyn said, memories of his father rushing through his head. "He was always a fair man, but expected everyone, even his children, to always adhere to the rules."

"He must have become more mellow as he aged then," Grant replied, his face lighting up with a crooked smile that reminded Gwyn of Radolf.

"Your father, Radolf, is much like our father was. They both had a great deal of responsibility put on their shoulders and, being the men that they are, they strive to ensure that things are done correctly, fairly and honestly. I hope you appreciate all the knowledge and wisdom that you can learn from your father, and that you take it to heart for the future."

Lora's home was nearer the palace, where the houses and the areas around them were cleaner and the air was fresher than it was as they approached the bowels of the city where the inn was located.

Grant sighed heavily, ignoring the misting rain falling on them as they walked along the dirty streets, shoving their way through the crowds and trying to ignore the beggars that accosted them constantly.

When they first started encountering them, Gwyn felt like he needed to give out coin to each and every one and Grant had to be quite firm with him while explaining they could not possibly save each of those blighters, and that it was in their own best interest to get back to the inn as soon as possible.

Stepping around one beggar that had fallen down, presumably just drunk, right in front of them, Grant got back to the subject at hand.

"I love my father, and I know he is a great man and he has already taught me much. But I am young and feel stifled always being trapped at the castle. I will do my duty, but first, I want to see the world and test my skills on more than a practice field. He refuses to understand that."

"Radolf's obligation is to his family and to the shire. It is paramount that he prepare you to take his place one day. If you leave to find your adventures, mayhap, you will not want to return and pick up the responsibility of your duties."

"I would never do that."

Grant stopped and held his hand up in front of Gwyn, then put his finger to his lips and listened, sure that he could hear the faint jangle of chainmail around the corner that they were approaching.

With no further words, he motioned to Gwyn and led him across the rutted dirt street. Once there, Grant whispered, "Stay here, hide yourself in this doorway till I return."

He looked back behind them and saw a large wagon being pulled by two oxen coming down the roadway. He waited impatiently until it reached him and then walked along beside it, hidden from view by anyone on the other side.

Once he passed the intersecting street where he'd heard the chainmail and sensed danger, he let the wagon continue on and quietly stepped back.

As he suspected there were two German knights standing just around the corner, their swords were drawn and they appeared to be waiting for someone, he assumed those someones would be him and Gwyn.

Grant was barely able to see them and they had no interest in what was going on in this part of the street, so he hurriedly crossed the road again and went down the next alleyway so that he could sneak up on them from the other direction.

They had gotten frustrated at the delay and were now standing in the roadway looking back in the direction that he and Gwyn had been coming from.

Their faces were red with anger that, somehow, they had missed the two of them, and now they would have to face Jakob's ire. Reluctantly, they stepped back into the alleyway to determine their next course of action.

"Looking for someone?" Grant asked, just as he leapt towards them, his sword wasting no time in engaging theirs. The Germans were worthy adversaries, but Grant had practiced his whole life for this very moment and was able to hold both of them off while inflicting various wounds to them.

The chainmail made it difficult to wound them badly enough to stop their charges, but when Grant's blade finally sunk into the throat of one of them, the other turned tail and ran.

Wiping the sweat off his brow, Grant took a quick look around to be sure there were no watchman or constables that might have seen what happened, then slid the body further down into the alleyway and left it. Beggars and thieves would strip it of any valuables, and he had no time to properly attend to it just now.

Such crimes were, unfortunately, an everyday occurrence in the bowels of the city, and rarely were there any watchman in the vicinity until after a crime was reported.

Grant then hurried back to Gwyn, who was shaking a bit, and not from the cold.

"Is it safe?"

"For now, but they will be back and there will be even more of them, we must hurry to the inn."

Grant and Gwyn made haste through the cold, dingy streets, Grant taking as many narrow, hidden alleyways as possible so they could not easily be followed while they made their way back to the safety of the inn.

Draco stayed close to Naomie as she entered a nearby shop. There was not a great selection, but she chose a plain white linen undertunic and a bright red, long-sleeved tunic to wear over it.

"I'm not sure red is the most obscure color, Naomie. Mayhap, you'd like something a little duller, something that won't attract so much attention."

"No," she replied, hugging the piece of clothing to her chest, her eyes open wide as she stared at him.

"Please," he said, the woman unnerved him for some reason, he had never met anyone like her and still couldn't get the thoughts of what she done with Beorn the night before from his head. He had to try desperately to keep his gaze from wandering down to her full breasts as they spoke, her mantle not even able to completely hide them.

Draco's pride was injured, knowing she chose his older brother over him, but he took a deep breath and forced those thoughts from his mind. He did not think badly of Naomie, mayhap he would have if she were English, but she was not and he knew nothing of her culture.

The only thing that he was sure of was that Naomi could be in danger and, having been charged with her safety, that is what he chose to focus on.

He tried to grab the tunic from her hands but, somehow, she was able to maneuver the dirk from her pocket and set it painfully against his right forefinger which was gripping the material.

She pressed down with the knife and a droplet of blood rose from under it.

"God's tooth, wench, I'm only trying to help you." He pulled his hand back away from her and put the bloody digit in his mouth. Removing it and grimacing at her, his patience at an end, he said, "Fine, bring it to the front so I can pay. Whatever happens to you while you wear it is of your own doing."

Naomi had a very self-satisfied smile on her face as they left the small shop.

"You know they are more likely to see you in that bright color, do you not?"

She stopped and turned to him. "Draco, red is the color of good health and happiness. I always wear something red and was very pleased to find this tunic. I have a mantle that is grey and will cover me so, mayhap, I will not be so bold and bright as to attract all the knaves in the city, after all."

Draco's heart skipped a beat when she said his Christian name in that lilting voice and looked at him like that, her eyes lit up like handfuls of diamonds and onyx sparkling out from her face.

He tore his own eyes away from her, suddenly feeling flushed and, wishing above all else that it was he that had discovered her first, not Beorn.

But that was obviously not to be, so Draco shrugged his shoulders and escorted her back to the inn, keeping an eye out the entire time for any potential danger. All the while contemplating how to clamp down on the feelings that he seemed to be developing for her.

Beorn was not altogether pleased when he returned from meeting with his mercenaries. Daegal had not been successful in getting very many additional knights, but they would have to make due with what they had. They agreed that Daegal would collect the others and they would meet up at the inn to confirm all of the details, hopefully, they would know by then when they could make the journey across the channel to the continent.

When he and Verne returned to the inn, Beorn was surprised to find Draco, Gwyn and Grant all hastily downing hefty cups of ale. Something, apparently, had them in quite a state.

"What is amiss?" he asked, as he took a seat at their table.

The others looked to Grant to explain and he drained his cup before beginning.

"The Germans are here and they have found us."

"How?"

"I'm not sure. After Gwyn and I met with the Archbishop, we went to see Lora. I think they may have been watching for us there."

"Christ's fingernails," Beorn swore softly, ignoring the look of reprimand from Gwyn. "It's Jakob, I should have killed him when I had the chance. He knows me and knows my family. Was there an altercation?"

"Yes," Grant said, a proud smile lighting his face and his chest puffing out just a little more than normal. "I took care of one of them, the other turned and ran."

"We'll have to go to ground for a bit, try to keep out of their sight. What did you learn from the Archbishop, Gwyn?" Beorn asked, waving over the serving girl and asking for another ewer of ale along with two more cups.

"Nothing good," he replied, after she left. "Henry has already left Germany and is on his way to Rome with his army. We must make haste or this will all be for naught."

Beorn was quiet as contemplated Gwyn's words.

"An army travels slowly," he said. "They must stop and make camp each night, especially with the King traveling with them, they will ensure it is a leisurely, comfortable journey. We, on the other hand, can push through without such pomp and can ride hard to reach Rome before them. Are you up for that, Gwyn?"

"Yes, God rides with me."

"And pigs might fly," Beorn murmured, having given up on God quite some time ago. "Grant, what of your missive to your mother and father?"

"That is why we went to Lora's house. She ensured us that she will get word to my parents."

"Are you sure this is what you wish to do. Your father will tan your hide when you finally do return home, and mine as well, if our paths cross in the future."

"It is, Uncle Beorn, and I promise I will return to Wyndymshire as soon as the mission is completed, and I will make it up to my parents."

"As you wish. How does Lora keep, Gwyn?" he asked, she was his youngest sister and he had not seen her for many years. It was still hard for him to envision her as an adult, managing her own family now.

"She is well, her husband is a Duke and they split time between London and in Normandy on their estates there. We were fortunate to catch her in the city."

"Pity that I cannot see her before we leave," Beorn said, his face filled with regret. "but, if Jakob has men stationed by her home, I do not think it would be wise."

"Lora was quite distressed about not seeing you, as well, but I told her where your estates in Normandy are and, methinks that, come spring, she will most likely show up on your doorstep."

"I would like that very much," Beorn replied. "And Draco, where is Naomie? Did you run into trouble, as well?"

"She went to her room," his voice was a bit surly, "and the only trouble I ran into was from her."

CHAPTER 11

Naomie was deep asleep when Beorn entered her room at the inn. She had bathed and climbed into the bed naked. Naomie was a restless sleeper and had partially kicked off the blanket, so Beorn was able to gaze at her soft, creamy skin, more beige than white, and offset by the reddish hue at the peaks of her full breasts.

The long, black lashes rested on her cheekbones and Naomie's face was more relaxed than he recalled ever seeing it before, mayhap, because she did not know he was looking.

He gently drew the backside of his finger along her jaw and paused to let it circle around her full lips, feeling his own physical response when they parted, and Naomie let out a soft sigh.

Beorn laid down alongside of her, wishing there was enough time to do what his body was craving, but there was not.

Still, he could not resist allowing his fingers a few more moments to explore the expanse of naked skin available to him, but even with just the feathery light touches, Naomie came full awake, her body ready to surrender while her mind was still grasping what was happening.

With those silver orbs staring into his eyes, calling to him, he had no choice but to lean forward and gently capture her lips, letting his hands roam even further abroad over her body.

Teasing her breasts and drawing a low moan from her, his fingers traveled further south, finding her ready and, as she writhed against his hand, he could not douse the fire of passion burning within and would restrain himself no further.

Removing his belt, sword and linen pants, he moved atop her body, his beard tickling her bare skin, his lips moving from hers down to her breasts and then to her sensitive belly.

"Please," she whispered, aching to have him inside of her, and he gladly granted her request, riding her to heights of pleasure neither of them had heretofore ever reached.

Still holding each other tightly as they lay waiting for their breathing and the rapid beating of their hearts to return to normal, someone started pounding on the door.

"What is amiss?" Beorn roared at the intruder.

"Everyone is here and waiting for you," Draco yelled back at him. "Time enough for your games another day, Beorn. Your mercenary friends do not look very patient."

"I will be there, anon."

"Will you?"

"Cry off, Draco, I will be there anon."

When there was nothing further from the other side of the door, Beorn kissed Naomie's shoulder and caressed her cheek before standing up and getting dressed.

"Draco tells me you cut him," Beorn said, unable to hide the smirk on his face.

"Yes, I wanted the red kirtle."

"So he says. I am sure it will look lovely on you but, please, try not to hurt anymore of my knights if you can help it. Makes them look bad."

"Ma-sha-llah," she replied, stretching her arms up over her head and giving him one last look at her wares.

"Methinks, you may be the death of me yet," he murmured, his dark blue eyes sparkling with admiration. "Get dressed and join us for our meal. The mercenaries are here and we will be making our final arrangements for the journey to the continent."

"Yes, Beorn," Naomie replied quietly, feeling content and satiated as she watched him square his shoulders and walk out of the room.

The talk and laughter at the table came to an abrupt halt when Naomie made her way over to it. The red tunic hugged her curves well and all eyes were fixed on her as she sashayed her way between the tables nestled together in room.

The tunic was a little large for her, but she had made it more her own style by adding colorful silk scarves, which called attention to the swell of her bosom and her tiny waist.

Several of the knights stood and indicated an opening next to them for her to make herself comfortable, but Naomie ignored them all and went to Beorn's side. He kept his face an emotional blank as he stood up and reached behind them to grab an empty stool.

"Hold up," a large, brutish man said, as Beorn snaked the stool away from his table.

"You would refuse this lovely lass a seat?" Beorn asked, and when the man looked her over from top to toe, the look of annoyance on his face changed to lust and Beorn was hard-pressed to keep from slapping the look right off of his face.

The man then looked over the group of knights and, seeing their set faces, their hands close to the hilt of their swords, he said nothing further and went back to his own business.

Their group had the largest table in the room and there were several men sitting at it that Naomie had not seen before.

The leader of the new group of knights was a tall, swarthy, man who Beorn addressed after making sure Naomie had a cup of ale in front of her. "Will there be any others joining us?"

"I've engaged all I could find who had no other offers," the man replied, his voice was low and deep, his eyes boring into Naomie. "She will not be on the ship with us, yes?"

"She will be with us on the crossing and for part of the journey once we land. Is that a problem?"

"Mayhap, it is," he replied, glancing around the table.

One of the mercenaries, whose brown eyes were always open wide, making him look to be in a perpetual state of surprise, said, "Everyone knows women on board a ship bring bad luck."

"They only cause bad luck because they distract sailors from their duties. We're traveling in the middle of the night, we'll be down below and she will not present any problems for the sailors."

He looked around the table again to see if there was anyone else that had something to add, but no one would meet his eye or contradict him.

Beorn knew well that Daegal, as well as the mercenaries that he had enlisted, were hard men that knew only battle. They were not to be trifled with and had little respect for the niceties of life.

Some had no conscience at all and would commit crimes not included as part of the duties they were paid for, simply because they knew no better and cared not for the consequences.

Beorn wished Naomie did not look quite so enticing in her bold, red tunic but, the damage was already done so he took his time and made sure to look each one of the new men in the eye before he began to speak.

"This woman is in my charge until we can get her safely back to her own people. She is off limits and no man here will touch her or he will answer to me. If that is not within your capabilities, I'd ask that you leave us now. I will give no quarter on this."

Beorn was a well-known warrior, he had been fighting for the King and as a mercenary for many years and his skill and fearlessness were renowned throughout most of the continent, as well as in England.

The men sitting around the table had a respectful wariness as far as he was concerned, but Beorn knew that may not be enough on a journey such as this.

"What say you?" he asked, when the men dropped their eyes from his and picked up their cups.

Daegal raised his cup towards Naomie. "We will honor your request and will do our best to ensure the girl's safety, as well. Good Health."

"Good Health," all the others chimed in before taking a long draught from their cups.

"Millard, what luck did you have with a ship?"

"If we can have everything on board by high tide at midnight tomorrow, the Glorianna will take us across the channel."

"Why not tonight?"

"The load he will be carrying to the continent will not arrive until mid-afternoon tomorrow. The next high tide after that is midnight."

Resigned to the additional delay, Beorn looked around the table once again. "Do you all have your own horses?

The men nodded.

"Good, have them, and yourselves, at the pier well before midnight so we can be prepared to head out. You all understand what our mission is?"

Daegal replied, "Aye, I've told them we go to defend the Pope, which is laughable, since most of us know we are so far gone that even he cannot save us from Hell when we die."

"Mayhap this good deed will count for something when it comes to that," Beorn replied absently. "Do not be late tomorrow night, men. We sail at high tide whether you are on the boat or not, and we need every man we can get."

He tossed a heavy bag filled with coin to Daegal. "Distribute this amongst the men and make ready for the journey. They will receive the rest due to them after our work is done."

"Aye," Daegal replied, grabbing up the bag, swallowing down the last of his ale and lumbering towards the door, the others right behind him.

"Do you trust them?" Draco asked.

"I trust them once the battle begins but, until then, they have us by the curlies and we must watch them carefully to ensure that we aren't betrayed by someone with a richer purse.

But let us turn back to the issues at hand, everyone must be prepared to catch the ship tomorrow night. The Glorianna sets sail at midnight so be there with your horses and your gear well before it's supposed to leave. Best lay low until then, Jakob and his knights are looking for us, so have a care if you do go wandering."

Food was ordered and shared amongst them. As the men chattered around them, Beorn leaned over towards Naomie and tickled her ear, as he whispered, "You must eat, you cannot wait for us to finish."

She looked at him curiously, wondering how he knew of their traditions. "It is difficult for me to change who I am and how I have lived all my life till now."

"I understand that, but we need you healthy and well-fed. Me, and my men, would give up our own food for you, need be. Never concern yourself about that, understand?"

Once their eyes locked on one another's everything around them seemed to disappear and time stood still as they entered a world unto themselves.

"I understand," she whispered quietly.

He raised his hand and buried it in her soft, thick hair, brushing it back off her neck, watching the pulse at the base of her throat beating rapidly, her lips partially open, begging to be kissed.

His brought his lips down so that they just barely touched her ear and she shivered in reaction to his touch. "You are more beautiful than words can describe but have a care on the ship. If any of the men give you trouble, you come to me or one these men at our table, yes?"

She turned her head and lifted her face at a coquettish angle, her eyes a sultry grey in the smoky light of the inn as they studied his.

"I have a dirk, I am not afraid."

"I did not expect that you were, but they are many and there is just one of you. Do not be so brave that you get yourself in a situation where you cannot get away from them."

She lifted her hand and stroked his beard, her eyes flickering from his intense blue ones to his hard, full lips. The others at the table tried not to stare, but the charge in the air around the two of them was difficult to ignore.

Draco, in particular, found it uncomfortable to witness and bellowed for another cup of ale.

"As you wish," Naomie whispered, ignoring Draco's outburst and with a little half-smile creasing her face, she turned to her food and began eating.

Naomie returned to her room after she had eaten. They all watched her walk away and Beorn felt his ire rising when they didn't even bother to hide the desire on their faces.

"I hope all of you will adhere to the tenets of knighthood and will remain chivalrous and keep Naomie's safety foremost in your mind as we travel across the continent."

"As you have?" Draco asked, his eyebrow raised and a look of disbelief on his face.

"What does that mean?"

"You have made no secret of the extent of your relationship with her. She is young woman, you are an old man, and you have not been treating her with the respect you are now asking of us."

Beorn stared hard at his little brother, whether the words he spoke were truth or not, he would not be spoken to in that manner.

His voice was soft when he responded, but even Gwyn felt the chill of his words. "This old man can fight circles around you, and what happens between Naomie and me is consensual and most enjoyable. If you would like to take issue with it, you say so now and come first light, we'll resolve this out of doors, with our swords, as grown men should."

Draco's mouth was set, his face white with anger and he was about to accept his uncle's challenge when Gwyn stood up so quickly that his chair fell over backwards, making a loud crack which startled them all.

"I will not have this. You, Beorn, are an adult, now grow up and behave as one. He is your brother, not your enemy.

You, Draco, stop acting like a spoiled child. If you are man enough to join this fray on behalf of the Pope, be man enough to know when you've lost the girl. Get over it and find yourself another one."

Gwyn's voice and his hands were shaking. He did not like confrontation, did not enjoy having to scold his two brothers. "This journey is troublesome enough, particularly for me, I will not continue on if this tension between the two of you is not resolved."

He turned and stalked out of the room. Beorn watched him go, a look of bemusement on his face as he did so, then he turned to Draco.

"I will try to hold my temper in check, if you will try to get over your anger and your jealousy."

Draco's green eyes were like shards of ice he stared at his brother, a brother he knew very little about. He didn't answer for a moment and his face mirrored his thought process, allowing Beorn to see how he was struggling.

The choice, Draco realized that he must now make, was whether or not he wished to continue on this mission. If he did, he would have to swallow his pride and get past any feelings he might have for Naomie.

If he did not, his only other option was to return to Wyndymshire and never gain the experiences he would have by continuing on this journey.

"I will try to do so, if I find I cannot, I will no longer continue on with all of you. You best take proper care of the girl though, brother."

"I intend to." Beorn swallowed the last of the ale in his cup and left to seek out the woman in question.

Now that the drama was done here, Radolf's knights left to visit another establishment where they could engage in some substantial gambling.

Verne tried to talk some sense into Draco, but it was not easy, he could be as hard-headed as Beorn. "You must try to understand your brother."

"No," Draco responded, "he must learn to live in today's world. Times have changed since he was the top cock in the henhouse."

"The question for you, Draco, is," Grant asked, "do you trust him to lead us on this venture?"

"I do," Draco replied.

"Then stuff it for now, we get the job done and then you go your own way."

"Mayhap, that is what will happen," he replied, grabbing for his own cup of ale. "We shall see."

When Beorn entered Naomie's room, he found her sitting atop the featherbed, running a brush through her heavy mass of black hair.

He quietly moved over behind her, grabbed the brush from her hand and started running it through her hair with long, smooth strokes.

"I'm not used to such pampering," she said, leaning her head back and relaxing under his touch.

"Interesting that there is a W etched on the wood of the brush, much like my mother has on hers back in Wyndymshire," Beorn said, his voice was calm as he continued to rhythmically stroke her hair.

"You wouldn't have pinched it from my family home, would you?"

Her shoulders moved up and down noncommittally. Beorn wasn't angry, in his opinion, if that was all she took they were probably ahead in the game.

Once her newly brushed hair was gleaming, he stepped in front of her and handed her the brush.

Naomie set it down beside her on the bed but continued to hold his hand with the other. She turned it palm up and then raised her gaze to meet his.

"May I?" she asked, as always drawing him in with her scintillating gaze.

"You may, but know that I don't go for any of that claptrap," he replied, sitting down beside her.

She raised an eyebrow at him, almost as a challenge, and then turned her attention back to his palm.

CHAPTER 12

With a featherlight touch Naomie traced the lines within his palm, sometimes hesitating, sometimes going over the same line several times, and occasionally frowning down at whatever they were telling her.

"What's the verdict?" he asked, when she finally raised her eyes back up to meet his, although she still continued to hold his hand in both of hers.

"You have large hands which means you are energetic and physically engaged with the world."

"I am, but you already knew that."

A slight smile came to her lips as she continued, "The ball of your thumb is also very large and full. Again, that shows that you have strong, physical vitality and indicates you sometimes have more energy than you know how to deal with, which is probably why you drink so much. It also indicates that you tend to get angry quickly and that you have an overactive sex drive."

A full smile now blossomed on her face and he wondered if she had overheard his argument with Draco a few minutes before.

"I will agree with you on all those things, but again, you knew of them before you looked at my palm."

"These are the three major lines in you hand," she said, ignoring his comments and turning his hand again, so that the palm rested upward. She continued to hold it while she gently traced the lines she was explaining.

"Your headline, your heartline and your lifeline all started out deep and strong, but there is a break in each of them which indicates something happened to change the direction of your life not so very long ago." Beorn tried to pull his hand away, but she held tight and shook her head.

"Listen, Beorn, please."

Frowning, he reluctantly nodded his acquiescence.

"Your headline," she traced the line running across the center of his palm, "is level and shows that you are focused and logical and tend to follow time-honored traditions. See the break here?"

"Yes."

"After that, the headline arches up toward your smallest finger. It means that you have trouble bringing together your head and your heart, you try to disconnect from your emotions."

He said nothing, just continued to watch her face.

"This is your lifeline," she took her nail and dragged it lightly along the line that ran around the base of his thumb and he could feel the hair on the back of neck rising in response. "it shows the nature of your energy. Once again, yours is long and deep, indicating strong physical reserves. But here is a break in the line where something traumatic occurred in your life. After that, it thins out and becomes fainter."

"And what does that mean?"

"It suggests a time when your life force thinned, when your life was filled with angst, with sorrow and with loneliness."

"But, look it gets deeper again."

"It does, but not as deep as it was before the break, so there are still issues that you need to resolve, or you will never be the same man that you were before that event happened."

"I never expected that I would be," he replied softly, knowing the event that completely changed the course of his life, but unwilling to share any bit of it with her.

Naomie could see the pain filling his brilliant blue eyes and was surprised he was allowing her to continue on with this.

"And this is your heartline."

"For which I am quite surprised, as I thought mine would be long gone by now," he said, trying to bite back the sadness that was suddenly enveloping him.

"You have a deep, strong heartline, which indicates that you are emotionally passionate, you love and you hate intensely."

Their eyes met again and Naomie had to drag hers away from his, which now looked like brittle blue chips of ice.

"But, then the break occurs and the line becomes shallow and pale. In combination with the unusually high heartline after the break, it indicates that you are uncertain about your feelings and afraid to invest yourself in them. You guard your heart."

"I don't disagree with what you are saying, Naomie, but it matters naught."

"It does though. The lines show how your life will go if you stay on the same road you are traveling. If you change how you think, and how you live your life, the results will change, as well. It is showing you the consequences of your choices. You are not bound to the past, Beorn, you are free to open your heart again."

He pulled his hand from her grip and began to pace around the room. For some reason, her words were causing his emotions to roil and he found himself unable to come to grips with them.

Beorn wished his flask was full so he could bury those feelings in an alcoholic haze, but it was empty and would be of no help.

Naomie watched him as he strode back and forth around the room, she knew he was full of conflict, the extent of which was well beyond any issue he had as far as she was concerned. "You are a brave, passionate man, Beorn, you just need to choose to live again."

"I want to hear no more from you." He stepped towards Naomie and pulled her to her feet. Burying his fingers deep into her thick hair, he pulled back on it, lifting her face towards his so he could look deeply into her eyes. He needed to be sure she would listen well and heed his words.

"I am what I am and no good will come from trying to change that. What I've lost in the past will stay gone regardless of what I do and, yes, I do guard my heart as best I can, so that it will never happen again."

He hadn't realized how hard he was pulling on her hair until he saw the tears glistening like jewels in her eyes.

"Nothing can or will ever come to fruition between us. You are a beautiful, courageous woman and I have never felt such utter helplessness as I do when I'm captured by the look in your eyes, and I've never lost myself as completely as I do when buried inside of you.

And that is why I must get you back to your family as soon as I can. I have nothing to give you."

The tears were now starting to trickle down her cheeks, although he had completely loosened his grip on her hair. He stepped back away from Naomie and she slapped his face as hard as she could, the sharp crack resounding throughout the small room.

"I never asked you for anything."

Naomie's face was set, her eyes almost black as her rage smoldered, while at the same time tears continued to flow freely down her cheeks.

She raised her hand to strike out at him again, but Beorn caught it in mid-air and forced her arm behind her back, bringing her body into contact with his own as he did so.

For a brief moment their eyes met and locked, then he swooped down and took her lips with his own, crushing them as he pulled her up even tighter against his body, loving the way the softness of hers yielded to his.

Mayhap, their anger drove them to madness for a time as they tore off each other's clothing and threw them to the floor before they fell onto the featherbed together.

Groping each other in a frenzy, their kisses hard and deliberate, every sense in their bodies heightened. Beorn nudged her legs apart, unable to wait one more second before possessing her.

Naomie's tears had stopped and her nails raked down his back as she sought to pull him even deeper inside of her. With an irrepressible fervor their bodies came together time after time, bolstered by all the power of their emotions erupting from within, both the good and the bad, until they reached an explosive climax that left them both completely spent and exhausted, mentally and physically.

They had found the relief their bodies needed, but both chose to hide in the arms of Morpheus until they could untangle their dissonant emotions.

They fell fast asleep, still wrapped in each other's arms.

Beorn was gone when Naomie woke the next morning and was not with the others in the main room of the inn when she made her way there.

"Join us, Naomie," Gwyn said, "we were just about to take our morning meal."

She felt her heart start beating just a little bit faster when Beorn returned while they were mid-way through their meal. He looked around the room, spotted their table and made his way over, never looking directly at Naomie.

"I've checked in at the stable and the horses are being well-cared for, they are aware we will be picking them up late this evening in anticipation of boarding the Glorianna."

He waved the serving girl over and asked for an ale, then helped himself to a chunk of bread from the trencher placed in the center of their table.

Beorn paused as he went to take a bite of the bread, lowered it down to the table and looked around with a frown on his face. "Where is Arnell?"

The others shrugged their shoulders.

"I have not seen him since he lost a pile of coin playing dice last night," Jay stated, grabbing another piece of cold chicken and tearing into it.

"I've never known him to have any luck when he gambles," Millard added.

"Does he have family in London that he would have gone to stay with?"

"I do not believe he does, he's a bit of a loner," Millard replied.

"Could he have run into trouble with the Germans?" Grant asked.

"Mayhap," Beorn said, looking thoughtful as he bit into a piece of the rye bread and then washed it down with ale. He glanced up and couldn't help but notice Naomie, who was sitting across the table from him, her eyes staring down at the trencher in front of her.

She did not exude the same vivacity as she normally did, and he knew the fault was his for crushing her spirit. He pushed his guilt down deep and refused to dwell on it just now, knowing it was a problem he would have to address at another time.

"I will wander and see if I can locate Arnell, or mayhap I will spy our German friends who are on the prowl for us."

"What shall I do today?" Gwyn asked.

"You are a grown man, Gwyn, you will have to make that determination yourself. I would only suggest you not travel far from the security of the inn."

He popped the last of the bread in his mouth and drained the remaining ale in his cup. When he stood up, he couldn't help but notice that Naomie was watching him closely now, and finally he deigned to meet her gaze.

"You should go back to your room and stay there, it will be the safest place for you."

Their eyes were locked but she refused to even acknowledge his words. The black splinters in her eyes glittered like chips of onyx and her face reflected the anger she still carried towards him.

"I'll come with you," Verne said, hoping to ease some of the tension at the table.

The two of them turned and left the inn together. "Seems you are at odds with several of our traveling companions. Is that wise at this juncture of our journey?"

"In all our years together, have you ever known me to take the wise path, Verne?"

"Not that I can recall, M'lord."

"Then all is how it should be. I worry about Arnell and would like to find where he's hidden himself."

"Worry about him in what way?" The two men continued down the side of the road, their broad bodies walking side by side, forcing others out of their way as they passed.

"I still cannot understand how he missed the Germans' approach on our way here. They were so close, it would be almost impossible to not see or at least hear them, yet he did not give us warning. If it were not for Naomie, we may well have ended our journey right there."

"And now we learn that he loses coin frequently while gambling."

"Indeed, and only came to Radolf's shire a short time ago. Jakob knows much about his adversaries here in England and he is a worthy foe. It would not surprise me if he had the foresight to set spies within any castles that he thought would provide aid to the Pope. This issue has been ongoing for almost a year, giving the Germans plenty of time to prepare."

"Where do we even begin to look for him? Or the Germans?"

"Let us stop here, it is a busy area, with much through traffic. If the Germans are on the lookout for us, mayhap, we might want to stay right here and watch for them. If Arnell is a spy, we may catch him in their company.

You go to that corner down there and I will wait here. Stay back against the building and keep your hood up so it's not obvious who you are. Give me the signal if you notice anything suspect and, together we will track them."

Being so close to the docks, there were many alehouses along this stretch, but also cookshops and bakeries. Depending on where the Germans were staying, they may well come this way to feed their bellies before continuing to search for him and his men.

The cloudy skies finally broke open and let loose a drizzling rain to accompany the cold breeze blowing in off the water of the channel. The cold did not bother Beorn and allowed him to keep his hood up without appearing suspicious.

They stood in the miserable weather for a time, but saw nothing amiss, not until Beorn spied someone that he had not anticipated and his entire body tensed.

He let out a whistle loud enough for Verne to hear and then waved him over. It was still raining but had tapered off to just a light mist now, as Verne hurried over to his side.

"Methinks, I just saw Naomie heading down that alleyway. I have no idea why she would be here and only saw the back of her as she hurried that way. We best follow to ensure her safety, if it is indeed Naomie."

As they hurried down the alleyway, Beorn became more and more uncomfortable, it was too easy to set a trap in these narrow confines, but he needed to be sure that it was not Naomie, and if it was, to take her back to the inn where she would be safe.

He threw his mantle over one shoulder and kept his hand near the hilt of his sword, ready in the event of an attack. Verne did the same as he followed right behind.

Turning a sharp corner, Beorn jumped back, almost knocking Verne to the ground, but managing to avoid the stroke of the sword meant to behead him, the blade instead burying itself into the clay and timber wall.

His own sword was already firmly in his grasp and he thrust it into the German's chest before he could get his sword back into position. Then Beorn looked around at the small circle of men in front of him.

He tried to keep his face expressionless when he saw Jakob holding Naomie in front of him, the point of his dirk pressing into her throat. Besides Jakob, there were only two other knights standing next to him.

Beorn hesitated, if he attacked, Jakob could easily slide the knife through Naomie's skin and kill in her seconds. "What do you want, Jakob?"

"What do you think? Throw down your weapons and you will find out."

"Let the girl go, she's not a part of this."

"But she is, she was a big part of the reason we were not successful in our first engagement with you. So, she must die along with you and the others."

"Have you sunk so low that you fight women now?"

"Need be, I do."

Naomie was standing completely still, she did not appear to be afraid although her eyes were open wide as she met Beorn's gaze. She seemed to be trying to communicate something to him and looked ready to take some action, he was not sure what that would be, but knew they must be ready when it occurred.

He took a step back so that he was standing beside Verne, and quietly said, "Be ready, protect her at all costs."

"Are you preparing to run like a coward?" Jakob asked, watching as Beorn moved back away from them.

Jakob had relaxed his grip on Naomie when Beorn and Verne appeared, so he could be ready for their attack.

Naomie had her hand in the pocket of her mantle and, in the blink of an eye, she pulled out her dirk and spun around in Jakob's arms, thrusting the blade deeply into his eye.

With his screams splitting the heavy cold air, Beorn and Verne closed the distance between them and took on the two German knights. The space was small and it was difficult to maneuver but, in the end, Verne and Beorn were the better swordsmen and easily dispatched the Germans.

Jakob lay writhing on the ground, he was still screaming in pain when Beorn reached his side. Beorn squatted down beside him and held him still, gripping the dirk and yanking it out. Jakob screamed even louder, and people were now beginning to take an interest in what was happening and were sidling down the alleyway. Beorn knew they needed to get out of there quickly.

"I showed you mercy once and still you came after me and mine. I will not make the same mistake twice." He plunged his sword into Jakob's heart, leaving him to die alone in the alley as they made their way back to the street.

They managed to get back onto the main stretch and blend in with the mob of people on the street, just as a portly constable passed them, hurrying in the direction they had just come from.

There was no talk amongst them until they reached the inn and then Beorn escorted Naomie straight to her room.

"What was that about? Why did you leave the inn and go to the Germans?" He did not want to believe it, but the appearance was that, mayhap, it was Naomie that was the spy.

"I went because you were in trouble and asked for me."

His face was filled with confusion. "How so?"

"I was a fool," she said, shaking her head, looking down at her hands folded in her lap. "I should have known that you would never call for me should you have troubles."

"What are you talking about?"

She raised her eyes to his and he was not sure what he saw in them, but it caused Beorn some concern.

"Arnell came to my room shortly after you left. He said the Germans had waylaid you and that you were hurt and had called for me. He said that he and the others would be going after them and told me where you were so I could go to your aid."

"I should have known he was a liar, but," now he could see the tears collecting, and her voice broke as she finished, "I thought only of you and hurried to where he said you were. I apologize for putting you in such danger."

Beorn sat down beside her and wrapped his arm around her, pulling her in close to his side.

"What am I to do with you?" he asked, kissing the top of her head as she rested her cheek against his chest.

Neither of them wanted to shatter the little bit of peace that had sprouted up between them, so they sat quietly for a bit and then Beorn knew he must deal with the Arnell situation before any more time passed.

He gently placed his fingers under Naomie's chin and raised her face towards his. "Thank you for being so brave and for being willing to put yourself at risk on my behalf. You are a woman unlike any I've known before."

His blue eyes reminded Naomie of a warm summer sky and she wanted to stay lost within them, listening to his soothing baritone voice and being held in his strong embrace.

He saw her lips part and knew she wanted the same thing that he did and slowly lowered his own towards hers, caressing them gently as he buried his hands in her thick, luxurious hair.

It was with great reluctance that he separated from her and stood up. "I must see to the traitor in our midst before he causes more trouble."

"I understand."

Just before reaching for the handle on the door, he turned back towards Naomie. "I meant what I said last night. I have nothing to offer you, yet, the thought of you in danger earlier, seeing you with a knife to your throat, filled me with a desperate worry that I might lose you forever.

I know naught what to do with these feelings, but I pray you do not allow yourself any expectations from me. I will only hurt you in the end."

He left the room and closed the door behind him, leaving Naomie to ponder her own feelings, wondering how she could continue to care more for Beorn each day, while with her next breath he inevitably left her with no choice but to come to terms with the knowledge that their time together would soon be over, and she would be returning to her own people and marrying Ninga.

She shut her eyes tight as she tried to get the old man out of her thoughts and a single tear escaped down her cheek.

CHAPTER 13

Beorn found Verne and Gwyn sitting in the common room of the inn.

"Where are the others?"

"Draco and Grant went off to the stables to see to their horses. Apparently, they are not completely comfortable with the quality of care promised in this part of the city."

"And Millard and Jay, never mind, there they are now."

The two joined them and a few moments after that Draco and Grant returned.

"Now that we are all here, there is something of great importance that we must discuss."

"Arnell is still not back," Millard said.

"I know," Beorn replied. "He was responsible for luring Naomie into the hands of the Germans this morning in an attempt to ambush me, and anyone with me."

"Arnell would not do that," Jay said, his cheeks flushed with anger at the thought of it.

"How long have you known him?"

"Only these past couple of months since he joined us in Wyndymshire, but I have never witnessed him being anything but loyal and honest."

"I appreciate that you have developed a friendship with the man, but he has chosen his side, and it is with the Germans. If you feel a greater loyalty to him than you do to me and our mission on behalf of the Pope, I suggest you leave us now."

Jay was a fairly young man, older than Draco and Grant, but not by much. He pushed his long dark hair away from his face and ran his fingers nervously through his beard as he tried to come to terms with what Beorn had said about Arnell.

He knew all of their eyes were on him as they waited for his response to Beorn, but he did not take any of this lightly. To go along with what Beorn believed about Arnell, was to sign his death warrant.

His raised his eyes to meet Beorn's and opened his mouth to respond, but Beorn lifted his hand, silencing him.

"Arnell just came in and is making his way to our table. Your answer will be obvious depending on how much you give away to him. The rest of you, let us pretend to be ignorant of what happened for now."

He did catch Verne's eye and nodded towards the exit. Verne understood his meaning and as soon as Arnell reached the table, he made his own excuses to leave.

Arnell was older than all of them except Millard, he was tall and broad, but his face was sallow, as if he did not get out into the sunshine and fresh air often. His brown beard was sprinkled with grey hair and his eyes were often red-rimmed and watery.

Beorn had originally put that down to their having to sleep outside in the cold, but it hadn't changed since they'd arrived in London so he now suspected that Arnell either suffered from a severe lack of sleep or, mayhap, a particular fondness for ale.

"Welcome, Arnell, we were worried about you. No one knew where you had gone," Beorn said, noting the confused look on his face. He had not expected to see Beorn here, not alive anyway.

"I was gaming all night and never thought to send word." He seemed twitchy, uncomfortable, as he looked around at the others.

"And were you a winner?"

"Nay," he said, "not this time. Where is Naomie?"

"Still in her room as far as I know, why do you ask?"

"No reason, I just expected she would be here." His hand shook when he lifted his cup of ale, but he held it steady enough to almost empty it in one pull.

"So, we will be meeting at midnight then?"

"Yes, you know where the ship is docked?"

"No, mayhap, I'll go take a look for it now." He finished what little ale remained in his cup and stood up, his eyes darting nervously to the others sitting around the table. Neither Millard nor Jay could look him in the eye and kept their gaze down towards the tabletop.

The Wyndyms all had the same hard look in their eyes, even Gwyn, and Arnell realized that his ruse was up, and that his only hope was to get outside and put as much distance between himself and them as possible.

"I shall see you all this evening then." He stood up quickly, almost knocking over his chair in his haste to leave the establishment.

Draco went to follow him, but Beorn reached out and grabbed him arm. "No need, I will handle this."

Beorn leisurely made his way outside and turned down the first narrow passageway, barely able to make out Verne and Arnell in the murky light.

Arnell was violently trying to escape Verne's grasp, but with his arm twisted severely behind his back, he was not successful.

He stopped struggling when Beorn stepped close enough to look him in the eye. "Did you think we would not find you out?"

He spit in Beorn's face and Beorn backhanded him before wiping the spittle from his beard.

"Will they be coming for us tonight at the ship?"

Arnell refused to answer.

"Will they be coming for us tonight," Beorn asked again, his words spaced far apart, "at the ship?"

Still no response, but his eyes widened and his resolve wavered when Beorn pulled a dirk out and tossed it from hand to hand in front of Arnell's eyes.

"I have dealt with traitors like you before. Whether you talk or not is your choice. The amount of pain you suffer is also your choice. What shall it be?"

Arnell was a coward, as most turncoats are, and so, he chose to speak, hoping Beorn would leave him with his life.

"I told them about the Glorianna, but the plan was to get you all today, during the day."

"Why not tonight when we will all be together?"

"That's why, they are afraid of you and your knights, they wanted to try to catch you when you were not together. Take care of a few of you at a time."

"And you were to use Naomie as bait?"

"Yes, once you were dispatched, I would go back and tell some of the others that she was in danger."

"And you are sure they will not ambush us at the docks?"

"Yes, the sailors will be there, as well, and they won't take a chance fighting them. Their only opportunity to stop you from continuing your journey is today."

"Was there no plan in case they failed?"

"They will also follow you onto the continent, need be."

Beorn contemplated what Arnell had shared, it made sense, but they could not be completely sure that any of it was the truth.

"Let him go, Verne."

Verne hesitated, then released his arms. Arnell's face crumpled in relief and he held out his hand to shake Beorn's.

Beorn grabbed it and pulled the man close, then ran his dirk across Arnell's throat, as he whispered, "For your treachery."

Arnell fell to the ground, grabbing at his throat, trying to staunch the flow of blood, but it was all for naught, he was dead within moments and Beorn and Verne hurried away from the scene.

"What do you mean, we cannot leave tonight? It is imperative that we get to the continent as soon as possible."

Beorn's face was red with anger and frustration. All of his men were at the pier and ready to board the Glorianna, but Captain Haslet had his sailors blocking their way.

The sailors were bulky, strong men themselves and were not afraid of the knights standing before them. They faced greater danger every time they took to the sea and these bad hats caused them no distress whatsoever.

Gwyn was more agitated than Beorn had ever seen him. He strode up to the Captain to try to reason with him.

"Captain, please understand, we must get across the channel and beat King Henry to Rome, or the Pope's very life could be forfeit. Help us, I'm begging you."

"Father, I would sail her if I could, but there's a storm blowing out in the middle of the channel and it could result in the forfeit of all our lives. That won't help your Pope and I won't lose my ship. We wait till mid-day tomorrow to try again, if the storm has passed by then."

Gwyn looked like he was about to cry from frustration and Beorn had enough.

They had managed to evade the balance of the Germans that afternoon, and they had not shown up at the docks tonight, however, should they have to wait any longer, it would only give them more opportunity to stop Beorn and his knights before they even reached the continent. In addition, it would be a serious impediment to their arriving in Rome in time to come to the Pope's aid.

He walked over to the Captain and threw his arm around the man's shoulder, walking him away from the others.

No one could hear what he said but when they returned, the blood had drained from the Captain's face and his hands were shaking as he adjusted his hat and started to speak to his men.

"We will sail with tide, men. Make ready now, we cannot miss it." He turned towards Beorn with a look of fear mixed with hatred. "Get your horses on board in the cargo hold and secure them. They'll be knocked around if the storm is as bad as the ships coming in are describing, and some of them may end up with broken legs, or worse."

Beorn nodded to his men who began leading their horses into the hold of the flat-bottomed ship.

Gwyn hesitated, but then asked, "What did you say to get him to change his mind?"

Beorn clasped his brother on the shoulder and walked with him towards the ship. "Nothing you or your God need to know about."

With the clanking of the anchor being brought up and the yells of the sailors as they got the sails prepared, the ship groaned as the water rose around it and slowly moved out into the channel.

No others were leaving, all of them listening to the warnings about the storm and willing to forgo one day's worth of trade rather than risk their entire ship.

Gwyn and the knights stayed below, out of the bitter cold wind, but Beorn needed to be up top. Threatening the lives of the Captain's wife and daughters had been extreme, but time was their enemy and he could not afford to lose another day.

He was torn between his duty and his worry about Naomie, Verne and his family members. There was a small niggling of doubt eating away at him that, if this storm was indeed as bad as had been reported, he may have jeopardized all of their lives

Should he be responsible for any of their deaths, particularly Naomie's, he acknowledged reluctantly, he could only hope that he did not survive himself, otherwise the guilt would eat him alive.

Beorn was surprised when Naomie suddenly appeared at his side, almost as if he had, once again, summoned her with his thoughts. Her heavy mantle was wrapped tightly around her, but the sea air blew her thick black hair all around and the cold breeze caused her cheeks to flush.

She sidled up against him and he wrapped his arm around her. "You should have stayed below where it is a bit warmer."

"Nay, I want to be where you are."

"Why?"

"It is where I feel safest. How long will the sea journey take?"

"Depends on the wind, I've crossed in as little as three hours when the wind was behind us but, with this storm, I'm not at all sure."

The two of them stood quietly for a bit, enjoying the bite of the cold sea breeze, watching the moonlight reflect off the water, ignoring the sounds of the sailors going about their duties, feeling once again as if they were in a world unto themselves.

It wasn't long before the clouds blocked out the moonlight and the whole atmosphere changed. The ship began to rock violently as the current increased and waves started to crash against its sides.

"And so it begins," Beorn said, turning Naomie in his arms so that she faced him, her eyes unreadable in the now dim light. "Please go below now, it'll be safer for you there."

"You also."

"Nay, I must stay here and help if I can. We will reach land safely, but I cannot watch over you up here while we battle the storm."

He lowered his lips onto hers, relishing their warmth against his own. If he were a praying man, he would have asked that they make it through the storm, simply so that he would have a chance to caress them with his own just one more time.

"Please, go below." Beorn had to yell to be heard above the wind now, as the skies opened up and the downpour began in earnest.

He watched Naomie stumble off, fighting her way against the strong wind. Once he saw that she was safe, he made his way to the Captain to find out what he could do to help.

Naomie joined the group of men sitting around in a circle down below but found that she was unable to sit still and paced back and forth in the small hold.

"Damn, wench," Daegal called out, "stop that, you are making this worse for all of us."

The strong, brave knights were a pile of nerves right now. They would take on any foe with a sword, but knew they were powerless against the Gods of the sea.

Gwyn sat off to the side of the others, his rosary in his hands and his lips moving silently as he prayed for their safety.

Naomie took all of this in and wondered why it was that Beorn had to be the one above deck, why was he risking his life when these gadje did not have the courage to do so?

The sea got angrier and the swells caused the boat to rock back and forth. The horses were nervous and having trouble keeping their feet. Naomie went to them and did her best to reassure the frightened creatures, stumbling herself occasionally.

They could all hear the wind roaring outside, the sounds of waves crashing against the side of the boat and men yelling up above. One of the mercenaries couldn't stand the constant motion and vomited off in a dark corner, much to his chagrin.

It felt as if time had stopped while they sat in the middle of the storm, feeling the ship heave and groan in response to the huge waves hitting it time after time.

They all jumped when there was a large crash up above as something very heavy must have been blown over up top. Naomie could sit still no longer and ran towards the opening that would take her up to the deck.

Draco grabbed her arm. "No, you cannot go up there, it is too dangerous."

She yanked her elbow from his grip and hissed at him. "Beorn is up there and could be hurt, even if none of you have the ballocks to help him, I do, so leave me be."

At that moment, Beorn was lying on the deck, one of the wooden spars that was used to support the rigging had blown over and caught him as it fell. He was pinned down and unable to move the heavy post. The sailors were busy doing everything they could to keep the ship from listing and had no time to help him just now.

He continued to try to squirm out from under it, ignoring the pain in his shoulder where it had struck him, but he hadn't the strength to do so.

He would have been safe enough, had the water not continued to careen in over the side of the ship. Beorn was lying on his back and with each massive wave, he choked on more sea water and feared he may actually drown if he was not able to get up soon.

He wasn't sure if he was relieved or even more worried when Naomie appeared at his side. She tried to lift the heavy mast, but even with Beorn helping, they could only move it a few centimeters and not enough for him to get free.

Another wave crashed in on them and Beorn sputtered and coughed. Naomie tried to use her body to keep some of the water from getting in his face, but Beorn could feel that he was losing his strength and another heavy wave might be enough to fill his lungs completely.

"Go," he said to Naomie, his voice was hoarse and she could barely hear him over the wind screaming around them.

She shook her head and continued to try, unsuccessfully, to move the post. Tears filled her eyes as she stared down at his pale face, she was frustrated and very scared.

Suddenly, Grant, Draco, Verne and even a couple of the mercenaries, braved the storm and appeared at their side. Effortlessly, they picked up the post to free Beorn, and he was able to scramble out from underneath it before they dropped the heavy pole back onto the deck.

Naomie breathed a sigh of relief and started to follow the others back below when an exceptionally strong gust of wind blew across the deck. It caught her in its vortex and she screamed when she was flung into the side of the ship. Naomie grabbed hold as tight as she could but worried that she might be blown overboard.

Fortunately, Beorn and a couple of the other knights were close by and heard her screams over the roaring wind, rushing to her side in such a panic that one of the large, clumsy knights stepped on her ankle as they all tried to grab for her before she went over the side.

She was carried down below by Draco and set down gently onto the wooden floor. Beorn slid down the wall onto the floor beside her and grabbed her hand while Gwyn tried to determine how badly the two of them were injured.

Other than being soaked to the skin, and colder than he could ever recall, Beorn had only a badly bruised shoulder. Naomie, on the other hand, ended up with her ankle either sprained or, perhaps, broken. It had doubled in size and Gwyn could not say for sure how bad it was.

They sat quietly, listening to the storm continue to rage, and Beorn pulled her up close against his side.

"Thank you," he said, to the men sitting around him. "Methinks, I may have drowned had you not come when you did."

"Naomie shamed us into it," Draco admitted. "She somehow knew you were in danger and went to help. After insulting our manhood, we had no choice but to follow her lead and go up, as well."

"I'm glad that you did," he replied. Naomie's body was already up tight against his own, her head leaning on his chest, her hand resting on his waist and he gently kissed the top of her head.

The Glorianna managed to limp into port a few hours later, not the port they had originally headed for, but any landfall was satisfactory after the night they'd just spent.

The bag of coin that Beorn handed the Captain was double what normally would have been required. "Thank you, sir, I hope there was not too much damage to your ship, but we appreciate your courage in making the passage and the Pope will know of the assistance you provided."

The Captain's eyes had dark circles and his face was drawn under his flowing white beard. He simply nodded, took the bag of coin and walked away, hoping never to see any of them again.

Beorn was in quandary as to what to do now. They needed to get to Rome quickly, before the Germans did, but he had Naomie to consider.

She was barely able to ride, and then only if someone assisted her in mounting and dismounting. Her ankle had swollen even more and he feared the injury may be serious enough to warrant a physician.

He pulled Verne, Gwyn, Draco and Grant aside to discuss their next move.

"My estate is just a few kilometers away. Naomie's injury will hold us up and I would like to take her there. I know we need to get to Rome, anon, so I would like you to ride on without me. I will get her taken care of and then ride like hell to catch up with you. With luck, that will be well before you reach your final destination. Is that acceptable?"

"Aye," Draco replied, "we'll be fine, the hard part is over. And I doubt we'll have any trouble between here and there."

"Have a care for the Germans. Although Jakob's group will be far behind us now and should no longer be a problem, there could be other bands of them along the way."

"We'll keep our eyes skinned for any trouble."

"Good," Beorn said, clasping him on the shoulder. "Go then and be safe."

"You, as well," Draco replied.

With a brief word to Daegal to let him know what was happening, Beorn and Naomie headed off in the opposite direction of the others.

Initially, the ride was slow and quiet, but Naomie finally broke the silence. "What will happen to me now?"

"I will leave you at my estate. I have servants who will care for you and can call for a physician to help heal your ankle."

"There is no need, I will care for it myself."

"I forget that you are a healer, but are you able to heal yourself?"

"I will manage."

"I can see that you are taken care of so there is no reason to make it more difficult than it need be."

"I will manage," she repeated, giving him a sidelong glance. In reality, the jolting motion of the horse and the pressure from the swelling in her ankle was causing her quite a bit of discomfort, although she tried her best not to let Beorn know that.

"You were very heroic to come up top and help me during the storm. I admire your courage and am sorry about your injury."

"You speak with pretty words when you want, Beorn, but you don't always speak the truth."

He looked over at her and raised an eyebrow. "How so?"

"I think you know well enough," she replied, in no way daunted by the look he gave her and determined to get an answer to her initial question. "When my ankle is healed, what then?"

Beorn did not reply immediately because he did not know. He didn't want to think about her being gone from his life, not yet anyway, although it was inevitable.

He knew she must be worried about the delay in meeting up with her people and so, he thought he would ease her mind about that.

"We will find your people for you, it will just be a bit delayed."

Naomie turned her eyes towards the ground in front of her horse, not wanting him to see the disappointment in her face. The thought of seeing her people again made her very happy, but what was foremost on her mind was Beorn.

She had intended to travel all the way to Rome with them, never anticipating an injury like this, and she was not prepared to leave him, definitely not now, and maybe not ever.

CHAPTER 14

They arrived at Beorn's estate a little while later and Naomie was surprised at how grand it was, even in the barren winter landscape. It was certainly not the life that she had envisioned Beorn living and it caused her to look at him in a different light.

Bellowing for the servants as he went, Beorn carried Naomie to his bedchamber. Gretchen, the housemaid, hurried in right after them.

She was a young girl, blond and blue-eyed. She looked much as her mother, Karla, had at that age. Karla was now the head cook and also managed the household for Beorn.

"Gretchen, is all well here?"

"Yes, Milord."

"This is Naomie, her ankle is badly injured and she will let you know what she needs to treat it. Get her anything that she asks for."

"Yes, Milord, shall I have food prepared for you?"

"Not for me, thank you. I will be leaving in just a few minutes and will be gone for some time. Naomie will be staying here until I return, have some food prepared for her. Please see to it that she is well taken care of."

"Yes, Milord," Gretchen replied, with a quick glance over at Naomie.

"You may leave us now."

Once she'd left them alone, he turned his attention back to Naomie. "Are you comfortable enough? I cannot dally and must catch up with the others anon."

"Yes." Naomie's eyes were wide with confusion. "You know that I cannot stay, do you not?"

"Naomie," he said, feeling the pressure to leave as soon as possible, but first wanting to be sure she understood what was on his mind before he left.

She turned her eyes towards his, taking him in once again with their pure gemlike beauty and he paused, not sure how to even begin.

"You must stay here until your ankle heals. You cannot wander around the countryside while you are injured."

"And then?" She hadn't wanted to ask, hadn't wanted to appear at all needy, but she couldn't let him leave without both of them knowing how this would end.

"You have nothing to fear, I will come back for you."

Her face softened at his words, and she raised her hand to run her fingers through his beard and caress his face. She had come to care for him a great deal and did not want him to leave her.

"You will come back for me, you promise?" she asked, her eyes wide as she looked deep into his, trying to find the truth.

But the truth that she sought was not what came out of his mouth.

"I promise," he said, his brow furrowed as he tried to find the right way to explain, and to ease her worries about being back with her people.

"As soon as I return, we will go together and find your family. If any type of explanation is needed, I will handle that. I will get you home safely and you can carry on your life as it was before you were torn away from it."

He was taken by surprise when he saw unshed tears fill her eyes, shimmering as they threatened to spill down her cheeks. "I don't understand, isn't that what you wanted?"

Beorn's heart was already twisted and damaged by the thought of her leaving, he wouldn't be able to bear it if she cried. He knew the real cause of her tears but refused to acknowledge it.

Naomie tried to control her sorrow, but a single tear managed to slip down her face before she was able to sniff back her sadness.

"I understand and I will be ready to go, you need not concern yourself about me any longer. I will not be a burden."

"You've never been burden, Naomie, and I wish that things could be different for us."

"How so?"

"I wish we could stay together always. You have become very special to me."

He reached out to run his fingers through her thick hair, but she slapped his hand away.

"There was no need for that."

"Mayhap, there was."

Beorn knew that she cared for him, as he cared for her, but seeing the despair on her face, he realized how deep her feelings ran and that her concern was not about getting back to her tribe, after all.

"Did you believe I would marry you? Even after the things I said to you in London?"

"Of course not. I know such a thing could never be."

She refused to meet his eye any longer and looked down at her hands that were now sitting in her lap, her fingers entwined so tightly that the skin around them was white.

"You are correct, it could never be, but I think not for the reasons you believe."

Naomie raised her eyes towards his once again and, this time she allowed him to sit on the bed beside her and take both of her hands in his.

"Hear me out, will you?"

She nodded and he took a deep steadying breath. "There are things about me that you do not know. I was married once before."

Naomie did know much more than he realized but gave him no indication of that.

"My wife's name was Anna and she was a kind, gentle woman. I loved her very much and I had to listen to her screams of agony for hours and hours while she gave birth to our child. In the end, she wasn't strong enough to withstand the ordeal and I lost her. That is what caused the breaks on the lines of my hand.

And even though she is gone, her screams continue to haunt my dreams most nights and I know that she died because of me. I will not put any woman through that again and that is why those lines will never get as deep again as they were before she died."

"You have such foolish pride," Naomie said.

"Yes, I do, but what has that to do with my decision?"

"God chose the time she would lose her life, not you. Whatever you do, or do not do, does not change that."

"You are catching hold of the wrong end of the stick," he replied, slightly annoyed, and could tell by the look of confusion on her face that she did not understand his words.

"You are missing the point that I am trying to make. I loved Anna and I was badly hurt at her loss. I will not do that to myself again, nor will I cause the death of another lass in the same fashion."

Naomie pulled her hands from his and stood up, limping badly, and he wanted to assist her but his movements in her direction froze when she turned her eyes toward him, this time they were slits of silver ice that looked as if they could freeze a man's very soul.

She wanted to hiss at him, to rake her fingers across his face and leave scars that would never fade, it took all of her resolve, but she managed to hold back from doing so.

"You are a coward," she murmured, limping over to the window to look out onto the barren, frosted landscape, and thought how well it reflected the way she felt inside right now, knowing that Beorn had never cared for her and that she must leave him.

Naomie heard his heavy boots crossing the room towards her and took a deep breath, steadying herself, refusing to allow herself to show any fear, any sorrow.

Beorn turned her around and she stumbled forward into his arms. He gently grasped a handful of her hair and pulled her head back until he could look upon her beautiful face.

"Listen well," he said, his voice sounding hoarse and jagged, "I loved Anna and it nearly killed me when I lost her. When I am with you, I cannot even recall her face, let alone how I felt when I was with her. When I am with you, all else in the world ceases, you enchant me, you consume me, you own me.

I cannot let whatever this is between us go any further because if I do, should I lose you after that, I have no doubt that I would die, if not from the heartbreak, then by my own hand.

Mayhap, I am a coward. I will accept that, but I would not be willing to face a life without you in it, so hear me, Naomie, I love you too much already, I will not risk what you could do to me if we stay together."

His sapphire blue eyes bore down into hers, he was angry at her, angry at himself, angry at the world for putting her in his life, only to make her have to walk back out of it.

Another solitary tear made its way down her cheek and Naomie reached her arms up around his neck and plied him with a devastatingly, thorough kiss, rubbing her body along the front of his, getting the reaction that she expected, just before she backed away from him.

"I would never marry a stinking gadje like you," she said, her eyes changed like quicksilver and now resembled storm clouds. Beorn could not recall ever seeing such pure rage on her face.

"My family warned me from the time I was a child how evil the gadje were, you almost made me believe otherwise, Beorn, until today. You are unclean, your soul is polluted and cannot be redeemed. You are spineless and your weak excuses make no sense, as well you know.

Go away with you and save yourself. I will not be here when you return."

She turned her head and spit on the floor.

"Leaving on your own is not the right thing to do. I will return soon and get you home safely." His voice was flat, emotionless, as he sought to contain the tumultuous feelings coursing through his body.

"But the choice is yours," he added, before turning and stalking out of the room.

Naomie stood at the window and watched him ride away, and it was not until he was so far gone that she could no longer see him that she threw herself onto the bed and allowed herself to cry out her grief and anguish.

Beorn rode his horse hard, allowing the crisp winter wind to clear his head of all thoughts of Naomie, or at least try to.

The clime here in Normandy right now was a little warmer than it had been in England, and he had less fear of hitting an icy patch and possibly injuring his horse. However, the winter snows could still come at any time, so he cantered on effortlessly, eating up the miles between him and his knights.

But, no matter how hard he tried, Beorn was not able to keep those brilliant silver eyes from crawling into his mind and taking over his thoughts.

He was angry at her response before he left, however, he realized that he shouldn't have expected anything different. In the short time that he'd known her, Naomie had always done what he least expected.

He knew that if there was ever to be another woman that he allowed into his life, it would have to be her, but Beorn also knew that he would never open his heart like that again, it was not an option.

He had trained for knighthood from a very young age and during that time, and his subsequent knighthood, his life was based on discipline and control.

When he met and married Anna, he was forced to give up that control, he laid his heart open for her and was very content when they were together.

She was a good woman, kind and loving, so unlike the silver-eyed minx trying to worm her way into his heart right now. With Anna, he was finally able to get past the nightmares that he had lived with for such a long time.

No man can easily get past so many years of violence, of bloody battles, of killing other men and of watching his friends die, and Beorn was no exception.

With Anna's patience and quiet acceptance of who he was, the nightmares became few and far between. Beorn found himself changing, finally able to put the beast to rest and enjoy his quiet life in the country.

When Anna died, it killed a part of him, as well, the human part, the part that allowed him to feel something for others. So the darkness found its way back into his life, but she was gone now and could no longer help him find the light.

He turned to drink so that he no longer had to deal with thoughts of his past and of his loss, or to acknowledge the emptiness that had been left inside of him.

Still he could not think of his child, the one that caused the death of his beloved Anna. In his mind, if he refused to accept the child as even existing, then he could harbor no bad feelings towards it.

The extent of Beorn's grief had been so deep when Anna passed that he feared he could cause the babe harm and had sent it away for its own safety. He still felt that same way today, more than three years later.

Thinking back to how difficult it had been when he lost Anna, Beorn found that his biggest regret as far as Naomie was that he could never fully explain how much he cared for her. If he could, maybe then she would understand why she could not be allowed to remain in his life.

But she was bloody-minded and had insisted all along that she be returned to her family so she could marry that disgusting old man that wanted her, leaving him to wonder why she was making such a fuss now that it was time to actually do so.

"She has only been playing me, biding her time until she could return to her own people and her old thieving ways," he said, to no one other than the horse beneath him. "For what reason, I know naught, but Naomie kens exactly what she wants, and it is not of my world."

In his mind's eye he could see her bright smile, rare enough that it made a man's heart swell when she bothered to toss it his way, those dazzling eyes unlike any he'd gazed upon before, and her full, ripe body, always at the ready for him, and only him.

When his own body started to respond, just at the thought of her, Beorn knew he was bewitched and needed to get her out of his head completely.

But that was easier said than done, for then he pictured some swarthy old gypsy man running his wrinkled, dirty hands over her pristine body, Beorn could hear the soft mewling sound she would make when he entered her, and a slow rage started to build inside of him.

He was so consumed by his thoughts that he was almost taken unawares when two vagabonds rode out of a copse of trees to his left, their blades already drawn.

Quickly unsheathing his own, Beorn took the offense, barreling towards them with a battle cry that made them both hesitate, but it was too late. Beorn was on them in seconds, his broadsword swinging wide and strong, bringing it down on each them again and again, ignoring their cries and pleas for mercy, he continued venting his rage on them until they both fell to the bloody ground beneath their horses.

It was then that he realized they were not warriors, just poor thieves who had picked the wrong man to try to rob that day. Feeling no remorse, he moved them off to the side of the road but would not take the time to bury them. Grabbing the reins of their mounts, he dragged them along behind him as he continued on his way, his rage now fading and his head finally clear of thoughts of Naomie.

He caught up with the others a few days later when they stopped for food and rest. Sliding off his horse's back, he took a chunk of the freshly roasted venison that Verne offered him and followed it down with a healthy draught of cider from his flask.

"Venison, someone got lucky today, didn't they?"

Grant smiled proudly. "The blooming fool ran right out in front of us on a long, clear stretch. It had nowhere to run, so we can finally fill our bellies well."

"Best enjoy it now, good meals will be few and far between on our journey."

"How long will it take us to reach Rome?" Draco asked.

"It could be as much as several weeks, longer if we run into bad weather."

"That is a long time, Beorn," Gwyn said. "I fear we will arrive too late."

"Mayhap, but word should have been sent much earlier then. We will ride hard, with few breaks for rest. We'll have to have a care for the horses, for we cannot lose any. I did manage to pick up a couple of spares in case we need them, because those with no mount will have to be left behind."

True to his word, Beorn did push them hard. They would ride all day with but short breaks to grab food and drink, for themselves and their horses. At night, by the time the fire was going and food cooked and eaten, the men just curled up around the warm fire and fell into an exhausted sleep.

Even so, it turned out that Gwyn was correct and by the time they rode into Rome, they were too late.

Robert I of Capua was the papal protector and Beorn went to his residence directly, bringing Gwyn along with him.

The place was a flurry of activity, knights, as well as clergymen, coming and going, everyone in a panic. It took a bit before Beorn and Gwyn were able to obtain an audience with Prince Robert and, even when they did, they were hard pressed to keep his attention.

"Your Excellency," Prince Robert said, when they were finally allowed to enter the room, "I am glad you have arrived safely, alas, the unthinkable has already occurred."

"What has happened?" Beorn asked, and Robert looked at him in confusion.

"Who are you?"

"This is my brother, Sir Beorn," Gwyn said. "He has helped me gather the knights that we've brought. I regret we were too late to join in the battle."

"There was no battle, but there may be one now. Every knight will be of tantamount importance."

"Can you tell us what has happened?"

Robert stopped rifling through papers and maps and turned toward the two brothers.

"King Henry arrived two days ago and presented himself at St. Peter's Basilica for his coronation as the Holy Roman Emperor, and for ratification of the treaty agreed to last year with Pope Paschal.

There was such displeasure by the other Princes and clergy that the Pope refused to crown him, therefore, Henry refused to renounce the right of investiture and seized Paschal and sixteen of his cardinals. We know not what his ultimate mission is, other than ensuring that the Pope crowns him emperor."

"Why was he allowed to take the Pope and the others without a battle?"

Robert's dark brown eyes were filled with anger when they met Beorn's.

"Henry had an army, we did not. Since then, more and more knights have been arriving and we are planning to head out shortly to liberate the Pontiff, by whatever means are necessary. How many ride with you?"

"An even dozen."

"That brings our number to somewhere around three hundred men. Get some food, take care of your horses, we will head out late this afternoon."

"Have you any idea how many you will be up against?"

"Doesn't matter, the Pope must be rescued and we will have God on our side."

"That cock won't fight," Beorn said, as he and Gwyn stomped down the steps outside of Robert's home, elbowing his way through the throng of people still waiting to get inside for a few moments of Robert's attention.

"What do you mean?"

"I mean that plan won't work because it is no plan. He has no idea what he is riding into and has not sent scouts out in advance to get any information. He is no soldier."

"He is what we have, and we must have faith in him."

"You can do as you please, but I have faith only in myself and in my sword."

CHAPTER 15

They headed out later that day, Beorn and his group were towards the back and tried to keep together as best could in the throng of men heading into this battle.

It had been a long, arduous journey to Rome and Beorn and his men were still weary and saddle-sore. As hard as he pushed them all, Beorn still had trouble during their travels trying to keep thoughts of Naomie from creeping into his head, catching him unaware and leaving him with a sense of dread, fearing she may have already left to find her own people.

With nothing to plan or prepare for this battle and with nothing to view but the backsides of hundreds of horses, he found that he was struggling now to keep his mind off Naomie and on the mission at hand. Tired of fighting it, he needed to find another way to bury those thoughts.

"Gwyn," he said, pulling his horse abreast of his brother's as they plodded along behind the huge band of riders and wagons spreading out in front of them.

"Yes?"

"Why did Robert call you 'Your Excellency'?"

"You noticed that, did you?"

"Indeed, I did, is there something you would like to share with us?"

"Before I left to engage you in this endeavor, the Pope made me a Bishop."

A smile blossomed on Beorn's face. "I am proud of you, Gwyn, congratulations. But why the secrecy about it?"

"Both Robert and the Pope thought I would be safer traveling as a lowly priest rather than a bishop. Since Henry deigned to kidnap all those bishops when he took the Pope, I tend to think they were right about it."

"I knew from the time we were children that you would become someone very important within the church. There is a peacefulness in your soul that allows you to accept the good in all people, not many have that particular gift."

Gwyn was surprised at his brother's turn of phrase and glanced over at him, their two sets of dark blue eyes meeting in understanding. "It truly is a gift and I'm glad you are able to see that. I only pray that someday you will let me share it with you, so you no longer have to carry such anger in your heart about Anna."

"I've told you before that we will not discuss her, Gwyn, and that has not changed."

Gwyn watched as Beorn's face transformed at the mere mention of Anna's name, and he whispered a quick prayer that God would find a way into Beorn's heart once again and let him finally release all the anguish that he carried there.

"And what of Naomie? May I speak of her?"

"What is there to speak about?" Beorn asked, staring straight ahead at the people spread out so far ahead of them that they could not even see the front riders.

"You took her virtue, did you not?"

"I did."

"And will you marry her now?"

"No." Beorn turned his head to meet his brother's eyes once again. "That will never happen."

"Why not, how can you leave on her own like that? You've put her in a horrid position and it's your responsibility to take care of her now."

"Even if I wanted to, which I do not, she would not marry me. I am a gadje, I am unclean and not good enough for her."

"I do not believe that is how she truly feels."

Beorn shrugged his shoulders. "I don't care what you believe, brother. This is a situation that she and I will resolve on our own. It is not your business."

"I think," Gwyn began, but Beorn held up his hand to stop him.

"I appreciate your concern, Your Excellency, but I will speak of this no more and am going to sneak off for a bit to do some hunting. We will be stopping for the night soon and it would be good to have fresh meat to eat."

The conversation had been uncomfortable for Beorn, but he knew it was important that Gwyn have his say about the situation.

Their battle would most likely take place the following day and one never knew if they would come away from it alive, so he decided it was time to clear the air between himself and Draco, too, before he ended up never having a chance to do so.

"Draco, come with me, let's go kill something for our evening meal."

Grant and Verne offered to go, as well, but Beorn shook his head.

"Nay, stay here, best if just a couple of us try to slip away, else they will think we are deserting and will then be hunting us."

The two knights found an area rich in game and sent their horses off to graze while they waited for a good shot.

"I knew your namesake, Draco, pity you never met him. He was a great man, a great knight, and you should be proud to wear his name."

"I've heard much about him from our father," Draco replied. "But, methinks you did not bring me out here to talk about my namesake."

"I didn't, but I find myself quite nostalgic today and I want to clear the air between us. You are my brother and, should something untoward occur to one or the other of us on the morrow, I would not want there to be any words left unsaid between us."

Draco was surprised and needed a moment to collect his thoughts. He stared out at the rabbit that had just hopped into the open, carefully sighted his arrow and let it fly, killing the creature instantly.

He turned to Beorn before heading over to collect his prize. "I respect you as a knight, but have trouble agreeing with who you are as a man because of the way you treat Naomie."

Beorn had assumed this was the direction their conversation would take and was ready to let Draco know his place in that particular situation.

"I've done nothing to her that she did not want me to do."

"She is a young woman, naïve and inexperienced with men that are not her own kind. You took advantage of her and from what I can glean, you have no intention of doing the right thing by her."

"What happens between Naomie and me is our business, you get no say in it. I know you care for her, but you cannot change what has happened or what may still happen yet between us.

Whether you trust me to do what is right for her or not, you must step out of it because you have no way of knowing all that she and I have been through, both together and apart."

"I know that she has a good heart and does not deserve to be left alone, alienated from everyone and everything that she knows, having to fend for herself."

"Once we finish with this, I will see that she gets back to her family safely."

"And you think that is good enough?"

"It will have to be."

Draco's green eyes glittered with a very strong emotion that Beorn could not define. At first, he thought it was anger but after further consideration, determined it might actually be disappointment.

"You and I," Draco said, "can be brothers, but never think that what you've done to Naomie is acceptable to me."

He stood up and went to get the rabbit. They stayed there a bit longer, but there was no further conversation of any merit between them.

Beorn kept to himself that evening, running the words he'd shared with both his brothers over and over in his head, but coming to no resolution as far as their opinions were concerned.

As they prepared themselves for the battle to come, the men ate and drank around campfires, some of them gambling, some wrestling, and others sharing stories of great battles from the past.

Unfortunately, it was all for naught and the drama was resolved by the following afternoon, much as Beorn had anticipated.

The army, three hundred strong, rode into the town of Ferentino, which was about sixty-five kilometers east of Rome, about mid-day. They were met by a much larger army being led by Ptolemy I, Count of Tusculum. He had always been loyal to the papal authority but now rebelled against it and sided with Henry, who was to be the Holy Roman Emperor.

Robert and Ptolemy shared some heated conversation which the knights were not privy to, then Robert turned and led them back to Rome. The fight was over with not one weapon drawn and no explanation of why.

Beorn was disgusted and, once they got a short distance from Ferentino, he led his small band away from the larger group.

"This was a farce," he said, angry sparks flashing from his eyes. "Apologies for having you come all this distance for naught. The good news is that you live to tell about it and you were paid well for little work. There is no need for you to return to Rome unless you would like to. I'll leave you to your own plans now and thank you for offering your services."

He tossed another bag of coins to Daegal, who caught it easily and gave a nod of acknowledgement to Beorn before leading the other mercenaries on their way.

"Gwyn, we will help you catch up with the others, I do not think it wise for you to be riding alone at this time. Once we do that, we'll be heading out. I see no reason to stay here and stooge about uselessly."

"I understand," Gwyn said, with a long look at his brothers and his nephew. "I thank you all for agreeing to come and help. I've enjoyed spending this time with you, getting to know the three of you all over again and I hope we will meet again."

Then he turned to Verne, who had become a real friend over these last weeks. "I've enjoyed our conversations, take care, Verne, and look after my brother when he hasn't the wits to do so himself."

"I will, as always, and safe travels to you, Your Excellency."

One by one, they moved their horses over close to his and extended their hand in a good-bye handshake, then they galloped off to help catch him up with Robert's army, so that Gwyn could travel safely with them back to Rome.

"Take care, brother," Beorn called after him before turning his horse and riding north, suddenly anxious to be home. Verne, Draco and Grant followed along behind him, frustrated that there had been no battle, but full of youthful exuberance and looking forward to other adventures still to come.

Beorn could have no way of knowing at that time, but he made a most prudent decision. King Henry would keep Pope Paschal and his bishops imprisoned for the next two months and there would be no further attempts to rescue him.

The harshness of the conditions and treatment were such that the Pope was no longer able to continue defying the King, and finally crowned Henry as Emperor on April 13, 1111.

It was almost a month before Naomie's ankle was well enough to even be able to walk comfortably on it. Beorn's servants had treated her pleasantly enough, even though she had not been overly friendly in return.

She would be leaving soon and would not allow any more of these gadjes to worm their way into her heart, even though Gretchen and her mother did their best to be kind to her.

Each morning she rose, hoping that would be the day Beorn would return to her, but he did not. She knew his travels would take him far, but she had hoped that, somehow, he would put her above the priest he was going to protect. That it would mean more to him that she might leave his life forever than his duty to a man he did not even know, and who represented a God he did not even believe in.

Every night when she went to bed alone once again, she fought the tears that threatened, and tried to steel herself for the journey she must soon make.

The thought of seeing her family filled her heart with warmth and she knew that they would make her feel welcome, make her feel like she was finally home once again. She wanted that above all else, or so she thought.

Sometimes, in the dark of the night, she could feel Beorn's arms around her, could feel him moving inside her and when she woke from the dreams, reality would hit and she would be overcome with dread.

Naomie was not sure how she would ever be able to tolerate another man touching her body, particularly Ninga, with his hairy wrinkled fingers.

It was said that if a dream was remembered in the morning, then it would come true. But even though she found her way into Beorn's arms most nights, she still woke up cold and alone every morning, with a deeper realization that he would not be returning for her, after all.

Not only was she having to struggle with her thoughts and emotions about Beorn, now she was questioning beliefs that she had been taught and carried for her entire life. So many of them had been proven wrong over these last weeks and months that she had been with the gadje, that sometimes she was no longer sure of what to believe.

Naomie had no cards with which to try and see what the future held and so she relied on tea leaves. They were usually accurate in seeing what lie ahead, but lately the signs were not clear.

When the leaves result only in unreadable clumps, it is generally a reflection of confusion on the part of the reader or the person who was being read.

Being both in this case, the results worried Naomie more than she cared to acknowledge, and so she stopped trying to see what they held.

Her ankle continued to heal and she began to get restless and wander around inside the Manor. The stone house was very large and built in the shape of an L, with two floors and many different rooms to search out.

Naomie began her explorations on the top floor, most of the rooms remained empty, although some were apparently used for storage. Finding nothing of interest, she eventually made her way to the main floor.

During one such excursion, she found clothing in a trunk in one of the unused rooms and could only assume they must have belonged to Beorn's wife.

Naomie, like many women in her tribe, was a drabardi, a fortune teller able to predict the future, in part because she could read the signs on one's palm or in their tea leaves, but she was one of the few that also was able to see and feel pieces of the past and present.

Her gift did not present itself often, but when it did, the signs were very strong and she knew that they should not be disregarded.

As she picked up the pieces of Anna's clothing from the trunk and held them in her hands, flashes of the past came to her, the visions were nothing that she could put into any specific order, but as they faded away, she was left with a sense of peacefulness and knew it was right for her to use the clothing for herself.

Naomie knew Beorn would be very angry if she pinched anything from him, particularly if it had belonged to Anna, but when the time came and she could find no further excuse to stay, she would help herself to that clothing with no regrets.

She could not wear the bright red tunic as she wandered the countryside by herself, it would be much safer if she did not stand out in such a way.

As her ankle continued to heal, she worked on strengthening it by walking further every day, knowing it would have to carry her a great distance once she left here.

The weather was warmer here in Normandy, but the days were still brisk, even with the sun shining down upon her. Naomie would wrap her mantle tightly around her body and spend as much of the daylight hours as possible exploring the outbuildings and the barren orchards.

She would walk as far each day as she could before her ankle swelled again and insisted that she rest it.

Every morning, Naomie would rise and find another reason to stay. However, it was inevitable that enough time would pass that her ankle would no longer swell at all, leaving her with no further excuse to remain at the Manor, which led her back to the chests with Beorn's dead wife's clothing.

Naomie looked through it hurriedly, before any of the servants happened in on her, and grabbed two long sleeved tunics, one was woolen, the other linen, and both were soft, muted browns.

She did not like to think bad thoughts of the dead, but these colors were for old women, young women needed to wear bright, vibrant colors that brought out their beauty and their high spirits.

Naomie thought of Beorn then and wondered what it was that made him love this plain, unexciting woman who was so different than herself. Or, mayhap, that was the answer to another of her questions and, instead it explained why he could not love her.

Mayhap, he preferred his women more sedate, more demure, but Naomie could never be those things, not even if she wanted to, and Beorn knew that well.

She wrapped the tunics under her skirts and hurried to her own room. Naomie would have preferred to not steal from Beorn but there were items she would require and so, she placed the tunics in a sack that she had found in one of the outlying barns along with the colorful silk skirt she had on when she was kidnapped. She would need that material for her journey.

There was a chest in this room, as well, but this one held Beorn's clothing. She opened a drawer and ran her hands over the items in it, picking up a white undertunic and holding it up to her nose, breathing in the faint scent of him.

With a rush of emotion, she threw it onto the bed as if it burned her hands and then went to stand at the window. No one seemed to be about on this cold, winter day. The orchards were off in the distance and the bare arms of the apple trees looked like old men beckoning her, letting her know that it was time.

Naomie fought the feeling, initially, at least, but was filled with an overwhelming sense that this must be the day that she remove herself from this place. She had wandered through the orchard earlier but froze in place when she heard an owl hoot from somewhere nearby.

The hair on the back of her neck and on her arms rose in fear, hearing an owl in the daytime was a very bad omen and did not bode well for her departure, but all of the other signs told her that today must be the day for it.

Besides, if she did not follow through now, when her mind was set, she may never have the courage to so in the future.

Naomie ate a hearty dinner and, after the servants had left for the day or had gone to bed in their quarters, she tiptoed to the kitchens and found whatever food would travel well. Those items were wrapped up and stuffed in her bag along with the clothing.

Naomie made to leave Beorn's room, but stopped to look around one last time, her heart aching at the thought that she would never see him again. The undertunic was still on the bed where she had thrown it and she ran over and grabbed it, stuffing it into the bag with her other treasures.

Then she threw her mantle over her shoulders and made her way out into the cold, winter night.

CHAPTER 16

"Will you stay at the estate for a time or head back to England?" Beorn asked.

They were sitting around a small fire, they'd been traveling hard and all of them needed some food and some rest, as did their horses.

Grant and Draco looked at each other. Finally, Grant pursed his lips in disappointment and turned to his uncle. "I think I should return home and deal with my parents' anger before it gets overly developed."

"That sounds like the right thing to do. How about you, Draco?"

They had come to a sort of truce since their heart to heart talk. The anger had dissipated, but more work would be required before all of the damage between them was repaired.

"I would like to find some adventure. There is nothing for me in Wyndymshire. Radolf is the Baron and Grant, his heir. All I am useful for is to walk the towers and rarely is there anything of note that requires a knight's sword."

"I can talk to some people that I know and may be able to get you set up with a good group of knights who are picky about the jobs they take on, unlike the mercenaries that just left us."

"Would you do that for me?"

"Of course, I will send word with you, so you can speak with them when you return to English shores. I have one request though."

"What is that?"

"Before you leave with them, you go back to Wyndymshire and you give our mother a proper good-bye, so she will not worry overly much about you."

"I will do that."

"Promise?"

"On my word."

"Good, then I will get that dispatched as soon as we return to my estate."

Verne usually kept his thoughts to himself but he had enjoyed being out with the other knights and had a request of his own to make.

"Milord, is there a possibility that I might be made a knight in the near future?"

Beorn looked over at him fondly. "I have neglected you, Verne, haven't I? I find you so satisfactory as my squire, I fear that to let you become a knight, I will lose my right hand."

Verne looked down at the ground, he did not want Beorn to see him blush.

"How old are you now?"

"Twenty and two."

"Time seems to have gotten away from me, Verne. You have more than earned your knighthood and I will address that as soon as we return to the Manor. Mayhap, you want to ride with Draco and Grant?"

"Aye, if that is acceptable."

Both men nodded their acquiescence.

"Fine, I will add your name to my missive. I will miss you, Verne. You've been with me most of your life and I know naught how I will get along without you." Verne was the closest thing to a son that Beorn would ever have and, although proud of the man he'd become, Beorn would be very sad to see him go.

Verne's eyes were a little misty as he threw a sidelong glance at Beorn. The knight had been more of a father to him than his own had ever been, and Verne felt he was being disloyal by wanting to leave and have some adventure.

"I can stay for a time, Milord, and see to training a new squire for you before I leave."

"I won't have that, my friend," Beorn said, using a stick to stir up the fire and sending sparks shooting up into the winter sky. "No, it is your time and I will not hold you back from it."

"Thank you, Milord. For all that you have provided me with."

Beorn just raised his cup towards Verne, feeling his loss already and the young man was not yet gone.

He turned towards the flames then, losing himself in them until Naomie's eyes appeared, like silvery moons staring out at him.

They'd been away for a long time and Beorn wondered, once again, if she would be at his Manor when they returned. He desperately craved her body, wanted to feel her in his arms, wanted to crush her lips with his own yet, in the back of his mind, he hoped she would be gone.

He'd always prided himself on his strength and his courage, but he was not sure if he had enough of either to let her go completely out of his life.

Beorn's emotions ranged from one extremity to another when he arrived home and found that Naomie had slipped out in the middle of the night not long before he had returned. He was relieved, he thought, yet something shut down inside of him and left an emptiness that he could not define or drink away, try as he might.

They filled their bellies with home cooked food and Gretchen was kept busy running back and forth from the kitchen to refill the ewers of ale and cider.

"Will she be safe?" Draco asked, well in his cups by then.

The three men turned and looked towards Beorn for an answer. Naomie was an enigma to them all and, although their feelings for her did not have the depth of Beorn's, she was someone that they all had come to care about.

"I know naught," he mumbled, before raising his cup back to his lips.

"Mayhap," Draco began.

Beorn wasted no time interrupting his thought before he could vocalize it. "No, I asked her to stay until I returned so I could get her home safely. Naomie chose to leave me and now she must take care of herself. I will hear no more about it."

He stood and, with an unsteady step, made his way to his bedchamber and fell onto the bed, snoring lightly just moments later.

Beorn's head was a little fuzzy the next morning, as were the other men's, but his heart was lighter. He'd woken up with a new resolve and, because of it, could ignore the headache.

He had not slept well at all, visions of Naomie had burrowed constantly into his head during the darkest hours of the night. It was not until he granted himself permission to take his leave and find her, to ensure himself that she was safe and back with her family, that sleep finally came to him.

He slapped his younger brother in the back of the head as he walked past him and Draco almost pulled his sword in response. Not being used to the potent cider that was made on Beorn's estate, he was not able to ignore the pounding in his own head.

"Why so happy this morn?" Grant asked, his voice a little raspy and his eyes rimmed in red.

"I am going to try and find Naomie."

Both men raised their heads to stare at him curiously.

"Do not look at me like that, I only want to assure myself that she arrived safely. Draco, you seemed to have concerns last evening, would you like one last adventure in Normandy while we track her down and make sure no troubles have found her? And knowing her as I do, I half suspect they may have."

A slow smile spread over Draco's face. "Indeed, I would."

"And you, Grant? Verne? Should you prefer to head back now, I will prepare the missive we discussed."

More than happy to postpone the scolding that he anticipated receiving from his parents, Grant agreed.

As much as Verne wanted to move forward into knighthood, as always, his first priority was looking after Beorn, so he enthusiastically nodded his head.

The four of them saddled up and set off a short while later. It was early in the spring by now and, although it rarely, if ever, would hit freezing temps, the days and the nights were still cold and the travel quite miserable when the rain began to fall.

It was lightly drizzling when Beorn pulled up his steed to halt in the middle of a crossroad about mid-afternoon, and a smile of satisfaction lit his face. He quickly dismounted and threw his reins to Verne.

He stepped over to a thick evergreen bush and snatched the red silk ribbon that had been left on one of the branches, returning to the others, he held it up with a smug look on his face.

"I do not understand, what is its importance?" Grant asked, looking at the twigs wrapped within the ribbon.

"The Romani are travelers, each clan has a sign, a way of communicating where they are going to their other members. Naomie told me that her clan leaves a small bundle of twigs wrapped in a ribbon at a crossroad and points it in the direction they are heading."

"Did she leave that for you, then?" Draco asked.

"I think, mayhap, she did," he replied, trying to hide his pleasure at the thought. He felt like the icy buildup around his heart might be thawing a bit and was suddenly anxious to get moving forward.

Naomie had been walking for a few days before she ran into any trouble. It escaped her why she had not pinched one of Beorn's horses when she left. She would be much further on her way by now if she had.

She had considered it, but the penalty for stealing a horse was severe and, although she did not truly believe Beorn would report her crime, she could trust no one and so she left on foot.

Naomie had tried to leave signs at each crossroad, for her clan, she assured herself. Even though, in the back of her mind, she acknowledged that Beorn may also remember what she told him about them and, mayhap, he would find her before she found her family.

But she could not assume that he would even try to locate her and knew she must keep moving forward. Naomie would hide amongst the trees whenever she heard horses approaching, not wanting to take a chance on the motives of whoever might be riding those mounts.

It was a busy rode and there were frequent travelers in wagons, as well as on horses. She considered trying to get a ride on the back of one of the wagons but did not trust any of these gadje and wouldn't take that chance.

She continued to trudge along, heading south, her people never came this far north so it was unlikely she would find them for some time still.

Naomie ignored the cold and the aching in her ankle that had just recently healed, and with her head bent down to block some of the wind from her face, she placed one foot in front of the other for as long as she could before resting in a copse of trees off to the side of the road.

As she rested, she could hear the sound of hooves approaching and realized there must be several horses. Growing curious, she hurried over to determine if she could see the riders they carried, while still hiding herself amongst the trees. Her heart beat a little harder in her chest when she noted that the riders appeared to be knights.

Could it be that Beorn had come looking for her? Could this be him and Draco and the others?

She stood frozen, unsure of what she should do because she could not tell whether or not it was Beorn. If not, she did not want to let them see her, however, if it was him, how would he know to stop? They were approaching quickly, and she had no time to think.

If it was Beorn, he had followed her signs thus far, so she quickly ripped off a piece of red silk and wrapped a stone in it so it would have weight. Then she tossed it out towards the road, knowing Beorn would know who put it there and, hopefully, stop to inspect it.

She hid herself back behind a large tree as the knights reached the roadway in front of her. Naomie was deeply disappointed when they continued on. At one point, it sounded like they might be stopping but no one returned her way. It was not Beorn, after all.

Waiting a few more moments, giving the riders ample time to be out of sight before she returned to the road, Naomie swallowed her distress, refusing to acknowledge how much she had wanted that to be Beorn.

There was a deep ache in her chest that she could not lose and she knew it was because of Beorn, because of how deeply she cared for him.

Naomie could not understand why though, not only was he a gadje, he was not even a particularly kind one, he was selfish and cowardly, there was no reasonable explanation for the way she felt.

She kicked at little pebbles in the road, her head down, the hood drawn over her hair to keep the light drizzle off of her, as his handsome face came unbidden into her mind yet again; the hard lines in his face when he was angry or set for battle, the warmth in his blue eyes when he was talking with his comrades; the way his face only completely relaxed when their bodies were merged into one.

Her musings were violently interrupted when she was grabbed by a large man who sprinted out at her from a copse of trees. She fought him as desperately as she could, but two others ran out to assist him. Both arms were now in their ironclad grip and the other was trying to get hold of her legs so he could stop her from kicking out.

A fourth man walked calmly towards them, they were wearing the same armour that the horsemen that had passed a short time before had on. They must have seen the rock being thrown out with the red silk and just waited to see who would appear after they'd hidden themselves away.

The man that came over last was taller and broader than the other three, his eyes were dark and bored into her.

"She'll do just fine," he said, his voice was low and Naomie felt a little shiver go down her spine in reaction to his words.

Beorn was getting frustrated, they'd been riding far too long without seeing any further signs from Naomie. He worried that they may have missed something and were traveling in the wrong direction.

"We're approaching a village," he said, pulling back on the reins. "I'm not sure she would go there, it might not be safe. I'm flummoxed as to where we should look now."

"There's a small farm just up ahead, let's ask if they saw her. She wouldn't have seen the town yet and may have passed them by."

"Good thinking, Draco."

The four men rode up to the small farmhouse and a wary old man came out onto the steps.

"Good day, sir," Beorn said. "We are looking for a friend, a woman with thick, black hair and silver eyes. She would have been walking along this road. Have you seen her?"

The man looked them all over carefully, his eyes narrowed as he tried to determine their motives.

"We only want to ensure no harm has come to her."

"Ain't seen anyone today but a day or so ago, the Baron's knights rode by with some woman screaming to high heavens, she had black hair, didn't see her eyes though."

"You didn't do anything to help?"

"I'm an old man. I can't fight a horde of knights for a woman I don't know. 'Sides, they bring women in all the time like that."

"What do you mean? What do they do with them?"

"If the Baron or his men want them, they keep 'em, otherwise, they sell 'em."

"Where do they hold these women?"

"At the Baron's castle, four, maybe five, kilometers out the other side of the village."

"Why do you help us?" Beorn asked suspiciously.

"Baron Beignet is a robber baron, killed his own father to get his estates and now he pillages and robs from anyone within his reach. Most of what I grow goes to him and his men. You look like you might give him trouble, so I help you, hoping that you will."

"Thank you, I shall do my best," Beorn said with a nod, as he and the others turned their horses and headed towards the nearby town.

Once there, they found an inn and settled at a far corner table to make their plans.

Beorn sat quietly, running his fingers through his beard as he contemplated the situation. Draco, Grant and Verne all bandied about ideas of how they might come to Naomie's rescue, but their words barely registered with him.

"Nay," Draco was saying, "we must sneak in at night, overpower the guards and take her that way."

There was a rage burning inside of Beorn so intensely that he needed to quiet his thoughts before being able to logically think this situation through.

He slid back his chair and stood. "I'll return anon."

They all watched him curiously for a moment as he walked outside, then turned back to their heated discussion.

They were in a good-sized village and Beorn found himself wandering through the streets. The rain had stopped completely and the sun was struggling to peek through the clouds.

He was a knight, a warrior, and it was time to think like one, but he found himself having trouble doing so because of his concern for Naomie. She was a beautiful, young woman and there was no telling what those brigands may have done to her.

Unwanted images of what could be happening at this very moment plagued him and he struggled to get them from his mind so he could focus.

What had happened already he could not change, but he could be sure that she would suffer no more under their hands and that is what he filled his head with instead.

Wandering around the dirt roads, he ignored the noise and activities of the villagers and focused all of his attention on what they needed to do. He was so engrossed in his thoughts that he almost passed by a flyer nailed to a tree in the town square. It was partially hidden amongst the others calling for information on thieves and vagrants in return for rewards and read: 'Call to arms for Baron Beignet, bring your own weapons.'

The missive had been there for some time, it was ripped and torn, and the ink ran in spots due to the rain and the wind, but Beorn saw this as their chance to get inside the Baron's castle and find Naomie. He tore it from the tree and carried it with him back to the inn.

CHAPTER 17

Naomie paced back and forth in her cell. There had been but little harm done to her as of yet, but Baron Beignet had made it clear when she was presented to him, that she had very limited choices as to how her future would go.

She could tell that he was intrigued by her, he was not a young man, although it was difficult to pick out the greys amongst his blonde hair and beard. His brown eyes were small and dark and there was no compassion in them, no kindness, and she knew he would show no mercy.

He had walked around her as she was forced to stand before him, her hands bound behind her back with a long rope being held by one of his knights.

The Baron had run his well-manicured fingers along her arms and then her breasts, letting them meander down her lean stomach. Naomie held her breath, her blood boiling at the invasion of his touch and she had to force herself to remain calm and not react.

The Baron grunted in apparent satisfaction and his beady eyes stared into hers.

"I believe you may do nicely," he said, his voice was as coarse as his conscience.

"I will take a closer look and then we'll get you a bath and you can wait for me in my quarters." He reached toward her again and, this time, he tore open the front of her kirtle and undertunic, exposing her breasts for all of the men in the room to view.

"What say you?" he asked, turning to his knights, all of whom stared at her with lust in their eyes, some actually licking their lips in anticipation.

"Fortune looked upon us when she happened into our path," replied Mason, the knight that was holding the rope attached to her wrists. "We look forward to our chance at her once you've finished."

170

"Mmm," the Baron replied, "that may be some time, my friend."

He pinched her nipple and Naomie could take no more. They'd made the mistake of leaving her legs unbound and she kicked the Baron in his groin with all her strength and he doubled over in pain.

Instantly the knights had their swords unsheathed and circled the girl as the Baron stumbled back out of her range.

Mason hit her in the middle of her back with the flat side of his sword, knocking her forward. Naomie couldn't break her fall because her hands were tied and her right cheek smashed against the solid wooden floor.

They all reached down at her, grabbing her arms, lifting her roughly to her feet, several groping at her exposed breasts as they did so. She snarled at them, her eyes cold and metallic, and some of them backed away from her.

The Baron had regained his equilibrium by then and stood near her, but not too close, ensuring that he was no longer within her range.

He stared at her with his pig-like eyes for a moment and she met his gaze with a fury that sent a little shiver down his spine. He'd always taken whatever woman he wanted and was able to subjugate them in short order. This one might prove to be his biggest challenge yet, but the thought of breaking her stirred his passion and filled him with desire.

"What is your name?" he asked, but Naomie refused to answer.

"I will name you then, I will call you Jezebel, because by the time I am done with you, that is what you will be. Take her to one of the cells in the tower until I am ready to begin her lessons."

Naomie was filled with disgust and not just a little fear when she remembered his words. They'd left her in the dark, cold cell all night with no food or water. She wasn't sure how long this particular torture would last but she knew that whatever was to come after it would be much worse.

She stopped her pacing as the slotted opening in the center of the door creaked open. A chunk of bread and bowl of soup were slid through along with a cup which she assumed was filled with water. She wanted to scream and throw it back at them, but knew she needed all of her strength.

"What did you say?" Naomie asked, when she heard whispering from the other side of the door.

"It will not go well for you until you submit."

Naomie peeked out through the slot and saw a young woman standing outside her door.

"Why would I ever do that?" she asked, and the girl moved a little closer so they could speak easier.

"They bring many young girls here, those that won't submit stay in these cells for months and they only bring them out to use them, as forcefully as they choose to. Some never leave on their own again."

"You give yourself to them willingly?"

The young girl cast her eyes to the ground, shame and disgust evident on her face. "I cannot bear the pain they inflict if I do not so, aye, I give myself willingly enough and do anything they ask of me."

"What is your name?

"Celia, and you?"

"Naomie, and I will never submit so, methinks, that I'm in for a long, difficult time here."

The girl looked at her with sympathy, then turned and walked away.

Naomie greedily drank down the water and then dipped the bread into the soup, she ate most of it that way and when the bread was gone went to pick up the spoon that Celia had slid through along with it.

As Naomie went to pick it up, the spoon slid through her fingers and dropped onto the floor. Her heart skipped a beat and she jumped up and ran to the slit of a window that was in her cell and which looked down onto the courtyard below.

She was instantly crushed, there was no one there other than Beignet's guards walking across the mud. She didn't understand, if a spoon drops from your hands, it is a sign your lover will come. She fully expected Beorn to be out in the courtyard, but he was nowhere to be seen.

Then she did throw the bowl with the remains of the soup in it and watched as it splashed against the moldy, dark walls. She wanted to weep but was too devasted for even that. If Beorn did not come to save her, she would most likely have no recourse but to take her own life. She would wait till she was sure there was no other way, but she would not live her life as Beignet's sexual plaything.

Sitting on the cold, hard floor, Naomie fought the tears that threatened and suddenly heard a familiar sound down in the courtyard below. Listening closely, she was sure that it was the jangle of bridles and a knight's chainmail, along with the sloshing of horses' hooves making their way through the mud. Trying not to get her hopes up, only to be crushed again, she went to the window slit and stood on her tiptoes, peering down into the courtyard.

A smile lit her face and her body sagged with relief when she saw Beorn, Draco, Grant and Verne riding across the muddy ground below. But her relief turned immediately to fear because Beignet would not take to their demands for her release lightly, and he had many knights available for his defense.

And Beignet might just lie and say she was not here and Beorn would never know the difference. She needed to bring herself to their attention as soon as she could, and ran over and began pounding on the door, screaming for Celia, or for anyone in the vicinity.

Beorn and his followers rode slowly towards the Keep, the ground in the courtyard was muddy and slippery and Beorn made note that if they had to leave in a hurry, there could be issues because of it that they would need to take into account.

His hand itched to grab his sword and leave a swath of dead bodies in his wake as he tried to locate Naomie, but he restrained himself. Even if they were able to convince Beignet they were here to serve as his knights, it still may take some time before they were able to locate Naomie, the castle was large and there were many places they could be stashing her. He must be patient, however difficult that may be.

Several knights stepped outside to greet them. Beorn nodded and stepped down off his steed, the others did the same and came to stand by his side.

"We've come to offer our services to Baron Beignet."

"This way," one of the knights replied, before leading them into the Great Hall. This was obviously a common occurrence and Beorn breathed a little easier.

The Great Hall was filled with knights, none of whom looked friendly. They formed a large semi-circle behind the four of them as they stood in front of a large older man who was sitting on what appeared to be a throne of sorts, and Beorn knew this man thought a lot of himself and would not be easy to deal with.

With a respectful bow, Beorn stepped forward.

"I am Beorn Wyndym." They had debated whether or not they should use their real names but saw no point in unnecessary deception. Beorn had the respect and the backing of the King of England and Normandy and would use that to his benefit, if possible.

"Wyndym," Beignet spit out, mulling over the name and why he knew of it. After a moment, he continued, "I had heard you were no longer in the service, that you were now a simple landowner."

Beorn allowed himself a slight smile. "I was for a time, but I fear that was a bit too tame for me."

"Why come here then?"

"We saw your inquiry for knights as we passed through the nearby village. Need for mercenaries is getting few and far between, hard to earn a decent wage at it anymore. Your inquiry seemed to be something of a more permanent nature."

Beignet's eyes narrowed as he studied Beorn, he had heard of him and Beorn was a knight to be reckoned with. He would be a great asset, if he was telling the truth, although Beignet could not come up with any reason why he wouldn't be.

"What brings you to this part of the world to begin with?"

"You have heard of the drama involving the Pope and King Henry?"

"Some, what do you know of it?"

"We were called to help protect the Pope, but he was already taken when we arrived. We marched on them and Robert of Capua had heated words with the leader of Henry's army, then we turned back with no battle, leaving the Pope in Henry's hands. It was frustrating and boring and we are ready to do real battle, should you have need of us."

Beignet had heard of the futile efforts by Capua and knew Beorn was telling the truth, at least about that.

"We can always use men of your competence. Do you speak for these three?"

"I do, they are brave and strong and will do as they are ordered."

"Good, we can always use men such as yourself. Let us share a cup of ale and discuss terms."

The other knights relaxed and stepped back. Tables were brought out along with plenty of ale. The four of them smiled and engaged with the others, all the while learning as much about the layout of the building as they could.

"There are untold riches to be had, if a man is willing to take them," Beignet was telling Beorn. "But you are used to being a leader, will you take issue with following my orders?"

"Not a bit, Milord, I tire of battling only for a just cause and am ready to reap some of the rewards in this life."

"Excellent."

Beorn stood then, the castle was large and they would have to be sufficiently ensconced within the group before being able to explore it and find where the prisoners were kept. "We shall collect our gear and return on the morrow if that is acceptable to you."

"It is, I look forward to spending more time with you. I think we could learn much from each other."

With a brief bow in Beignet's direction, Beorn and the other three headed towards the main door.

They had almost reached it when one of Beignet's knights came over and whispered in his ear. Beignet paused long enough for a thin-lipped smile to cross his face.

"Hold up, Sir Beorn," he called out, and Beorn stopped in his tracks, his hand snaking down near the hilt of his sword, not knowing what this could be about.

"There are other benefits, as well, that you might be interested in."

"Such as?"

"Bring her in here," he told his knight, then turned to Beorn, waving him back to his side. "We have some of the most beautiful women in this part of the land available to us."

"How do you manage that?" Beorn asked, returning to his seat next to the Baron.

"We have ways of making them learn to love the attention that we bestow upon them. This one that you will now see may well be the prettiest of them all. I thought she would fight harder, but women are weak and it doesn't take much to break their spirit."

Beorn clenched his hands together on his lap under the table, it was difficult for him to restrain himself from knocking the smug look off of Beignet's face. He knew it must be Naomie they would be bringing in and needed to quickly come up with a plan.

He gazed at the others in his group one at a time, they had been following Beignet's conversation, as well, and knew the time was upon them. They kept glancing around the room, gauging where the most danger would come from when they tried to make their escape with Naomie. Their hands were itching to pull out their swords, but they knew enough to wait for Beorn's signal.

He swallowed hard when he saw Naomie dragged into the room, her wrists were tied together in front of her by a length of rope, her beautiful thick hair was knotted and in disarray, there was a large bruise on her swollen cheek and her kirtle was torn down the front.

She walked tall and proud, ignoring the fact that most of her body was exposed to the men in the room because she could not use her hands to hold the pieces of her kirtle together.

Beorn tried not to let any emotion show in his face and hoped the others were able to do so, as well. Naomie met his gaze for a brief moment then she turned her hardened eyes in the direction of Beignet.

He had a smug smile on his face as his eyes devoured her. "I hear you have come to terms with your position."

"I have, I see no choice but to give myself to you."

"You were a spitfire when first we spoke, why the change of heart so soon?"

"I am not simple, I know there is no other way for this to be resolved."

"You see, my friend, Beorn, the beauty that awaits us. This one is mine, at least for a time, but there are others that you may all share in."

"Well," Beorn said, standing and moving away from the table. "I will leave you to your business with her. We shall return once we've collected our weapons and gear."

"I look forward to working with you," Beignet said, barely able to pull his eyes from the creamy skin peeking out from Naomie's torn kirtle.

Verne, Grant and Draco stood, as well, and moved over near Beorn. Naomie was on the opposite side of the table and Beorn had to find a way to get closer to her.

"Would it be impertinent if I requested an opportunity to run my fingers over that silken skin just one time, so I know what I have to look forward to in the future?"

Beignet's eyes narrowed. He wanted her only for himself but, mayhap, it was another lesson for her, that he could allow any of his men to touch her in whatever manner they chose, and there was naught she could do to prevent it, other than striving to please him.

"As you wish."

Beorn walked towards her slowly, trying to communicate to her with his eyes, hoping she understood what he was doing.

He slowly reached his hand up and caressed the skin on her neck, sliding it down around her breast and then to her taut stomach. Her skin quivered under his delicate touch, but she stood stockstill, their eyes caught in a silent conversation.

Draco, Grant and Verne had looked away and were relieved to see that Beignet's knights were all caught up in watching what was transpiring between Beorn and Naomie.

Beignet was not happy about the complaisant way the girl was responding and was about to order Beorn to stop when he reached behind her and grabbed the length of rope, yanking it out of the knight's hands, Beorn tossed it to Naomie, and pulled her in close behind him.

With just a couple of long strides he was at Beignet's side and yanked him up out of his chair, positioning the blade of his dirk against the man's throat.

Beignet's knights were not sure what to do and, since Beignet was not a knight himself, he was powerless to do anything.

The tip of the dirk dug deep into his throat and drops of blood oozed out onto his bejeweled tunic. Beorn used him as a shield until he could reach his knights who were making their way toward the outer door.

Swords had been drawn by Beignet's men who were scattered around the room and all were positioned to attack.

"Hold," Beorn yelled, catching all of their attention, "stand down or your leader dies."

His knights hesitated but Beignet nodded to them and they stepped back, although their swords remained at the ready.

Naomie suddenly moved away from Beorn, hurrying over to a nearby alcove and they all held their breath, if she was grabbed by one of Beignet's men, they would no longer have the upper hand and all could be lost.

Naomie reached into the shadows and, because her hands were still tied, she had to grab the girl's tunic with only her fingers and pull her over near Beorn. Together the small group formed a circle around the two women and made their way closer to the large wooden doors.

Verne was closest to them and ran to open them wide, allowing the group to step outside.

"To the horses, hurry," Beorn yelled out. "I'll keep them busy and give you some time."

"No," Naomie screamed.

"Get her out of here, Draco." Wasting no time in following his orders, Draco grabbed her and practically threw her up onto his horse as he jumped up behind her and cautiously began to make his way across the muddy ground.

"Grab Celia," Naomie screamed out to no one in particular. Verne turned and saw the young woman looking around in confusion, so he lifted her onto his horse, leaped up behind her and kicked it into a canter.

Beorn had no time to look and see if they were able to get away safely before several men started pushing their way through the door. He was a talented and strong knight but soon there were more of them than even he could handle.

"You won't get out of here alive," Beignet said.

"Watch me," he replied, and then shoved Beignet with all his might into the crowd oozing out through the doors and, amid their confusion, he was able to leap onto his own horse and take off.

He hoped that he'd given his group at least a little extra time, and kicked his stallion's sides, urging him on even faster, praying that it would keep its feet across this muddy patch till they escaped the castle grounds.

CHAPTER 18

They rode hard for about an hour, but then had to stop and let the horses rest. They found a stream and Grant kept watch while the others watered the horses and let them cool down.

Beorn looked around and saw that the young girl was being assisted by Verne. He'd find out more about her later but, for now, his only concern was for Naomie. He took her hand and pulled her aside, away from inquisitive ears.

With a featherlight touch, he ran his finger along her bruised cheek. "How badly are you hurt?"

She looked at him with a mixture of gratitude and despair. "I fell, they did not beat me."

"I am so sorry this happened, why didn't you wait for me?"

Naomie's body tensed, she was filled with so much anger and humiliation at what she had been through, and she was still afraid, although she would never show it.

As grateful as she was that they had come to her rescue, Naomie could not get out her mind the fact she had ended up in that horrific situation because of Beorn.

Her eyes, like wisps of clouds in the moonlight, stared hard into his. "You never came back for me."

"But I did, it just took much longer than I anticipated."

"I need to be with my family. I appreciate what you've done for me, but I must go on alone and find them."

"No, Beignet has many men, they will find you again."

Still their eyes held each other's, both wanting to say so much more, but afraid of the other's reaction, and their own. So, they fought this battle instead.

"It is of no consequence, what will be, will be."

"There is a consequence, and it will fall on me and my men, so you will not walk away from us right now. Each and every one of us cares about what happens to you, else we would not be here. You will come with us to my estate and we will prepare for the assault that Beignet is most likely planning as we speak."

"Why is it better for me to be there, then?"

"As long as you are single and have no family nearby, he will take you and use you anyway that he wants. If you are married to a knight of the realm, a man wo has the backing of the King himself, Beignet will not have the wherewithal to try and take you."

Her look was incredulous, both eyebrows raised high over her wide eyes. "You intend to marry me?"

"Yes, it is the only way that I can save you from him."

His words echoed in her head, accompanied by an icy pick pounding into her heart and breaking it into small little bits as they repeated over and over again.

"I would not marry you if there were no other men left. It would be no better than marrying Ninga. At least his hairy, old man body wants me for who I am, which you do not."

She turned and walked away, not wanting him to see the tears forming in her eyes.

Beorn watched her go, his face contorted in anger, but he wasn't sure if it was at her or at himself. He stomped over to his saddle and pulled out a spare tunic. Then he stalked over to Naomie, who was staring down into the flowing water of the river.

Draco had given her his mantle to protect her from the cold but, whenever she relaxed her grip, the mantle would open, leaving her bosom and torso laid bare for all to see.

"Take this," he said, holding out the tunic, "and cover yourself."

Still she would not look up at him, her emotions too raw to even be near him or to hear his voice. She reached out her hand and he thrust the tunic into it, then stalked away.

Naomie watched as Draco and Beorn had a heated conversation on the other side of the clearing. She found herself very curious about it because of the sidelong glances that Draco kept throwing her way.

"Let's get ready to head out," Beorn called to the others, then made his way over to Naomie.

"You will ride with Draco," he said, lowering his eyes to the ground. "Hear this, you will not leave us, we will keep you safe in whatever manner we can."

"I will not marry you, gadje."

"You've made that very clear and I understand. But you will marry Draco."

"No, I will not do that either."

He raised his head, his cheeks flushed in anger, his eyes looked like brittle bits of sapphire flashing out of his face as they caught hers.

"I understand how much you hate me right now. I really do, but I care enough about you that I will not let you fall into Beignet's hands again. Draco will marry you and, as he is also a knight, you will have the full protection of the King should Beignet come for you.

I leave it to you and Draco to figure out what happens after that situation is resolved."

Naomie turned her gaze over to young Draco, who was sitting uncomfortably on his horse watching the two of them. She gave him a hesitant smile, he was a good man and none of this was his fault. She couldn't let him be brought into this mess that she had made of her life.

For now, she would go along with the plans they were making for her, but she would ensure that her life was of her own making again once they reached Beorn's estate.

Beorn's mood deteriorated as they got closer to his home. His thoughts continued to battle relentlessly back and forth, he knew that he cared for Naomie, he knew that she was a very special person and that he would be lucky to have her in his life. Naomie challenged him like no other had ever been able to do, not even Anna.

But he was not ready to put his emotions on the table so to speak. He had survived as long as he had by keeping them hidden down deep within himself and was not ready to change that.

Yet, the thought of Naomie in the arms of the old, hairy gypsy, or even handsome, young Draco, filled him with angst such as he had never before experienced. He thought that Anna's death was the worst thing that had ever happened to him, but now, he was quite sure it was having Naomie enter his life.

Not just enter it, but to completely beguile him and then be gone, leaving him with nothing but a dark hole in his heart to remember her by.

Draco was a nervous wreck for the rest of the ride home, he cared about Naomie, but the thought of being her husband actually filled him with terror. She was more of a woman than he had ever known before, and marriage itself was not something he anticipated happening for many, many years.

Although Naomie leaned closely against him as they rode and aroused him in a way that took his breath away, he was no fool. He knew how deeply Beorn cared for Naomie and how deeply she cared for him.

He would let Beorn think he would marry Naomie just so that they could continue their trip back to the estate without battling the entire way, but he had no intention of doing so.

Draco made sure to be the last in line as they continued their journey and fell back a bit, so that he and Naomie could have a long, confidential conversation about the future.

Beorn bellowed for the stable hands to take care of the horses and then began yelling at the staff inside the Manor as soon he entered.

"We need cider, food, bathwater and a priest. See that its done, anon."

The staff scattered to follow his instructions.

"What is it?" he asked, when Naomie approached and obviously had something on her mind.

"This is Celia, she was also stolen by Beignet and forced to do unspeakable things."

Beorn looked over at the girl, but she continued to stare at the floor and would not meet his eye. She was not as tall as Naomie and had long blonde hair, she was so thin that, even with a belt, her kirtle hung loosely on her body.

"May she stay here? At least for a time until we can get her to her home?"

"Of course," he replied, wondering how many other girls like this were still at Beignet's castle and his face flushed in anger at the thought of it. "Gretchen, please see our guest to her room before taking care of your other duties."

"Yes, Milord," she replied, as she led the young woman away.

"Thank you," Naomie said, then turned to leave.

"Where are you going?" he asked, seeing the direction she was heading.

"To prepare for a bath and put on other clothing."

"Not in my bedchamber," he replied, grabbing the cup of cider placed in front of him by one of the other servants.

She did not respond for a moment, then nodded and headed down one of the other hallways. She did not return to the Great Hall until sometime later.

Beorn's breath caught in his throat when she finally entered the room again, wearing the devasting red tunic that she'd left behind. Celia was at her side, but Beorn never even noticed her.

Naomie's skin was flushed with the heat from the water of the tub and her hair was slightly damp. Even the bruise on her cheek could not take away from the beauty of her face as her lustrous silver eyes sparkled from it like gems.

Naomie saw the look on his face, and she knew that Beorn belonged to her. He just didn't know it yet.

She sat at the opposite end of the table, next to Draco, and lifted a newly filled cup in his direction, then downed half of it. They ate and drank and relaxed a bit, but then the conversation had to return to Beignet.

"I will take the first watch," Beorn said. "I don't anticipate that he will be here much before tomorrow afternoon, at the earliest. He would have to get his men and his plans in order first, but we cannot take the chance of being caught unawares."

"I've had word," Beorn continued, staring down at Naomie and Draco, "that the priest will be here early in the morn, so you two must be ready for him. The marriage will have to take place before Beignet arrives."

"As you wish," Naomie said, standing up and moving away from the table. "Good evening, all of you. Before I go, I do want to thank you for saving me, and for doing battle to keep me safe. You'll never know how much you all mean to me."

She walked off then, slowly and seductively, knowing they were all watching her go, particularly Beorn.

Beorn paced back and forth outside, he had a torch with him, set into the ground at entrance to his estate. Only one road led to it, but he was not simple enough to think Beignet would boldly ride up to the front gate. However, it was a quiet night, there was no moon, no stars showed in the overcast sky and sounds carried far on the gentle breeze.

He sincerely hoped that they would not show this night because he could not manage to keep his head clear of thoughts of Naomie and feared he wouldn't survive a sneak attack.

He was frustrated and angry. *How could she so easily agree to marry Draco? She didn't care for him, so why would she do so? Had she come to hate him that much?*

As Beorn continued pacing, he finally acknowledged that the reason was because she did not believe that he cared for her. Because he had been so stubborn and so resistant to having her in his life that he had turned her away and had hurt her deeply in the process.

As a result, Naomie believed she had no other choice but to leave and, in so doing, she was captured, injured and humiliated, and it was all because of him.

Why then, he thought, *should I be angry at her for being true to herself, when that is exactly what made me care for her to begin with?*

He sighed heavily, he knew the fault was not hers for any of this mess that they had created, but the truth was not enough to ease his mind or the sharp pains ripping at his chest.

Beorn could only hope that the clash with Beignet would occur on the morrow, after the wedding, and that Draco would take her far away after that, so he would never have to see her or think of her again.

Sadly, he was not sure that even copious amounts of cider would ever help him lose the image of those shimmering silver eyes.

In the back of his mind, he thought maybe she would sneak out to see him, to spend her last unmarried night with him, but that was not to be, and his anger and frustration continued to build as the night slowly wore on.

Naomie had no intention of going out to visit Beorn, she was busy preparing for her wedding day.

Since she could no longer use Beorn's bedchamber, she had chosen the one with the trunk full of Anna's clothing and had taken her time digging through it until she found her wedding dress.

Celia was in the room next door and she ran over and knocked her door.

"Yes?" Celia said, her voice thin and frightened.

"Please open the door, it's me and I need your help."

"What do you need?" Naomie was approximately the same age as this young woman but, to Celia, she would forever be her heroic savior. There was nothing that she would not do for Naomie.

"Look what I've found." She grabbed Celia's hand, pulled her into her room and secured the door before holding up the lovely wedding kirtle.

"Where did you get that?"

"Beorn's wife died and this trunk is full of her clothing. This dress was buried down at the bottom, but I want to use it for myself tomorrow."

"Won't Beorn be angry?"

She shrugged. "Mayhap, but that is not my concern. We must find thread and needles to turn this into my proper wedding dress."

"Draco will be very pleased to see his bride in a kirtle as fine as this."

Naomie looked at her in surprise. "I will not be marrying Draco, I will be marrying Beorn."

"But I thought you were to marry Draco." The poor girl was very confused.

"It is difficult to explain, but Beorn and I are destined to be together. He fights that but, at close of play, he will accept what his heart demands and step in Draco's place on the morrow."

"How do you know what will happen?"

"The signs are clearer to me now and I feel it deep in my own heart. It will be as it should be."

Celia's brown eyes were wide with wonder as she gazed at Naomie, wishing that she could have just a small amount of the confidence that Naomie carried so easily.

"But I thought you were angry at Beorn."

Naomie paused for a moment, trying to find an appropriate explanation for how she felt.

"I am angry at Beorn, at his pride and his cowardice which led to my capture. But, because of what happened, we have both been forced to look deep within ourselves.

I've learned that my anger towards him is fading already, but that my love for him never will.

If he hasn't learned the same thing already, he will soon enough. Come, let us find what we need to alter the kirtle. All will be resolved in the morn."

They enlisted the aid of Karla and Gretchen to secure the items they needed, and Celia and Naomie worked until the wee hours of the morn recreating the kirtle to fit Naomie's figure and her style.

The priest arrived early the next morning and everyone met in the Great Hall. Draco and Grant, his best man, waited next to the priest while Beorn leaned back against the wall, sipping cider and acting as if this day was anything but one of the worst of his life.

Verne was one of the guests in attendance for the wedding and watched Beorn with concern. He knew the man well enough to know this marriage did not bode well for any of their futures.

All of the men stopped whatever they were doing when Naomie stepped into the room. Celia, who would act as her Maid of Honor, entered the room first and made her way over to stand near the priest. None of the men, save Verne, gave her more than a cursory glance.

All eyes were on Naomie. The white silk kirtle hung to her feet and somewhat shorter, colorful sheaths of bright silk were sewn over the top of it, as well as along the bodice.

Her hair was combed back, away from her face and held in place with a bright red scarf which was wrapped around her head. Dressed like this, Naomie felt like herself again for the first time since she'd originally been taken.

The bruise on her cheek had faded a little and her face positively glowed with happiness as she looked around the room.

Naomie could not miss the scowl on Beorn's face, but even that could not take away from her joy. She walked across the room and stepped up alongside Draco, turning to face the priest.

Father Montclair seemed a bit flustered but had performed many weddings and so he began, "Welcome, loved ones. We are gathered here to join,"

He leaned over towards Draco who whispered in his ear, and then he leaned over to Naomie and listened to her as well, then he stepped back.

"We are gathered here to join Draco Wyndym and Naomie Patrin in holy matrimony.

Draco, please repeat after me, I promise to cherish you always, to honor and sustain you,"

Draco opened his mouth to speak, but before he could get any of the words out, Beorn had stepped between him and his future wife.

"This farce must stop now," he said, his cheeks were flushed and his blue eyes snapped with anger.

"Are you objecting to the wedding, Milord?" Father Montclair asked.

"Yes, I am."

"On what grounds?"

He hesitated, unsure of why he was doing this, knowing that Naomie may well deny him, and she would be justified to do so.

Beorn then turned to look into Naomie's eyes, unable to read the emotions that he saw in hers and not sure if he wanted her to agree to this or not. If she did, he may well be opening himself up to some horrific hurt at her hands.

"She knows."

"I see," the priest mumbled, this had never occurred before and he was not sure of his next step.

Draco looked back and forth between them. "I will step down, but only if that is what Naomie wants, as well."

She was barely able to tear her eyes away from Beorn's to look over at Draco.

They all held their breath as they waited for her response.

"I will take Beorn Wyndym as my husband."

Draco tried to hold back his grin as he winked at Naomie and then stepped back, leaving just the two of them in front of the priest.

"Er, um, shall I start over?"

"Please, do," Beorn said, taking Naomie's hand and tucking it in to the corner of his elbow, not just wanting, but needing her touch at this moment.

His emotions were twisted as he listened to the words the priest spoke, and sorrow battled with joy as he recalled a similar scene when he had married Anna.

Trying to lose those thoughts, Beorn gazed at Naomie and wondered where this would lead them. Was it only a temporary respite to save her from Beignet, or would they be able to make this a real marriage? He knew not, but could only hope that the two of them did not do permanent harm to each other whilst they tried to find those answers.

He stumbled over his vows and his chest seized up when the priest asked for the ring.

"We have none," he said, leaving the priest flummoxed once again.

"We must have something to use to confirm this bond between you."

Beorn struggled with the decision he knew he must make now. "Hold up, we do have something, give me a moment."

Beorn ran out of the room and hurried back a few minutes later, holding up a beautiful gold band. Sliding it onto Naomie's finger, he said, "This was my wife, Anna's. Take it for now, but I will see that you get one of your own once all this other godswallop has been resolved."

Suddenly the warning bells began to ring and Beorn turned to the priest. "Finish it, quickly."

"I now pronounce you husband and wife, you may kiss the bride."

Beorn swooped down and took her lips with his own, not quite sure how he felt about being her husband now that the deed was done, but there was no time to dwell on it.

"Gretchen, show the priest, Celia and Naomie into the cellar where you will all be safe. Be sure to take your mother and any others working in the kitchen down with you, as well."

Naomie started to open her mouth to argue, but he put his finger over her lips. "Stay there until I come to get you, please. I cannot let them have you."

"As you wish," she whispered, and kissed him lightly before following behind Gretchen.

The others had already drawn their swords and Beorn followed them outside where they were met by several dozen knights, all still astride their battle horses.

CHAPTER 19

Baron Beignet sat in front of them all, his sword drawn and resting against the pommel of his saddle.

"What can I do for you, Baron?" Beorn asked, his own sword drawn and the tip resting in the dirt at his feet.

"I believe you have something of mine."

"No, I don't believe so."

"Enough games, Beorn, bring me the girl and we'll leave quietly, and you and friends will live to fight another day."

"That will be a problem, Milord, the girl, Naomie, is my wife, and you cannot have her."

"Your wife?"

"Yes, and should you try to take her, all the wrath of the King will fall on you, as well you know. You would not want that, would you?"

Beignet hesitated, he had not considered this particular situation and tended to agree with Beorn. Mayhap, they should forget about this girl, there were many that could take her place.

But then she walked outside and stood behind the four knights. His eyes narrowed as he took in her appearance, and those eyes, those incredible eyes. There were not many that could take this particular girl's place, after all. And there were only four of them, they could be beaten easily and, if they killed everyone else at the estate, there would be no one to report the incident to the King.

Beorn knew that Naomie had come outside and was standing a couple of meters behind him, he did not trust the look in Beignet's eyes, or the tautness of his muscles.

When Beignet straightened up and tensed his shoulders, firming his grip on his sword, Beorn realized with no small degree of shock that Beignet was willing to do battle to get Naomie back.

"Ready, men? This is happening. Naomie," he raised his voice a little, "go inside where it's safe, please."

"No, I stand at your side, for better or for worse."

Beignet was just about to give the order to attack when there was suddenly a rush of hundreds of men on horseback galloping towards them, hooting, hollering and yelling, waving their weapons as they approached through the apple orchards, swerving around the dormant trees, straight towards the group outside the Manor.

Behind them came wagon after colorful wagon across the fields, filled with even more people, men and women, all brandishing weapons.

Beignet's horse started to prance nervously, as did many of his men's. They looked to him in confusion, not knowing what to make of this turn of events.

"Gypsies," he bellowed. Initially, he wanted to scream out to his men, ordering them to attack, but seeing the approaching hordes and knowing he also had Beorn and his men behind them, he changed his mind.

He turned his small, dark eyes toward Naomie, realizing now that she was also a gypsy and they were here for her.

"Beorn Wyndym," he said, turning his wrathful gaze toward him, "this is not done between us. We will finish it another day, my friend, have no doubt about that."

Then he kicked his horse's flanks and led his men down the main road outside of the estate. Some of the gypsies continued to ride after them, but after a short bit slowed and returned.

Beorn and his men were also looking around in confusion, this was something they had never experienced before either.

"Luca," Naomie screamed, as she pushed past them, running into the arms of one of the men who had just dismounted from his horse.

His hair was as black as hers and they shared similar features, the young man then picked her up and swung her around with a broad smile on his face. Beorn could only assume that he must be her brother and walked over towards them.

The man set Naomie back down and turned to Beorn, his dark eyes narrowed into slits.

"Luca," Naomie began hesitantly, knowing this was not going to go well, "this is my husband, Beorn."

Luca turned to her and slapped her across the face so hard that she stumbled backward.

Beorn had his sword tip at Luca's throat before the man could blink and Naomie got up hastily and put her hand on his arm.

"Please, don't," she said, not because every other member of the tribe was ready to come to Luca's defense, but because she deserved the slap.

"Don't ever touch her again," Beorn said quietly, before lowering his sword.

The crowd parted then, allowing an older woman and man through. They stood quietly, looking back and forth at Naomie and then at Beorn.

Luca muttered something in another language and the relief on the old woman's face left it completely, and the man's cheeks flushed red with anger as he turned his eyes on Naomie.

He said a few brief words in their language that made Naomie hang her head and then he turned back towards his wagon. The old woman took a step forward and rested her palm on Naomie's stomach.

For a moment, Naomie thought that her mother might forgive her, but the old woman sealed Naomie's fate with the utterance of just one word, "Mahrime".

Then she spat on the ground and followed her husband. Luca took one last look at Naomie, then shook his head sadly before mounting his horse and turning away, the others all following along behind him.

Beorn stood by her side, with Draco, Grant and Verne just a few steps away. No one said a word or moved a muscle until every rider and every wagon was out of sight. When they were gone, Beorn turned to Naomie and was shocked to see the tears in her eyes, shimmering like the moon's reflection on an angry sea.

He held out his arms and she stepped into his embrace, the tears falling uncontrollably down her cheeks. Her body shook with the sobs racking it and the others all went inside to give them some privacy.

Once she quieted to a few sniffles, Beorn walked with her to a nearby bench. "What is mahrime?"

"Unclean and impure."

"Because you are married to me? Would it have gone better for you if we did not get married?"

"No, having any relationship with a gadje would make me unclean."

"But they would not have known."

"Yes, they would."

"Because you are no longer a virgin?"

"No, because I carry your child."

"You what? How?" He moved away from her so that he could look down into those incredible eyes.

"You need me to explain how it comes to be?"

"No, I just, I, when did you know?"

"A few days ago, I started to dream about mice."

"I don't understand."

Naomie ran her fingers through his closely cropped beard and then around his lips, she could see the fear in his eyes at the thought of her being with child.

"Dreaming of mice means you are or will soon be with child."

"So, you may not be right now?"

"My mother knew when she put her hand on my stomach. I am quite sure of it."

Beorn stood up and began to pace back and forth in front of her, tugging at his beard as he considered this new information. "The marriage and all that has happened has come upon us so quickly, I must think on it all."

"We have created a child together and now we are wed. What is there to think upon?"

Naomie was not completely surprised at his reaction, but she was frightened. She had just lost her entire family and could not lose Beorn, as well, it would be too much for her heart to take.

"This day had been full of strong emotions, has it not?" She nodded her agreement. "Then let us put those behind us for a short time and celebrate our marriage, shall we? We will talk more later."

"Yes, I would like that."

As she stood up to walk inside with him, a slight drizzle started, just a few drops sputtering here and there and Naomie held out her hand to collect them.

She wore such an unusual look on her face that Beorn was curious about her thoughts.

"What is it?"

Naomie looked at him with tears sparkling in her eyes. "If it rains on your wedding day, it means you will have a happy marriage. But this rain is not steady, as if it is unsure of what it wants to do. Mayhap, it has not yet been determined whether or not our union will be happy."

"Only time can tell us that, Naomie, not your silly superstitions."

Her beliefs had been ridiculed by the gadje many times throughout her life, but some events were certain portents of what would be, and even Beorn's disdain could not dissuade her from her concern over this particular omen.

Naomie swallowed her sorrow and her unease and walked with Beorn back into the Great Hall to join the others. Karla had managed to provide a grand feast with very short notice and they all enjoyed the broiled venison in a spicy pepper sauce which was served with root vegetables, cabbage and pears that had been cooked with a fruity wine and white vinegar and then stored for a time, ready for just such an occasion as this.

The food continued to be paraded out to the guests, mushroom pasties and braised beef; poached fowl and bacon with pudding, nuts and various cheeses that were made on the estate itself and, finally, the fruit and sweet pastries to end the meal.

Throughout it all, Verne and Draco were animated, talking excitedly about their future as knights, anticipating great battles still to be fought.

Grant did not join in, he knew where his duties lie and was begrudgingly coming to accept his fate.

"Grant," Beorn said, "you have great things in store for your future, as well, you know that, do you not? You will take a different path than these other two beggars and you will have great responsibilities put on your shoulders. But, I know that you will do well and bring honor to the Wyndym name."

"Thank you, uncle, I appreciate your words."

Naomie forced herself to eat some of the delicious food, but she was devasted by the actions of her family and found it difficult to share in the conversations at the table. It did not matter that she completely understood why it had to happen, the reality of their being able to completely ostracize her was like a knife being buried deep into her chest.

Beorn sat by her side but rarely looked her way and seemed much quieter than normal.

"I don't understand why your people just left like they did," Draco stated at one point. Beorn wanted to kick him when he saw Naomie lower her eyes to the table.

"My people believe that anyone who is not Romani is unclean and untrustworthy. If a Romani rule is broken, the person that did so is considered unclean and they are ostracized. The worst punishment that can be handed out is to be excluded from the family.

I broke our rules and ostracization ensures that the same mistake is not made by anyone else because our gypsiness is our most prized possession."

"How does being with Beorn make you unclean?"

Naomie's eyes were warm, glittering silver orbs as she reached out to take Beorn's hand with her own. Instinctively, he enclosed it within his own.

"Anyone who is not Romani does not know our ways and thus, must be unclean. They will contaminate us in turn."

"Will you at least be able to visit them in the future?" Grant asked, and Naomie shook her head.

"It is irreversible, once you are ostracized, it is as if you never existed. My name will not be spoken again and if I try to contact them, I will be stoned."

Beorn removed his hand from hers and gently pushed back an errant strand of her thick luxurious hair from her face, his emotions continuing to do battle. He cared for her very much and could not bear to see her so hurt, yet, he feared he may end up being the one to hurt her even more deeply.

"I knew what to expect," she said, seeing the concern on his face.

"Why then, did you allow things to happen as they did?"

She ignored the question and turned to the others at the table. "I thank you again for defending and protecting me. And now, my husband and I will be retiring for a bit of privacy."

The knights raised their cups in a silent cheer to the newlyweds as Beorn and Naomie left the room.

Once they were comfortably ensconced in Beorn's bedchamber, they sat side by side, neither sure of what to do next.

His body ached for hers, yet, they had issues to discuss first and once that happened, she may well completely reject him.

"I wanted to answer your question privately."

"Please do, we have many things to talk about."

They sat side by side, their arms touching, their hands clasped in their laps as if they were trying to keep from reaching out to caress one another.

"The first time that we were together, I did not plan on that happening, my body responded to yours and so I gave myself to you. With no regret," she added, turning to look up at his face, her worriment growing when he refused to look her in the eye.

"After that night, I craved being in your arms. I thought I would still be returning to my tribe but could not face being married to that wrinkly old Ninga without first laying with a strong, virile man such as yourself."

Beorn was frowning now. "Is that the only reason you came to me after that first night?"

"I was drawn back to you because I wanted more of what you had shared with me. You are handsome, strong and brave and you needed me."

"I, what?" Beorn asked, turning then to stare down into the glittering depth of her eyes.

"You needed me, but you didn't know it yet."

"Mayhap, I did," he responded, running his finger along her jawline and then around her mouth. Watching as her lips parted in anticipation and he wanted so badly to not think about anything, to let his body take over and join with hers once again, but he could not.

"Was I not truthful with you all along, Naomie?"

"You were, you made no promises."

"And now, we find ourselves married and you with child. I've tried to explain to you why I never wanted to find myself in this particular situation again. My thoughts on that have not changed."

"Why then, did you continue to couple with me, you knew that I would eventually become with child. Did you plan on having me back to my family by the time that happened so you would not have to acknowledge it?"

"Of course not."

Naomie was not angry, she was sad, very, very sad. She knew who Beorn was deep inside, she had hoped he would be able to reach down and find that person, but it appeared he would not even try to do so.

Instead, he would remain stubborn and cold and aloof, and refuse to let love into his heart, or his life.

"What do you want then, Beorn? I have no coin, I have no where to go. What is that you want from me?"

He took her hand into his own and held it tight. "God help me, I don't know, Naomie. I only know that I cannot be your husband and father to the babe you carry. I cannot do it and it would not be right for me to pretend otherwise."

They sat in silence, both crushed into despair, and now anger was beginning to simmer inside of Naomie, and his next comment made it explode to the surface.

"You can do spells or cause things to happen with the use of certain herbs, yes? Can you get rid of the child?"

She tore her hand out of his grip and stood up, pacing back and forth in front of the bed.

When she finally stopped and turned to him, he saw such a torrent of anger and hurt spilling from in her eyes that he was stunned.

It was even greater than he had imagined possible and for all his worry about hurting her, it was done now, and may well be irrevocable.

"I would never do that," Naomie said, her words brittle and harsh. "That you would ask me to do so makes me think that I never knew you at all. You are not the man that I thought you were. I will stay here until the babe is safely delivered and then we will leave, but you will in no way act as my husband while I remain here.

Now, I need you to remove yourself from my sight, my fingers itch to claw your eyes out and I would be hard pressed to continue trying to restrain myself."

"As you wish," he replied, his voice a monotone as he headed for the door.

Beorn had no idea how to make this easier for her, or himself, and thought it best he be away from her while he mulled over the issue.

"Ho," Draco called out loudly when Beorn joined them in the Great Hall, "that was awfully quick, Beorn. Mayhap, it should have been me to wed the lass, after all."

"Mayhap, it should have been," Beorn replied, grabbing a cup and filling it to the brim with his most lethal cider, hoping to bury all the thoughts swirling in his head, thoughts that were making him feel like a lesser man than he had always taken pride in being.

The men sensed something important was amiss and kept their thoughts to themselves.

"Verne," Beorn said, after taking a large draught of cider, "let us get you knighted this afternoon. I know you are all anxious to be away and find some trouble to stir."

"Thank you, Milord," Verne replied, half in the bag himself, but ready to go through the ceremony whenever Sir Beorn wished to begin.

"Once I have finished my cider," Beorn said, staring down into its golden depths, sadly acknowledging that he would, once again, be spending many more days well into his cups, "I will finish the missive for the two of you miscreants, we'll have the ceremony and then I will send you on your way."

"What is it?" Naomie asked, in response to the hesitant knocking on her door.

"It is me, Celia."

Naomie wiped the tears from her face and opened the door. "Yes?"

"They are preparing for Verne's knighting ceremony. I did not think you would want to miss that."

"No, I would not, thank you for letting me know. I will be there anon."

Naomie joined them in the Great Hall a few minutes later and the three young men could not help but notice how swollen and red-rimmed her eyes were, although she squared her shoulders and refused to show her despair.

"Verne," Beorn said, dressed in full armour, except for his helmet. "We should have had your knighting ceremony, the accolade, before the feast, so that we could all appreciate what you have accomplished in your life. However, this day has been filled with drama and I seem to be making a cock-up of everything."

His eyes travelled over to where Naomie sat, but she would not meet his gaze.

"You and I will share a cup of cider down the line, Verne, and you can regale me with all your tales of derring-do and then I will remind you of the adventures that we've shared in the past. In the meantime, be sure to brag of all your deeds to these two as you make your way to your new life with them."

Verne stood before Beorn, also in battle dress, his eyes positively glowing with pride and excitement.

"I will miss you, my friend," Beorn said softly, then let his voice rise, "but I know you will bring honor to your family and to my household, and you will live your life by the code of a knight of the realm. State your oath."

Verne had memorized the oath years ago and practiced it almost daily. He stood tall and proud and spoke the words clearly and with complete commitment.

"I shall obey the laws of England and honour my peerage; I shall defend the realm, its lands, King and people; I dedicate myself to the noble pursuit of Honesty and justice; I pledge myself to support of my fellow man; I dedicate myself to the persecution and cessation of poverty and hunger; I pledge myself to the protection of the weak; I dedicate myself to the cause of Good and the fight against Evil and Injustice."

"Kneel before me." Beorn did not have to ask him twice and, as the young man went to his knees before him, Beorn dubbed Verne on each shoulder, conferring his knighthood upon him.

"Good luck to you, Verne," Beorn said, holding out his hand and helping him up to his feet.

Naomie stepped forward then and gave Verne a warm congratulatory hug.

Once the others had shook his hand and offered their congratulations, Naomie touched Grant's arm to get his attention.

"Yes?"

"I do not wish to upset you unduly, however, I fell asleep and there were some signs in my dreams that had to do with you and with your family."

"Bad things?" he asked, his brown eyes widening as he felt a deep squeeze around his heart.

"Not necessarily, just signs that something will be happening at Wyndymshire and they will need you. Get yourself home soon, Grant, no more delays."

"I will, thank you, Naomie." He turned away but then stopped and looked back over at her. "Will you be alright?"

"Aye, I will be fine," she replied, her eyes sliding over to where Verne and Beorn were talking.

"Have a care for yourself." He kissed her cheek and called to Draco. "Let's pack up and go."

"Now?"

"Yes, now."

There was quite a commotion as the three knights prepared their horses and gear and got ready to head out. All gave a warm hug and a kiss on the cheek to Naomie.

For Beorn, they had a hearty handshake and much gratitude, and even Draco seemed genuinely sad to be parting ways with him.

"I'm glad we've had this time to get to know one another. Even though we don't see eye to eye on all things, I'm proud to have you for my brother."

"And I, you."

Naomie stood by Beorn's side as they watched the men ride out of sight, without thinking, he put his arm around her and pulled her up tight against his side.

She stepped away from him, her eyes narrowed in a glare that caused a shiver along his spine.

"May I ask a favor of you?"

"That depends on what the favor is," he replied.

"Celia has no home to return to, her family was killed by Beignet when they took her. May she stay here and work as one of your servants?"

"I have no need of more servants. Mayhap, I can get her a position with someone nearby."

"Please, she has been badly damaged by what was done to her and lives in a world filled with fear, even though she is now safe. It would cause her more consternation should she have to go to a place where she does not know the people, men in particular. I worry about her peace of mind."

He could not tear his eyes from Naomie's as she pled with him about Celia, they had softened and were no longer shooting daggers at him. He knew that Naomie still fought with her own memories of the short time Beignet had held her captive and could only imagine the horrors Celia had experienced.

He made Naomie wait for his answer, he knew that it would be for whatever she wanted, but he needed to keep her near him for just a few minutes more, so he could study her face.

They had much that would still have to be resolved between them. There was no way that he would be able to live in the same household with her and not take her into his arms whenever he felt the need for her.

Beorn looked out in the direction that Verne and Draco had gone and wondered if it may be time for him to head out himself, mayhap he could find mercenary work that might allow him to unleash his frustrations with the tip of his sword.

"Beorn, may she stay?"

"You are the Lady of the Manor, Naomie, if you need a servant to take care of your needs, you shall have one."

"Thank you," she said, hesitating for a moment and then finding her resolve, she turned and hurried towards the Manor. Celia would be greatly relieved to learn she could stay here.

CHAPTER 20

Beorn and Naomie managed to avoid each other for the rest of that afternoon and evening. Beorn drank cider until he passed out in the Great Hall in front of the roaring fire.

His head was pounding when he woke early the next morning and he felt a desperate need for some fresh air. He headed towards the stables, planning on taking a long ride in solitude to ease his woes.

Hearing an unusual noise, he had removed a dirk from his belt and was just about to throw it when he realized the man skulking around in the dim early morning light was none other than Draco. And then Verne appeared at his side.

"Good way to get killed, what are you doing here?"

They walked over to him and, even in the murky light, he could see the anxiousness on their faces. "Where is Grant? Has something happened to him?"

"Nay," Draco said, pushing his long brown hair out of his face. "He continued on to England."

"Why didn't the two of you?"

"We made it into the nearest village last night and learned of some disturbing news that we thought you should be aware of."

"What?" Beorn asked impatiently.

"The gypsies headed that way and were staying on the outskirts of the village. Beignet showed up and he and his men grabbed a bunch of their young women."

"Why would Beignet head in that direction? His castle lies to the south."

"We think he followed them deliberately, because they came to our aid earlier in the day."

"What are you are asking of me, then?"

"Naomie's brother tried to help the girls and killed two of Beignets knights. They knocked him out, trussed him up like an animal and took him, as well. They intend to hang him once they get him back to Beignet's castle."

"Damn," Beorn murmured, pacing around the stable. Naomie no longer owed these people any loyalty after what they did to her, but he knew her and when she cared about someone, she cared deeply. He also knew her family would be no exception, even now.

"Come with me inside, we need to let Naomie make this decision."

They found her eating alone in the Great Hall, her eyes were even puffier than the afternoon before and Beorn bit back his guilt, knowing that it was his words and actions that were causing her grief. And he was about to make it even worse.

"What is it?" She could immediately tell from the looks on their faces that something was horribly wrong.

"Where is Grant?" Had she misread her dreams then?

"He is fine and is continuing on home," Beorn said, striding over to her side. Taking her hands in his, he was pleasantly surprised that she did not pull away from him as she stared up into his eyes.

"There is no gentle way to say this, Beignet followed your tribe and kidnapped some of the women. When your brother tried to defend them, he killed some of Beignet's men and they intend to hang him."

"No," she whispered, staring down at the table. She thought she had cried herself dry of tears, but more found their way out and dropped onto the table in front of her.

Although their minds were at a discord, their hearts and bodies knew better. Beorn pulled her to her feet and opened his arms, Naomie stepped into the warmth and comfort of his embrace with no hesitation.

As he wrapped his arms around her, trying to ease some of her anguish, he rested his cheek against her hair, desperately wishing there was something more that he could do for her.

"It is all my fault."

"No, Naomie, it is not. It is only due to the pure evilness that resides in Beignet."

"You don't understand, bad luck only comes to the Romani when one of them is unclean and causes the bad luck. This has happened because of me and what I have done."

"We will go after him," Beorn said, his words surprising them all, including himself. But he knew that nothing he could say would dissuade her from believing she caused this. He could only ensure that he kept her brother and those other women from any further harm, so that she had no reason to continue punishing herself over this.

"Thank you," Naomie whispered, her voice cracking.

He stepped back and wrapped his large hands around her upper arms as he leaned down and looked into her eyes. "We are but a few and cannot take on Beignet's knights alone. Will the other Romani men help us?"

"To save Luca, yes, they will."

"Will you come with us to talk to them?"

Now she looked more frightened than upset.

"They will not listen to me. They do not acknowledge that I even exist."

"We need you to come with us, if they refuse to listen, so be it, but we need to try to enlist their aid or your brother and the girls they took may well die very soon."

"Yes, of course, I will try, but do not expect much."

Verne and Draco's horses were already saddled. Beorn took of care of his while Verne saddled one for Naomie and they left a short time later.

Beorn did not lead them towards the town, but by way of a different route that he anticipated would bring them directly to the Romani caravan, if they were already following Beignet's men.

His instincts were correct and they came upon the entire band later that morning. Tensions were high as they approached and men on both sides had their hands hovering near their swords, or whatever weapon they happened to carry.

There was an older man with long white hair riding towards the front of the group. He pulled back on the reins and bellowed out something in their language.

"I can go no further," Naomie said, and Beorn moved his horse over closer to hers.

"Why not?"

"That is Ninga, the man I was promised to. He warns me that my life will be forfeit if I approach any closer."

Her lips quivered and Beorn wanted desperately to be there for her, but there was no time.

"Go back to my, I mean, to our home. I will get some of these men to help us, but we must ride like the wind and catch Beignet before he gets to the castle. Once there, we will not be able to engage them or save your brother's life. Promise me that you will stay there until I return. This is not yet done between us, we have much left to discuss."

Naomie started to feel a little bit of hope expanding in her chest, but then she heard the yelling from her tribe and looked over at them, knowing she would never see them again. Even her own parents refused to look at her.

Naomie lifted her chin and sat proud on her horse as she turned away from them, finally accepting the fact that there was no one that she could count on other than herself, not even Beorn.

"As you wish." She kicked the horse in its sides and galloped off the way they had just come.

Beorn watched her for a moment but the yells coming from the gypsies were distracting and he quickly turned his attention back to them.

The sun had finally broken through the stubborn rainclouds and brightened the day around them. Beorn wondered if that was a good omen, but Naomie was far enough gone by now that he couldn't ask her.

Getting a closer look at Ninga, Beorn could fully understand why Naomie ran away to begin with.

All of the Romani men were long haired and most were thin and wiry. To a man, their faces were closed up, no emotion showing other than suspicion and mistrust.

One of the younger men rode towards Beorn, who also went forward and they met halfway between the two groups.

"We know who the men are that took your womenfolk and Luca and they are riding towards their castle. Will you come with us? We can overtake them if we ride like the wind, but we haven't enough men to fight them alone. If they make it to their castle, we will not be able to save your kin."

The young man listened quietly and then turned his horse back. A small group of men huddled around him and there was much discussion, all low enough that Beorn could not hear what was being said.

Only a few moments passed, but Beorn felt like it was hours before the young man rode back over.

"We will come, only men, only on horseback. The others will follow later. You know how they will go?"

"I do."

The young man turned his head and nodded towards to the older men who spat out something in their tongue and then dozens of men yelled into the open sky as they kicked their horses' sides and galloped over towards Beorn and the others.

"Let's hope their swordsmanship equals their enthusiasm," Beorn mumbled, leaning the reins against his horse's neck and turning off in the direction Beignet would be traveling.

Even though the Manor was a large building, Naomie still hadn't gotten used to living inside and felt closed in at times.

This day, she found it particularly oppressive and made her way out into the orchards. The days were still cool enough to need her mantle wrapped securely around her body, but the world was beginning to spring up around her.

More and more birds were appearing and, as she approached the cattle foraging for new shoots of grass, she spotted quite a few calves that had been born recently. With a bittersweet smile, she rubbed her own belly and watched them frolic under the trees.

Thoughts of her brother crowded into her head, taking away her briefly attained peace of mind. It mattered naught that he could disown her as he did, Luca would forever be in her heart and she could not see him injured or killed if it could be prevented.

Naomie wandered slowly back towards the Manor, finally forcing Luca from her mind, only to have Beorn take over her thoughts. She knew not what to make of him. Naomie knew that he cared for her, but he would not allow their love to be, and it frustrated her to no end because she could not find a way to get through that barrier he had set around his heart.

"Damn you, Anna," she whispered. "Please let him go."

She made her way back to the Manor and found Celia, Gretchen and Karla in the kitchen. Karla was preparing the mid-day meal and the other two were assisting her.

Their chatter came to an abrupt halt when Naomie walked in and she knew that she must have been the subject of their conversation but did not care.

"May I help?"

"As you wish, M'Lady," Karla said. She was a large woman, with her hair pulled back tightly, away from her broad face.

She always seemed happy and full of life, traits which she shared with her daughter, Gretchen, and which Naomie envied.

"These just got brought in from the cellar, you can cut them up if you've a mind to."

Naomie grabbed a knife and began to cut up the vegetables for the stew that Karla was preparing. She did not know the woman well, but assumed Karla would have the most knowledge about the subject that she needed to learn more about.

"What kind of person was Anna?"

Karla was surprised at the question and stopped what she doing, lifting the large knife she had been using to cube the beef for the stew as she contemplated how to answer.

"She was a kind, gentle woman, why do you ask?"

"Beorn cannot let her go and I am just curious as to the type of woman she was."

"Sir Beorn was a hard, hard man when first they came here," Karla said, lowering her knife and continuing to cut up the meat, as she thought back to her early days here with him and Anna.

"He could be a real devil, angry all the time, and he didn't care a pin what he said or who he said it to. It was Lady Anna who finally helped him let go of all that anger."

Naomie slowly sliced the carrot she was working on, she could easily see Beorn as Karla had described him.

A smile blossomed on Karla's broad face as her memories brightened. "For a time, it was a happy place here, do you recall Gretchen?"

"I do," the girl replied, as she energetically scrubbed one of the pots. "Lady Anna was always kind to me and taught me many things."

"She insisted that I bring Gretchen here with me, even before the girl herself was old enough to work. She loved children and was so excited when she finally got with a child of her own.

Her face positively glowed as the babe grew inside of her and they made a nursery in one of the rooms. Sir Beorn, himself, built a cradle with his own two hands for the child. I remember her teasing him about it, because he made it so big that a mere infant would get lost in it. But he was just so proud of it, anyway."

The smile on Karla's face faded as her memories got darker.

"The babe was twisted inside of her and they didn't think the child would survive the birth, but it did." Karla made the sign of a cross and continued, "Poor Lady Anna, she gave everything she had to be sure that babe would survive, but in the end, she had nothing left for herself."

"And where is the child now?" Celia asked.

"He sent the girl away to live with Lady Anna's brother. They aren't far from here, but he won't see the child or have anything to do with it."

Naomie continued cutting the vegetables in silence, not sure if she felt better, or worse, after learning what she had about Anna.

They rode hard all afternoon, stopping only briefly to let the horses rest. At one such stop, Beorn met with the young man he'd first spoken with and a couple of other Romani men, along with Verne and Draco, noting that the one called Ninga always kept his distance.

Beorn had been sending men off ahead as scouts and it finally paid off. Beignet's group of knights were too hard to hide and they now knew exactly where they were.

"We will wait until they bed down for the night, then we will surround them and kill each and every one of them, agreed?"

Not one person hesitated, and all heads bobbed in agreement.

Spring was barely upon them and it had been a couple of weeks since the ground had last frozen, however, the temperatures at night were just slightly higher than freezing and the daytime highs never went over 11 or 12 degrees celsius, so the ground had not thawed as of yet.

Beorn threw the stick he had in his hand off into the brush. It was no use trying to draw up their plan of attack in the dirt, so he would have to explain it to the Romani men and hope they could understand and follow orders.

They went over the details several times and then he told the men to rest a bit. Night would be falling soon and then they would be on the move again.

He did call Draco and Verne over for a private conversation. "I know naught how well these men will do in battle. We know that Beignet's men are hardened knights and should not be underestimated. Stay near me, these gypsies do not give a damn about us, so we three must watch out for each other."

After another night of tossing and turning, amidst very little sleep, Naomie woke with a new resolution. Her body craved Beorn's, she wanted him to hold her, to kiss her, to make her feel safe and loved once again, as only he could, even when he was trying not to.

She had threatened to leave him as soon as the babe was born, but that was no longer an option. Naomie was not going to let him destroy the joy that the two of them could share. All he had to do was to open his heart and let it happen.

Somehow, she had to make him understand that, and Naomie had come up with an idea that she thought might help her cause.

Realizing that this may well make things worse, initially at least, she was willing to take that chance in order to make this their home, a place where they could find the peace and happiness that she knew was waiting for them, for all of them.

Karla was surprised when Naomie appeared in her kitchen at such an early hour that morning.

Pulling up a stool and looking at the cook conspiratorially, she laid out her plan. Naomie no longer had her family or her tribe, so now, everyone in this household was a part of her new tribe and, although it took great courage on her part, Naomie gave her trust to Karla, to Gretchen and to Celia. She could only hope that they would not play her false.

"First, I need to know more about the child, is it a girl or a boy?"

"A girl." Karla had a guilty look on her face as she continued, "Please don't tell Sir Beorn, but I visit the child when I can. She is a sweet, young thing and my heart breaks that he won't see her."

"I am going to change that."

The guilt left Karla's expression immediately and fear replaced it. "He would not like that. On this subject he will not bend."

"No, he will not, at least to begin with. But I am now the Lady of the Manor, and I will be making some of the decisions. He will have no choice but to accept them. And have no worries, he will not know of your participation in this, it will be resolved between he and I alone."

Feeling a little drop of hope, Karla asked, "How can I help?"

"First, I want to see the room they prepared for her, what is her name?"

"Julianna."

Naomie nodded in satisfaction. "For her mother's memory, that is good. Call Gretchen and Celia. We will leave them to put the child's room together whilst you and I go find Julianna and bring her home."

It took most of the morning to prepare, but then Naomie had one of the stable boys take them in a wagon to visit Anna's brother's home. She had tied her hair back and dressed carefully, wanting to be sure to look respectable, so that he would have no doubts about her ability to care for the child. She tried to look anything but Romani, although she could never hide her wild gypsy eyes.

"Karla, what a pleasure, I did not know that you would be visiting today."

The Lord of the Manor was a bit portly, with greying hair and sad brown eyes.

With a brief curtsy, Karla said, "I apologize for not giving you advance notice, Milord."

She hesitated, not sure how he would take this news. "This is Lady Naomie, she is Sir Beorn's new wife."

"A pleasure to meet you," he said with courtly bow, but there was no friendliness in his brown eyes, just suspicion and, perhaps, anger. "I had not heard that Beorn remarried. Congratulations."

"Thank you," Naomie replied.

"I am George Cuvier. Excuse my manners, Charles," he called out, "please bring some food and wine for my guests."

Then he turned back to the women and offered them a seat on the chairs near the warm fire.

Karla and Naomie looked at each, neither of them knowing how to start the conversation.

"You have come for Julianna, have you not?"

"I have," Naomie said, letting out a long, relieved breath.

"I knew this day would come. I am not ready for it just yet, but I am an old man, and my wife has been gone almost as long as Anna has. Julianna needs to be with her father, with parents young enough to let her enjoy her youth. I have just one request of you."

"Yes?"

"May I come to visit? I have no one else and the child has brought a great deal of happiness to my life."

Naomie caught his eyes with her own and he was mesmerized by their uniqueness and gratified by her words.

"Karla tells me the child is happy and intelligent and brings joy to all who meet her. You have done a wonderful job taking care of her when she most needed it. I hope you will come often and help me learn how to be such a kind and loving parent as you must have been for her."

Tears collected in his eyes as he took in her words and he hastily wiped them away when the servants brought in trays of food and drink.

"Please, help yourself, I will make arrangements for Julianna's things to be packed while you take your refreshments."

CHAPTER 21

They waited until well after dark to begin their attack, although Beorn had a devil of time trying to restrain the Romani men from attacking as soon as they got into position.

He couldn't get them to understand the advantage they would have when most of the men around the fire were sleeping.

He, Draco and Verne, slowly made their way in a large circle around the encampment, looking for the men that were on watch.

Those men had to be dispatched quietly, with a knife if possible, before they could call out a warning.

The three of them could not wear their chainmail which left them vulnerable, but it could not be helped, its clattering would take away any element of surprise they might have.

Beorn sent Verne and Draco off in one direction and he went the other. Stealthily making his way amongst the trees, he spied one of their lookouts. The man was relaxed, not expecting any problems as he leaned up against a large tree. Beorn came around the tree and slit his throat with his dirk, preventing the man from making any noise before he slunk onto the ground in a dead heap.

He was able to dispatch one other lookout in a similar fashion before the gypsies could no longer contain themselves and, with the cacophony of all kinds of yells and calls, they descended onto the men asleep around the fire and all hell broke loose.

Beorn's most immediate challenge was to find Verne and Draco, he did not trust the gypsies and he had to see to their safety.

Running across the way, he could see the two of them were engaged by Beignet's knights. They must have been on watch, because they were not sleepy-eyed and scrambling to get to their swords, they were intent on going in for the kill.

Verne and Draco were holding their own, but were outnumbered and Beorn hurried towards them, only to be blocked by a large man who stepped out in front of him, swinging a battle axe with all the strength in his massive arms.

Beorn ducked and it just barely missed his head. He had no time for this one but couldn't leave him alive. As the man was trying to get his battle axe back into position Beorn swung wide and hit one of those bulging arms, blood spurting everywhere as the arm hung useless.

The man bellowed and his eyes were wide with anger and pain. Beorn sunk the tip of the blade deep into the man's stomach and the bellowing stopped as he fell back onto the bloody ground.

There was mayhem down around the campfire, the gypsies were nothing if not persistent and, regardless of the fact that they were out-manned and the knights had better weapons and training than them, they continued to dive into the fray with no hesitation, no fear.

Beorn could see Draco's parries were getting weaker, he was tiring and the two knights attacking him sensed it and became bolder.

With a battle cry to turn one's blood cold, Beorn leapt towards them before they could deal their final blows to Draco. With steel clanging against steel, Beorn took them both on and was able to move them away from where Draco was catching his breath.

Turning to block a blow from one of them, the other managed to catch Beorn's arm and his sword fell to the ground when his hand went numb.

He stood tall, showing no fear as he waited for the death blow to strike but, instead the man grunted and fell to the ground at his feet. Draco nodded at him and then turned to finish off the other knight they had been engaging.

"Where's Verne?" Beorn asked, once that had been accomplished.

"I know naught, we got separated when the gypsies attacked."

The two of them scanned the scene, the persistence of the gypsies paid off and dead knights lay scattered all around, those few that survived grabbed their horses and were high-tailing it from the scene.

"There," Draco called out, seeing Verne lying on the ground off to the side of where he'd been caught up with the two knights.

The two of them hurried over to him and Beorn found he was holding his own breath and didn't release it until he was able to feel a faint pulse in Verne's neck.

"Quickly, cut off part of your undertunic, he has a deep a cut along his ribs and is losing much blood."

Verne regained consciousness when Beorn tightened the cloth tight around his torso to staunch the flow of blood.

"Can you walk?"

"I think, mayhap, I can, but slowly."

The three of them made their way over to the group of gypsies.

Beignet, himself, did survive the attack and they had him tied up in the center of a circle of Romani men. Luca stood in front of him, a sharp dirk in his hand as he slowly drew lines along the man's face, releasing thin rivulets of blood to flow down his face and neck.

They were yelling at him and, although he didn't know the language, Beorn could easily imagine what they were saying.

Luca took the knife and stabbed him in the side, Beignet screamed but that was just the beginning. Luca handed the knife to one of the girls that Beignet had kidnapped and she stabbed him on the other side.

The knife was then passed on to each of the girls until they'd all had a chance to give him some pay back for what he had already done, and what he intended to do.

Beignet's screams faded and then stopped altogether as the blows continued, his soul was already in hell by the time each of the girls had their turn at him.

Luca stepped over to Beorn. "Ninga tells me you brought my people here to help us."

Beorn could see the same facial structure as Naomie's, but his eyes seemed to be completely black, perhaps because the only light was from the fire, but they reflected nothing.

"Yes, we did."

"Thank you."

"If you want to truly thank us, you could do so by talking to your sister, by accepting the fact that she is my wife."

"I have no sister and you should leave us before our bloodlust carries over and we look for more gadje to kill."

They stared hard into each other's eyes and, if Beorn were not so worried about Verne, he may have taken the man on right then, regardless of how many gypsies he had at his back.

Instead, he and Draco helped Verne onto his horse and with one last look at the group of them, they kicked their horses' sides and cantered away into the night.

Beorn was confused, he was suddenly standing in the middle of an apple orchard and the sun was shining down upon him. The trees were covered with pink and white apple blossoms and the warm spring air was alive with their fresh, floral scent.

He could hear the birds calling to one another in the trees and was sure he spotted the orange feathers of a Redstart as it flitted from tree to tree.

He turned in a circle, trying to take all of it in and make sense of it somehow. Beorn stopped when he saw a feminine figure approaching him and thought he might burst into tears when he recognized who it was gliding towards him, an ethereal smile on her face and love and adoration filling her soulful brown eyes as she looked his way.

"Anna, my love." His voice was only a whisper because his throat was clogged with emotion and it was the best he could do. "Am I dead, then?"

She was right in front of him now and her face held a serene glow that made her even more beautiful than she had been in life.

"No, Beorn, you are not dead."

"Then how am I with you? I prayed for that so many times since I lost you that I finally gave up praying altogether. Why

are you here now?"

"I have been with you every moment since I left, you know that, you've always carried me in your heart. I'm here now because you need me to help you find your way back into the light."

"I fear it's too late for that, my love."

Tears were running unbidden down his face and Anna gently rested her hand on his cheek and he leaned his head against it.

"I can feel your hand, Anna. How is any of this possible?"

"Come, walk with me," she said, and he took her hand in his and they made their way through the blossoming trees, breathing in the wonderful scents surrounding them, and Beorn found the closest thing to happiness that he'd felt since Anna had left him.

"I must confess something to you, my love."

"What is that?"

"I married another and gave her your ring. It was unavoidable, I had no other to give her at the ceremony. I do not believe that we will stay married but, even if we do, I will give her a different ring, no one but you should wear that wedding band."

"Tell me about her, your wife."

"No, I cannot."

"You must, she is why I am here."

He looked down at her curiously. "She is nothing like you, she is wild and stubborn-minded. You were calm and loving and helped me lose some of the ugliness that I carried inside of me."

"I did, but you've let it come back."

"Because you are no longer here to help soothe me."

"What is her name?"

"Naomie."

"Is she beautiful?"

"Very much so."

"Why did you marry her?"

"To save her from being kidnapped and being made into

someone's slave."

"That is the only reason?"

"That is the main reason, I had no intention of marrying again."

"But you are still a young, virile man, Beorn. What is your reasoning for that?"

"I loved you with all my heart, Anna, and I still do. I was crushed when you died. I cannot go through it again. It is selfish, I know, but I live with your screams of agony in my sleep every night. She carries my child and I cannot take the chance of that happening again, I could not live with it."

"Oh, Beorn." Anna's face was sad now, the light fading from it. "Those screams you hear at night are not my screams of agony, they are my screams of frustration because you left my daughter with others and she will never know the love of her own parents."

"No, that cannot be."

"But it is. She did not cause my death and should not be punished because of it."

"I know, but I fear I would not be kind to her."

"Beorn, you must reconcile yourself about our daughter, else you will hear my screams every night of your life."

"I will try, Anna, that is all I can promise."

"It is a beginning, at least. Now let us talk more about your wife. Do you remember when we talked about your days serving as a knight? We both knew that it was the depth of your loyalty that caused you the greatest trauma.

You felt that you needed to be there for each and every man under your command, but some of those men never made it back from the battlefield, and it took a long while for you to be able to forgive yourself about them. I think now you are suffering from the same problem now."

"How so?"

"You still feel that you owe your loyalty to me because I was your wife."

"Of course, I do."

"Till death us do part, Beorn, remember those words? They

set you free when I died, to live again, to love again. And now you must do those things. Do you love Naomie?"

He hesitated, he had never lied to Anna but did not feel comfortable telling her the truth on this particular subject.

"This is your dream, Beorn, you cannot worry about how I will feel. I am gone now, and it is you that has to face the truth about Naomie, about the child you created with her and about our daughter. Yours and my love will never die and you do not have to feel that you are being disloyal to me by choosing to live again."

They stopped walking and Beorn felt something shift inside of himself, perhaps some of that ice that had his heart in its grip had begun to crack.

He looked down at his beautiful wife and the horrible longing that had been part of him for such a long time started to dissipate. Their eyes met and there was much that he wanted to say to her, but she seemed to be fading and he began to panic.

"Anna, don't go yet, I still need you."

"No, my love, you don't need me anymore. You have someone else to love, someone else who loves you. Allow yourself be happy, Beorn."

Her voice was still there but she had faded away and all he could see were pink and white petals floating on the wind around him. Beorn cried in earnest then, cried away the pain, the loneliness and the hurt that he had been carrying with him for such a very long time.

Beorn woke a bit later, it was still dark, the moon had slipped behind a cloud and the cold bit through his woolen blanket. He could feel the dried tears on his cheeks and knew those, at least, had been real enough.

"Thank you, Anna," he whispered into the darkness. He slept no more that night, just thought about her, and about Naomie, and finally allowed himself to be honest about who he was and what he wanted.

CHAPTER 22

Naomie heard the commotion outside and knew that Beorn and the others had returned. Now would be their moment of truth and she was ready to do whatever battle was necessary to get through to him. But, first she must find out if her brother was alright.

"Celia, please take Julianna to the kitchen. Once I've let Beorn know she is here, I will call for you both. Thank you for all your help, you are a good friend."

"Thank you, Milady," Celia said, blushing a little with pleasure, then she reached down for the baby and hurried into the kitchen.

Naomie made her way out to the courtyard to find only Beorn, Verne and Draco. The stable boy was leading all of their horses away and the men looked bedraggled and tired.

She could not read the expression on Beorn's face as he studied her, which caused her some concern.

"You did not find them?"

He was now just a couple of steps away from her. "We did and they are all free now. Some of your people were hurt in the battle, but they will all live."

"And what of you men? Are you well?"

"Verne was cleaved quite deeply, methinks, you should take a look at his wound."

"I shall, please bring him into the Great Hall. I'll see to having food prepared for you and will get the items I need for his wound."

"Thank you." It was as if they were strangers and knew not how to talk to each other any longer.

Naomie took a deep breath and stepped closer to him, ignoring the erratic thumping of her heart, she ran her finger along his bristly jawline, and murmured, "I am happy that you are safe. It is good to have you home again."

"It's good to be home."

She gave Beorn a brief nod and hurried inside, wondering how she would be able to keep the child's presence hidden from him until they'd eaten and she was able to converse in private.

Fortunately, Julianna had fallen asleep in the warm kitchen and she asked Celia to put her down in the cradle in her bedchamber for now.

Naomie hurried back into the Great Hall with warm water and linen squares with which to clean out Verne's wound. It was deeper than any of them had realized and took some time to clean properly.

It was a long, jagged cut along his rib cage where the broadsword must have slid in because they did not have the protection of their chainmail. She used the water to clean it as best she could and then poured wine over the wound.

She wasn't sure whose cry was the loudest, Verne's because of the unexpected burning sensation, or Draco's, because of his despair at good wine being wasted in such a manner.

All the cleansing caused the bleeding to begin again and Naomie couldn't get it to stop. She stood and walked over to Beorn, who was staring down at the fire raging within the fireplace. She gently placed her hand on his arm to get his attention and was gratified at the look on his face when he realized it was her standing beside him, until she told him what she needed.

"I can do it, if you prefer," she said quietly, with a glance at her patient.

"No, all is well, let me get one of my dirks properly heated in the fire and I shall cauterize it. Be sure to get him a stick or a piece of leather, something to bite down on so his screams won't embarrass him later."

She ran into the kitchen and Karla provided her with a spare wooden dowel. She grabbed that and some herbs and another big piece of linen, then ran back to the Great Hall. Beorn lifted his knife from the fire, its blade now glowing red, and he nodded to Draco and the two of them moved towards Verne.

Naomie handed Verne the wooden dowel and stepped back. He knew what was coming and tried to mentally prepare himself, but nothing could have prepared him for the pain of the red-hot knife as it seared his skin closed. Fortunately, Draco was there to hold him still, he couldn't have remained motionless on his own.

Beorn removed the knife, ignoring the smell of burning flesh, and Naomie spread a paste of musk mallow and lesser periwinkle over the angry wound, then wrapped the clean linen around his torso.

"Thank you," he said, tears streaming down his face.

"You're welcome, you did well, and it should heal with no further problems, but I'll continue to check on it for you."

"You best look after Sir Beorn's arm now."

Naomie turned towards the man in question and raised an eyebrow at him.

"I have no wound, I was hit by the flat side of the blade and it numbed my arm for a time. I am fine now."

Food was brought out then, but the men only seemed to have an appetite for some strong cider and Naomie couldn't bear the thought of eating anything until she'd spoken with Beorn. Her stomach was in knots and she needed to resolve their situation once and for all.

"May I speak with you, Beorn?"

"Of course."

"Alone?"

"Certainly." He took her hand and led her into their bedchamber.

Naomie hadn't expected that and hoped Julianna would stay asleep until she'd had an opportunity to talk to him about her. The child was on the far side of the bed, so unless she made some noise, he wouldn't know Julianna was there.

Beorn sat down on the bed beside Naomie, he had done a great deal of soul-searching and thought he knew how this would go, but he could never be sure when it involved Naomie.

"Beorn, I know that you think I will be in danger by having a babe, but I am strong and healthy. I want to be with you, only you. Having children is a part of loving one another, they are inevitable and are a blessing."

She ran her fingers along his cheek, her eyes peering deeply into his, trying to read what was hidden within their dark blue depths.

"I love you with all my heart. What can I do to convince you that we belong together; that no matter how different we are, no matter what the past has dealt us; we can still make a good life with one another?"

Beorn was silent for a moment, his heart pounding hard in his chest, her words were what he had hoped for, what he wanted as much as she did and now he could tell her that, with no doubts, no fear, no hesitation.

"And I love you, Naomie, and I want to be your husband, not just in name but in every way possible, to have and to hold until death us do part."

"Beorn, please, you must listen to me." Naomie had certainly never expected those words to pour from his lips and had to stop and process what she thought she had heard. "What did you say?"

"You heard me."

A slow smile spread across his face and he raised his hand, running his fingers with a featherlight touch across her jaw and her lips, then sinking his fingers into her luxuriant hair and pulling her forward so that he could capture her lips with his own.

Naomie moaned softly and leaned into him for a long, thorough kiss. Then she slowly dragged her lips away from his and stared up into his brilliant blue eyes which were, for the moment, completely unguarded and full of emotion.

"Truly?"

"Yes, my love. I cannot promise that it will be easy for you, but I'm willing to have a bash at it, if you are."

"I have been ready for that since the first day I saw you."

"Shall we seal the deal properly?" he asked, leaning towards her again.

But, Naomie pulled back away from him, her heart skipping a beat, hoping she hadn't ruined their chance for happiness with her impulsiveness.

"There is one more thing to discuss before we do that."

His eyes narrowed suspiciously. "And what would that be?"

She took his hand and stood up, dragging him behind her as she rounded to the other side of the bed and there, sound asleep in the cradle that he'd built with his own hands, was his beautiful young daughter.

"This is Julianna."

Beorn raised a fist to his chest and tears filled his eyes as he gazed upon his daughter for the first time.

"I'm sorry," Naomie said, seeing how emotional it made him to see her. "I should have waited until you were ready."

"Shh," he said, putting a finger to her lips, still not able to tear his eyes from the sleeping child. "You were right to do this, I did not realize how deeply I would be affected by seeing her."

The little girl opened her big, brown eyes and looked back and forth between them, then she raised her arms towards Naomie.

Picking up the child, Naomie turned so they could both look at Beorn. "This is your daddy, little one. Would you like to hold her?"

"Not just yet, she and I will have to get used to one another slowly. She looks just like her mother," he said, swallowing hard.

"That is what Karla said, and she is a very sweet little girl. You have much to catch up on with her."

He exhaled loudly.

"You, Naomie, have a way of turning my life arse over tip so that I never know what will come next. Let us go join the others now, although you and I also have much to catch up on, and I will not wait much longer before sampling your wares once again, wife."

"Ma-sha-llah," she responded with a broad smile, as the three of them made their way out into the Great Hall.

Spring came soon enough after that, and over the summer months and into the early fall, Beorn fought with his fears and his worries about Naomie as her stomach expanded, and his babe grew within her.

There were rare occasions when he would come upon her unexpectedly and he could see the sadness in her eyes and knew she was thinking of her family.

But most days found Naomie calm, serene even, and her beautiful face glowed with happiness, although he still could not guess at what she was thinking at any given time.

She was never hesitant to disagree with Beorn should his position on a particular subject not agree with hers. On most occasions, they were able to discuss their issues, but there were times when the conversation became heated and neither of them would back down.

Ultimately, they would find their way back into each other's good graces and Naomie suspected that Beorn sometimes goaded her into arguments, simply because of the passion they shared while reconciling.

"Ma-sha-llah," she said quietly to herself, when such thoughts would come to her.

Draco had returned to England and was working as a mercenary for one of Beorn's friends. Whenever they came to the continent, Draco made sure to stop by, if possible.

Verne had had his fill of battles, his wound healed with no further complications and, although it took a bit of time for Beorn to get used to the fact that he was a knight now, no longer a squire, eventually they agreed on what Verne's duties would be and he stayed on with them, in the only home he had really ever known.

Naomie and Beorn tended to suspect the true reason he stayed on was because Celia was now working at the Manor. She and Verne had begun spending an inordinate amount of time together and seemed to be getting closer every day.

Julianna frequently accompanied Beorn on his daily rides to look over his estates, and together they checked out the apple and pear crops, as well as monitoring the cattle and cheese products. Her giggles inevitably put a smile on his face, regardless of the issues that would arise during their inspections.

Beorn found that sharing stories about Anna to their daughter was very cathartic and helped him feel that she was there with them, a part of their daughter's life. He thought that must be so because her screams in the night had stopped and he was no longer tormented by them.

There was much he still had to learn about being a father, but Julianna made it easier for him than he had ever expected it could be.

As the time for Naomie to deliver their child approached, it took all of Beorn's courage to remain strong and not let the fear drive his thoughts back into the darkness.

And when the baby boy was born and both he and his mother were healthy, strong, and extremely vocal, Beorn gave in to Naomie's vision of their future and accepted that this was just the beginning and their happiness together would know no bounds.

THE END

THANK YOU

I wanted to thank all of you for spending your time and your money on Winter's Knight. I sincerely hope you enjoyed reading it as much as I did writing it.

Please feel free to visit debbieboek.com to contact me or for more information about me and my books. I would love to hear any comments you have about the characters, the book, the storyline, anything that you would like to share.

You may want to also check out my blogs at debbieboek.blog where I talk about the writers who have inspired me, about books, and about the monsters and urban legends that keep our imaginations fertile.

If you did enjoy the book, I would appreciate it if you could write a brief review. Reviews aren't just beneficial for the author, they also help others find good books to read. So, please let the world know about whatever books you are reading, not just this one, by writing a brief review.

Thanks again and I'm looking forward to our next adventure.

Debbie Boek